The Abandoned

By

Sharon Thompson

First published in 2018 by Bloodhound Books

www.bloodhoundbooks.com

Print ISBN 978-1-912175-90-1

To the magic which keeps us all going.

Dublin, 1950s

I knew the stranger at my door would cry. All that curled blonde hair and her clinging to a navy handbag. I was surprised her type still found me.

'Peggy?' she asked.

'Yes.'

A gloved hand steadied her on the door frame, and I moved to let her inside. Thanks be to God she didn't embarrass us both on the doorstep. A busy Dublin street is not the place for a woman to weep and wail about her lot.

'I was sent by –'

I lifted my hungover hand to stop her. 'No names. You're lucky. My medicines room is free at the minute.'

Perfect curls danced under her fancy hat when she nodded. Then, sweet Christ, it started. Like I knew it would. Big tears, plopping down onto those pale cheeks, blue eyes begging me for sympathy. I know I'm hardened to a great deal, but tears are tough to ignore.

'How far along are you?'

'Not long.'

'This way,' I said. There was no sound from upstairs. My two girls must have been sleeping rather than humping.

This blonde one had a slim behind with no bulge out in front. A navy skirt snipped in at the waist and a grey jacket that I'd have liked myself over her cream blouse all ironed and silky looking. She knew how to look after herself, and someone had raised the money quick-smart; by the looks of her, she seemed much the age of myself. Hitting thirty, she was, and she should've had more sense than to need me.

1

She watched me intently, despite the tears; my bleached hair not to her standards and me with a tattered apron on to hide my tight knitted jumper and straight skirt.

'You sure you're in bother?' I asked, turning the key and creaking open the door to my medicines room.

That nodding started again and more snivelling. Slim shoulders rising and falling as she trembled to her very knees.

'Don't be crying.' I thought of the money. 'Please.' I became as gentle as you like and used the midwife's face that I've practiced over the years.

An odd time, I wonder why and how they have come to this. I know though that most of them are married and visit me more than once. Burdened with too many. Used to spreading their legs and having life or death removed from their groins. But these girls are different. They're damaged either by themselves or somebody else. I probably hurt them again, but, sure, that's business. I can't think of every one of them.

'It'll be grand. We'll sort things. Stop the crying.'

I pointed at the high bed in the middle of the room. Light for my work comes in the tall window, with the flash of an odd pigeon behind the net curtain. It's not a palace, but it will do for now.

The Angelus rang out, and we blessed ourselves. Looking down, I prayed to Our Lady and St Brigid for blessings and guidance. I've given up on forgiveness.

There before me when my eyes opened were expensive navy shoes with elegant straps. They were just the perfect height for dancing.

'Where did you get them?'

'Sligo town…' A handkerchief muffled the name of the shop. But sure, I wasn't going all the way back to Sligo for a pair of dainty shoes. She'd come as far as myself, but she'd most likely go back.

'Got money for this?'

The tiny gold clasp clicked open. She took out an envelope that bulged like my eyes. I tried not to snatch it. Country girls always have the right amount. Honest as the day is long. I left the twenty pounds on the dresser, under the mirror out of harm's way, and pointed again to the bed. The greyish sheet was changed – this morning had left its mark.

The modest way this one removed her skirt and panties made me chuckle. As if I'd never seen my own bits and pieces. Gently, she placed her hat on the chair where I usually plonk my basin. But I said nothing and went about getting my business ready. With my back to her, she sobbed, and I thought of the last time she might have had something inside her.

I never ask questions, but sometimes, they tell me it all, hoping to make it all better. But we all know it's never that simple.

There was a nice smell from her – calm as lavender, and smooth and fresh like face cream. You could tell the way she looked about the room that she was well raised. She knew her manners. That perfect nose wrinkled in displeasure but not disgust.

Her slim hands still trembled as I told her to come to edge of the bed. I lifted her knees and encouraged them to flop out to the sides. My syringe was full of the concoction that would either solve her ills or make them worse. Who knew?

Sometimes, it takes no time at all to prod the wire and the rubber tubing in. Many don't say a word or bless themselves and pray throughout. Others cry. Mostly, I don't notice anymore. But with this pretty, young one, something didn't feel right. She barely spoke. Even the rich one's ramble, making excuses for their decision. This one seemed sure in her quest. Her eyes held tears, but as she curled her fingers into a fist, I felt no remorse off her, and it dawned on me she needed this badly. Pity flooded me, and there's nothing I hate more than pity. I felt it wouldn't be the last I'd see of her, and this worried me. Something deep in my gut told me she was a bad omen.

'I'll have to get myself some shoes like those,' I said.

She sniffed and murmured her agreement.

'Do you dance?'

'Not much.'

3

'I love the dances in the Gresham. Haven't gone much since…I came here.'

'I don't feel like dancing,'

'Course.'

Her blonde curls splayed on the pillow, and she faced right towards the window. 'I hate everything these days.' She shuddered either with fear or cold.

'Those shoes, now, sure you couldn't hate them?'

She didn't answer me. I did what I could for her. It all went grand until she was readying herself to leave. I couldn't help staring and saw no ring on her finger.

Suddenly, she touched my arm. She came closer and said, 'Thank you. You saved me. You must save so many.'

Something cracked. All I knew about myself shifted. It was the way she did it. I couldn't look at her.

'You go now. Wait for the bleeding and the pains to start. Don't come back here.'

With a zip and a swoosh, she was dressed. Sheathed in the jacket, she reached for her hat; the loud wobble of the chair breaking the silence when the hat was moved.

I was worried for her more than most. 'My work is over, but sometimes, women need tablets for infections. You're a clever girl – you should know if things are right down below.'

Her voice shook as she sat to fidget with buckles. 'Yes. Thank you.'

I couldn't wait to get rid of her. A lingering sense of all that I knew shattered before me. She'd shaken me to the core of myself. I trembled and opened the latch on the front door. I couldn't speak. She got to the footpath and walked away.

Closing the door, I felt like a woman who steals souls for money. I normally don't think on it much at all. I just know I am a criminal bitch who lives in the gutter.

It was never about saving anyone; I just needed the cash, they needed the service. Now, my heart is split with the torture of them all. All of them who've needed me and them in a bad way.

Those who I thought nothing of at all. I can't cast my mind to it. I simply can't. That bitch made me a saviour and made it all too big a deal.

'God takes and gives life,' the priest says.

I was always told it was wrong, but this one muddied my waters, unstilled what has been right for so long.

'Women always do the best with what they are given,' Mammy would say.

I did my best, but now, I feel like I'm going fucking mad.

Chapter 1

'I'm sorry!' I shout in my half sleep. It's been a while since I had such vivid dreams.

My nightmares were few and far between…but since that one came from Sligo, I can feel it all again. I sense my best girl, Molly, has come to soothe me. She sings a lullaby of sorts. The only one she seems to know. The one she sang to Fionn. I'm sure she misses him, although she never says. It's wrong for women to feel so strongly. Why do we have these deep feelings and have no way to ease them?

Molly's emotions are complex, even more so than my own. The pout on her these past few days has annoyed me. They all want Molly's new buck to stay the night. But no. There's too much going on in number thirty-four. No men stay for the full night. Although, I've let a few of my own cuddle me to sleep over the years. But none have been totally mine, especially since we came here to the backstreets. Here, we're hidden away, like vermin.

Mountjoy Square is not far from Ranelagh, but I've fallen a heck of a distance. The four-storey building is still Georgian but decrepit, damp and dismal. The very top floor is habitable only to bats and pigeons; the basement is home to two families who've sunk even lower than ourselves. The high notions that are left in me have taken on the ground and first floor. We've a kitchen, tiny back scullery and a back yard that you might swing a cat in. There's also a rank parlour, a small downstairs medicines room and four small bedrooms to bed ourselves down with the odd man. I'm posh – there's a toilet and sink upstairs with room for a tin bath. We call that hole of a room the privy.

The street lamps all along the road are home to swinging children. But the lamp posts near number thirty-four are empty of their noises. Gossiping women fear harlots like us. I'm glad of the peace we get from the laughter of children. It seems insensitive some days.

I know I'm no angel, but what I do has been done for centuries. Women know themselves what they're capable of, know what they need to do for the best and how they must survive. I am merely here and need work. There's no great calling or falling in my eyes. What happens at number thirty-four happens because of life. That's it.

I like the streetlights so close to the house and how they light up the night. I hated the shadows and places where ghosts hide. The countryside of my youth was without light, the source of all my fears, and yet, the place where my mother howled me out of her.

'I roared in agony when you were born,' she had told me. 'But you were worth every pain. You're my little dreamer. Always want more, Peggy, but don't want too much.'

I'll always remember that about her. The fear in her eyes about everything.

'We must… We should… We can't…' were her standard ways of starting a conversation.

Finally, though, I broke free from the stifling farmland around me. Fled the village where women would swing in perpetual motion of wifehood, motherhood, gossip-hood and feckin' sainthood. I read and dreamed of Robin Hood rescuing me. I was Maid Marian. Robin would throw me up on his horse and take me away to Tír na Nóg where I would play with the fairies of legends and talk with Little John. It's probably why I haven't settled. I'm always waiting on someone to rescue me.

Romance and married love, I didn't understand. I got love. Yes, I was loved. Mother loved me until she was lost inside her mind.

'Disease of the brain somehow took her,' Father Lavelle said.

That hilly scrub and a few lush acres were all mine then.

'A slip of a girl cannot own land like that,' the priest muttered to anyone who'd listen. The tuts on market day that the law might let me have what was mine.

Father Lavelle tried convincing me: 'The convent is a place of respect and grace for the likes of you, Peggy. No kin left. It's the place for you.'

Whispers at Mass: 'Pretty price for them fields. She's got a good dowry.'

It wasn't long until Mammy was taken away, matted hair covering her face and the hunch on her back as she left me. The very next day, Father Lavelle tried persuading me again. 'Marriage, then, Peggy? It's the only way for a woman with means. The convent wants two hundred pounds to make you a nun.'

I'd been adamant. 'No.'

'Then, you'll marry John Herley? It's up to you.'

I was no convent girl, I was certain of that. So, there was nothing for it but for me to tie myself to "Him." I never called him anything else. He doesn't deserve a name. Names are nice. "Him" or "It" was good enough for that bastard.

The past swings with the present in my mind. Here on the bed, my Molly sings on, swaying to and fro with me. A large cushion sits up her dress. She rubs it, and I close my eyes to see my mother rub the side of the cow in the byre and smile.

She had a wonderful smile, had Mammy. Perfect teeth, dark hair, and skin that she washed in spring water. Mammy was nice. I can even smell that cow shed. The manure ripe and the morning air crisp.

But then, He appears, like he did when she left me.

'We need water,' Himself shouted at me that day.

I sighed, curling my tired hands around his bucket handle. Getting into the sunshine was a reprieve. No one at school mentioned how men like their crowns and kingdoms. My own father, lost in a war, was no example.

All the women were saying, 'You're lucky John took pity on you. You're married now.'

Married, me arse, I thought.

The nudges told me to accept my lot with dignity. Mammy had known poultry. She'd shown me cookery, darning and planting seeds, but she didn't know the art of farming men. That type of husbandry never passed her lips.

I had nothing left to love, then, except Dora, the cow. I used to think that at least she was happy, knee deep in the finest meadow, looking into the hills all day long. I patted her warm behind and made her follow me a step, ambling like a pregnant woman, her udder filling for me to pull on it. Mornings were my favourite time with Dora. He was snoring, and the birds chirped over the din of him. Steam rose when I squirted her whiteness into the bucket.

Dora had given him three calves since he'd put his claim on us. Three fine heifers, red like herself. She was always taken to the bull, and I was good at the calving. She depended on me. He just stood and prodded her with a sally rod. Thank Christ, despite all his prodding at me, nothing happened.

Dora walked on in the pasture, her head bowed low to graze, leaving me in disgust, her crunching audible despite the swings of my bucket. I loosened my hair and held my freckles into the sun, willing the expanse of blue to absorb me into the possible abyss of peace. I knew that I shouldn't dally for long.

Even now, while Molly sings in the present, I know I cannot linger long in this nightmare, remembering…but it comes on regardless. Like a child being born, there's nothing I can do.

Our water spring spilled into the deep heather and shimmered down the mountain like a young one's skirt. There's nothing like spring water for the milk or the poteen.

I thought then on his poteen still in the byre. A groan left me. I can feel it still – the dread and impending disaster. I failed to milk off the badness. The almost-ready batch was ruined.

It was the warning of the corncrake he unsettled from its bed that made my goose pimples rise. Fear that made me squint into the sun. But it was the sight of his march through the long grass, the flash his flailing stick made at Dora, and the sound of the water filling that made my own water leave me. The warmth wet my legs and drenched the dry heather under foot as my tears came.

'PEGGY!'

The hill echoed my own name and tossed water from the pail. Frozen, I stared at his contorted features and the sally rod getting closer. Closer still he strode as my pail rattled. The sun scorched the hill as his mad fingers tangled in my hair.

Down I bowed. 'You cow,' he roared. My face came level with the top of his boot as he slashed with the rod. The sting was long and sharp, and my scalp gave his fist another clump of me. Stumbling, he reached to get me.

I fell lower in prayer and howled, 'Please?'

Not sure of foot, he grabbed my dress, hauling me to him with such ferocity, he toppled. Backwards he rolled over and over. I went, too, watching the greens and blues flash by as my limbs met dull thuds. There was no sound. The sky was blue and the heather purple. The breeze was nice. Everything seemed the same. Straining and stiff to rise, the meadow's verge swished in the evening breeze.

Before me, Himself lay sprawled, gasping for me to save him.

Under me now, there is a coldness. Despite my thirty years, I have wet the bed again. Molly says nothing, but there's no more singing as she rubs her pretend belly. But here she and I sit, in my piss.

It was that girl from Sligo that did this. That blonde bitch who has brought all of this to mind. It is she who has made me remember that far back.

Chapter 2

The thumping of the bed on the floor above us is not helping my hangover. I've had quite a few now trying to drown the nightmares.

'That sounds like music.' Molly taps a spoon off a saucepan and grunts in time to the rhythm upstairs. A halfwit, they call Molly, but she knows what makes money. 'He had me last week.' She stands tall and twirls in her new dress from Clery's, Dublin's nicest department store.

I don't take as much money off Molly as I should. She needs every shilling, her only child farmed out to country folk in County Cavan. Sixty pounds a year is a lot of money for a girl like her. The men like her red hair and nice figure, but when she talks, many don't like "taking advantage." Little do they know that it's Molly who takes advantage.

'You're not as simple as you make out,' some of the other girls have accused her.

Those blue eyes shine above her creamy, smooth cheeks. Like silk, they are.

'She talks funny. Won't look us in the eye,' some say.

But I know Molly's as cute as a pet fox. She never did tell me who put her in the family way. It was probably some pig in that hellhole we were in together. I'm not even sure where Molly comes from or why she was in the cells. I know it must have been something odd, because she wasn't sent to the laundries and wasn't in the prison for too long.

I've always worried about Molly. But the way her belly contorted all on its own made me worry that she was carrying a demon. Even as a midwife, I was troubled by the way her dress moved so often. She rubbed her bump, stuck it out good and proper and hummed away to herself. It meant the other bitches left her and me be. Most people don't like what they don't understand.

Molly didn't give birth until we both got thrown to the streets.

The chaplain had winked after the hand job Molly gave him. 'They're letting you out together. You are both ready for release. I had a quiet word.'

I'm not sure if Molly had stuck with me, or I had stuck with her. Maybe she was sent to make me care. Like she fell out of somewhere safe, so I would have to protect her. Just like that wet Friday last year when her child fell out of her onto our kitchen floor. She must've been in labour but failed to mention it to anyone and me only in the door. I've never seen such a huge baby boy. We called him Fionn after the legend of the Irish giant. He hollered like one too.

'Fell into life, Peggy,' she said. 'I'll protect him.'

I'd tried to talk Molly into abandoning the infant on the side of the road.

'Like Moses in the bulrushes. We'll wait nearby, and we'll see him rescued. Once he's found, the state will pay for a mother. He'll be looked after. You'll see. I can make sure that Sergeant Bushnell has him staying with a nice family. Not in one of them big homes.'

All my protesting and bullying had no effect on Molly. Knowledge of Moses or not, she was having none of it.

I'd explain over and over. 'But when I had my own premises in Ranelagh, I did this often. Helped women give birth, and then, after a while, we'd leave the bundles safely where they'd be found. The likes of the sergeant would appear with what I'd just left out on some rural road. He'd give me instructions to see it housed with Catholic, God-fearing people.'

I do miss the joy of giving a bustling house or some barren woman a baby bundle. I also miss my fee. The Americans always paid well for the cutest babies to take over the Atlantic. The fucking nuns had a monopoly on that end of things, though. I found it dangerous to take on the church. I paid the price for being "insolent and immoral." Funny how the lay folk must bend to the will of God and not the fucking nuns.

Anyhow, I couldn't talk Molly into any scheme of mine. I didn't blame her really. I was only a criminal to her. She didn't understand what midwives were, and as I was no longer one then, it mattered little anyhow. All Molly saw was an older convict who talked big things but hadn't even the price of next month's rent.

Fionn was strong and healthy. I was sure that I could make Molly free again, and that her breasts would heal, and we would have some capital. But Molly stood firm.

'No. He's mine. We'll find him a good place, until I'm rich.'

I considered stealing him while she slept. But once Molly's breast left his mouth, Fionn wailed like nothing earthly.

'He cannot stay, Molly. I'm not allowed to house children.'

Molly wasn't far from a child herself in her mind. But no one wanted the responsibility of her, and we couldn't have her baby. So that was that. When I thought clearly about it, I realised, too, that I couldn't afford to be caught selling a child again. So, Fionn went to Cavan, legitimately, with Molly's money sent monthly.

Molly neither cried nor wailed. She was certain that she would see him again soon. 'Take care of him. I'll get him when I'm rich,' she told the foster mother who did look like Mother Earth incarnate. Round and fair faced with rosy cheeks, she was, as she promised she'd have him praying under the Sacred Heart gleaming on her wall when he was old enough.

Fionn just looked at Molly, and she kissed his little cheek and that was that. The pudgy little bastard knew when she needed him to be quiet. Molly hummed the whole way home on the bus and ate the bar of chocolate I'd bought her. My heart broke in two for her. It really did. Life isn't fair or good sometimes.

The girls are now fighting over the customers.

'You've all got your regulars, and Molly has hers. New ones to the door are for whoever wants them.' I'm repeating myself. I've been saying this over and over. 'Stop the whinging.'

Men about Dublin know that my girls are picky. They don't just take every man. Whoever he is gets a quick examination in the hall, and no girl does any man she doesn't choose. That's just the way I work. All girls are given the midwife lecture about the French letters and the pennyroyal. The doctor is a regular visitor (in more ways than one). He rarely helps me in my work, but does send on a few women in bother.

Men are told they must be clean, and I don't allow abusive fuckers back in. Of course, some idiots take any kind of creature upstairs. But, so long as all is quiet, I'm happy.

'Molly stole my regular cause I told her he was handsome and that he'd kiss her down below.'

I sigh. 'That's how it goes.'

This girl is from the country somewhere. She won't stay long. None of them do, apart from Molly and Tess. Also, if they give me any kind of bother, I get them to leave. My heart isn't into running a knocking shop. With only two or three girls at any one time, I'm not exactly a big business. I keep things nice and quiet with enough to do us. But I don't have the true heart for it. There are too many men about. Too many women fighting over blaggards who should be in the real world or with their wives.

'They're paying for a hole, nothing more.'

'And titties. I've got good titties. He was gorgeous. Tall, clean and young, he was.'

I think I know the buck she means now. He came knocking a few days ago. I presumed him a soldier, as his shoes were gleaming at me from the doorstep…

He stepped inside and said, 'Hello, I'm lookin' for a girl.'

'Good place to come.' I looked at his lovely arms and his high chest. Those blue eyes of about twenty-five were determined in their quest. 'All my girls are busy. Would you like a cup of tea?'

He shuffled his feet, wondering whether I was serious or not, and looked at my breasts, then at my face and grinned. 'Please.'

I swayed my arse ahead of him to the kitchen and pointed to a chair. Setting out the mugs, I noticed the trousers on him were pressed with a crease down the middle. The green jumper was tight with a crisp white shirt peeking over it. His hair shorter than short and yet slicked with something to make it gleam like those shoes.

'Soldier?'

'Yes. How did you know?'

The way he took the milk bottle from me to set it on the table stirred the place in my pants. It has been a long time since a man did anything for Peggy Bowden.

'I'm on leave.'

'It's not a bad day,' I said, but then, the rain started to pitter patter the kitchen window. We both smiled, knowing I wasn't one for the outdoors anymore. His handsomeness was smooth like his jaw, and his lips curled at me again.

'You're a handsome lad. No nice girls at the dances?'

He smiled gloriously at me, reminding me of how a young fella smiles at a statue of Our Lady. One of awe but also intrigue, as to whether she is really a virgin at all. 'I need one in a hurry.' That crooked look in his eye that made him respectful but lusting all at once.

'Why? Does love not take time?' I said, knowing full well men don't need love for nothing.

'It's only…I'm not on leave long. Nice girls are a bother.'

'Nice girls?'

It was his turn to blush. 'You know what I mean.'

'You're young. It shouldn't be too much bother.'

'It is. You've got to play games. I just want a woman.'

He made me curious. I rarely talk with the men that make their way to number thirty-four.

'Why pay for it?'

'Why shouldn't I?' Young and virile, his confidence was enough to make me shudder. 'I have the money and you have the girls.' He wasn't in the least embarrassed.

'Business.' I smiled and opened the top button of my blouse. 'What kind of girl were you after?'

Those blue eyes watched as my buttons opened and only then did he look at my face and said, 'I thought you were in charge –'

'I am. But I pick some for myself. It's been a while.'

'Well, if I'm not getting any tea…' His grin was wanting, and he stood to walk the few steps towards me.

I locked the door, but he lightly caught my wrist as I turned the key in the lock.

'How much?'

I put my finger to his lips and his other hand under my open blouse. His arm curled me into him like my Mick used to do. It was lovely the way he slipped that clothed arm in around my back. As I looked up at him, his mouth found mine. He knew how to open brassieres. He was under it in a flash, his fingers on my nipples and his mouth still on mine.

That tongue tasting like beer and cigarettes and the moans of him marvellous to a horny girl like me. My hands gripped his arse, and through his trousers, the bulge of him was against my leg. The kisses were passionate like in the pictures – full, open mouths with a frenzied breathlessness. He groped on until he had the skirt off me and the pants as well. The blouse and bra hung on me as he nuzzled my neck and his hand slid between my legs.

There's no way to describe the longing that was on me. None at all. Deep and fast his fingers felt. They slid around me, through me, melted me into the scratchy wool of that jumper of his.

'Here?' he asked, and I thought he meant the spot where he had his finger.

'Yes,' I moaned, never wanting him to stop.

'You want to fuck in the kitchen?'

'Yes.'

I opened his trousers slipping my hands inside. His trousers clattered on the floor, with a muttered 'Jesus,' as he toed off his shoes. To feel a young man hard for me again was better than anything.

'Jesus has nothing to do with this. Although you're an answer to any woman's prayers.'

The kissing he did to me then was animal-like. It's funny how men like to feel a woman has waited for them, prayed for him – her perfect man. Though, I suppose I had waited for him. He was worth the wait because, Jesus…He ran his tongue the length of me, down over my breasts, down my belly and into…into there. Tasting me and kissing me like he did on my mouth. I put my foot up on the chair, leaning to it, anchoring myself in case I'd lose my sanity with the feeling of it all. I thought of the nuns and wondered did they ever get to feel like this. I thought of the Virgin Mary herself and how disgusted she'd be about a man's head between my legs and me with a leg up on a chair. But he licked on, groaning away and driving me wild.

Suddenly, he stood to pull off his jumper and fumbled, cursing at the buttons on his shirt. I shrugged off my blouse and opened bra. I stood there in all my glory, watching him.

'Got anything to wear on himself?' I pointed to what was looking up at me.

'Don't the women get them?' he asked, still fussing at the shirt. Then, with one rip of a few buttons, his chest appeared. It was young and lean, with a good bit of hair to prove he wasn't a teenager.

The window got a glance, but he pulled me close to him and away from it. The kitchen table at my back was moving on the floor, scraping along as I tried to steady us both. That kissing and those hands taking me away somewhere wonderful. The table moved across a few more inches to lean against the cupboards.

'I need you now,' he grunted in my ear and lifted me to perch my naked behind on the table. He was inside me before I could blink and the thumping of him into me was like a dog at a fair.

It was over in seconds with him panting, heaving and cursing. I couldn't blame the young fellow. The heat off us made even me lose the run of myself. There was the usual spurt out of him and a sigh and that was it.

Over it was.

'Christ,' he said, cleaning himself with his underpants and pulling them on.

There were no words in my head.

'You're good for an auld wan,' he grinned at me and pulled on his trousers.

'Thanks,' I muttered, hauling my skirt on and finding my blouse.

'I'll see you again.' The shirt covered his hair. 'You're worth a few more bob for letting me fuck you in a kitchen.' His socks were still on, so he sat to open his shoelaces. 'How much do I owe you? Now, don't be bad to me – you enjoyed that too. I could tell.' He winked, and his blue eyes were full of pride.

'That one will be on the house,' I said, knowing full well he'd think himself a ram for sure.

'God, you're a good lay.'

His arms went around me and squeezed me to him. Those arms now annoyed me.

I squirmed out of his embrace saying, 'Only so much is free this time.' He seemed unconcerned, and I watched him tie his shoes. I had to turn my back on him to hide the tear that somehow found the corner of my eye.

The hallway felt long, and my arse didn't sway at him as I saw him to the door. I just wanted him gone. Didn't want to think about how I gave myself away because I wanted to feel like a woman and have a man inside me for a few seconds.

'What's your name?' he asked as he stood out into the street.

'Doesn't matter.' I closed the door.

I shook myself back into the present.

It must be that soldier who's still causing me heartache. The voice of Tess is tiring me. 'That young soldier was mine, Peggy. I saw him leaving. He said he was already seen to.'

'If you go out gallivanting, you cannot expect me to entertain your men.'

'I wasn't gallivanting. I went for cigarettes. Mary was busy upstairs with that new clerk in the bank, so it must have been that bitch Molly.'

'Must of been,' says I, wiping the edge of the kitchen table.

Chapter 3

I hear the familiar clip of our best punter's shoes on the tiles inside the door.

'Professor.'

There's a man with him, and he's hovering above all of us. He's a massive bulk of a man by anyone's standards.

'This is the Big Lad. We call him Tiny. He works for me.'

I smile. This beast has no teeth and is grinning.

'Russian or summat, he is, not a word of English but understands enough to do.'

'Off a ship?'

I should know not to ask the Professor too many questions, but he answers me with, 'Molly about?'

'She is. And waiting on you.'

'Tiny will wait in the kitchen.' He points up the stairs. 'Usual room?'

Those thin legs in their expensive stripy suit leap a few steps at a time. It's unlike him to show excitement – he usually pretends he's above the rest of us and lacks any emotion other than anger.

'So, how do you like workin' for himself?' I ask the big fella, thinking if I speak slowly he might get what I'm saying. A gummy smile greets me, and there's food stuck in the flaps of red weeping flesh.

'Teeth?' I motion to my mouth and hit my front tooth with my nail.

He makes a fist and launches it towards his own jaw. Sure enough, there are bruises on the underside of his chin that make his thick neck look colourful.

'Oh.' I raise my eyebrows and decide it's definitely potato in the gaps I can see. 'Tea?'

His bulky frame nearly fills the hallway as he ambles to the kitchen. The smell of him is odd but not unpleasant, and there's something nice about the way he waits to be told to sit. There is nothing to say, and he isn't fond of my tea. The way his large nose wrinkles makes me laugh. The silence is terrible for a chatty bird like me, so I leave Tiny in the kitchen.

I need a stroll. The air in the house seems stale, and although Dublin's chimneys don't worry about my head or lungs, I think the air outside will do me good.

The day, of course, doesn't know what kind of a day it is. Summer time that is deeply grey and mizzling with an odd good wetting skiff of rain. People always have a place to go, don't they? Flitting over the footpaths, rushing to somewhere or other, caring nothing for the poor fecker huddled in the doorway next to the pub. It's not often I take the time to think of the hoards that pass our door every day. Not often I take the time to catch the eye of a passing gentleman who bobs his head and holds his hat to greet me.

Molly will be flat on her back by now, letting that weasel inside her. It isn't good for the soul to have men do what they like to us. I manage to avoid it, and yet, I do miss the feel of a man on top of me. I find I long for someone to want me. It's seldom that men want a whore for a chat and a stroll. It's hard for us to shake the title. Yet, a man can call once a week – once a frigging day and be a beaut of a man. The injustice makes me sick. Some of them come just up the street from their wives and ask for it with little shame. Sometimes, the bastards even look for a discount.

Men like the Professor are rare. Boyos that can actually bring more than a cock to our lives. The Professor is dangerous. He's called the Professor because he stole or forged some paper from Trinity College to make out he was educated.

Tess mentioned, 'His father's a grocer. He's disgusted with him. He's a bad son of a bitch involved in anything shady this side of the Liffey. Kills and maims his own men, knocked bigger, more important men down to get where he is today. He's been top of the tree about these parts longer than most.'

He had taken a shine to Molly and ironically followed her home from Mass. Soon as I laid eyes on the weasel, with his signature trilby hat, I'd known him as the one everyone feared.

He'd sat on in the parlour, saying, 'All about here owe me money for…protection. No one mentioned you girls.'

I'd been told he would sooner or later find us, and luckily, he wasn't averse to my simple plan.

'Molly for free once a fortnight – if you look after us.'

'Once a week at least.'

'No.'

He jumped up and held my face in one of his slimy hands and said, 'No one says no to me.'

Through gritted teeth, I said, 'It's up to Molly.'

He'd flung me from him, and Molly had looked at him from head to toe, like he was a prize bullock. Walking around him like a man does to a beast at a fair or a man does to a woman. I loved her so much for that. Loved the way she managed to say nothing but treat him like an animal.

'Once a fortnight and I get presents.' She looked well pleased with her arrangement. Her red hair bounced as she tossed herself on the couch, he grinned and sat next to her.

'All the presents in the world for you, Molly. And if you're good, I'll pay you as well. Time is money, after all.' He rubbed his thin moustache down with his fingers and slicked back his hair. 'You girls will have no bother if people know I come here.'

He'd been right. We never really have any trouble. Even the Gardaí don't come knocking, unless they want a girl too. The peace he brings is grand, but as usual there's a price to everything: the guilt I have, for one thing.

'He likes her innocence,' Tess said. 'Some of them say she's like having a virgin all the time. Think she's like a child with nice breasts.'

'For fuck sake.'

I had thought it terrible until I thought of Mary-Ann at home who'd been sent away for mentioning that Father Lavelle's curate had liked to do things to her. 'Why would anyone want a child?'

But men like the Professor can have whatever they want, and there are no priests to destroy the likes of him.

When there were complaints about my black eyes years ago, he (the husband) had purred, 'Something for the church.' The priest had stuffed the bundles into his cassock and almost pissed himself with excitement – over my fucking money.

The bench is a little damp, but my skirt is thick so I sit to watch a few children kicking a football. By rights, I should've had a few of them by now, but thankfully, my body doesn't seem to want to make any.

If I could expand my business, there would be hope of me making something of myself. Moving more upmarket and getting better clients. Rich, paying boyos, like the Professor, would be good for us. Men like him have property or know people who have good places all over the city. Women like me need to be tough. I've been out of prison for a while now, so I'm stronger, ready to be the Peggy Bowden with fancy clothes and a car again.

I flick my hair out from under my collar and pretend I'm in the MG, leaning back letting the air into my scalp at the back of my neck, feeling my hair blowing in the breeze on the open road just like it used to do.

'Want more, Peggy,' Mammy used to say. 'Work hard and always want more. Not more than you should have, don't want too much.'

Tiny is sleeping by the range back in number thirty-four. All is quiet upstairs, and so I take the sweeping brush to the hall's tiles. It's unusual for the Professor to stay this long with Molly.

'Time is money,' he jokes when he's leaving here most weeks. He likes cigars and the smoke from them lingers like the impression he leaves. A bad taste in the mouth, he is.

I'd asked Molly, 'What's he like?'

She'd shrugged and hadn't seemed bothered either way about him. I'd only seen him without his clothes by accident when the door lay ajar once. His bony back was covered in funny marks, and he had a tattoo on his ankle.

'Do you hate fucking him?' I asked Molly.

She'd shook her curls, and I'd asked no more, pleased he didn't make her skin crawl like he made mine do sometimes. But he still prefers Molly. I keep sweeping, hoping to speak to him. The mop and the bucket clang, and Tiny doesn't waken. He is snoring soundly and scratching his balls occasionally.

The floor is dry by the time I hear the clip of the Professor's shoes on the stairs. I nudge the big fella and check my reflection in the small hall mirror and totter out to say, 'All good?'

To say the man looks pleased with himself is an understatement. The eyes gleaming, his dentist-cared-for teeth on show and the swagger of him painful as he says, 'Never better, Peggy. Never better.'

'Good.'

He glances at his pocket watch as Tiny appears at my elbow. He smooths out his waistcoat and brushes his sleeves with his thin hands.

I breathe deeply and say, 'I aim to move premises. Know of anywhere?'

He looks at me like I crawled out from under something. He lingers there for an agonising few seconds. Then says, 'Why move, pretty lady?'

'I aim to get more girls. More quality customers like yourself. I also have a side-line business...'

His eyes widen and my heart falls a little.

'Side-line? You never said.'

'It's not worth mentioning. But if I got better premises?'

'Oh yes.' His beady eyes squint. 'You went inside for selling babies.'

'I didn't sell them,' I stammer. 'I helped...'

'Course you did.'

'I don't go near children anymore.'

'So, what is this side-line business, then?'

'I give women…relief from…being in the family way.'

He laughs. It bursts from him like water from a long disused tap. 'Fuck! You're a butcher?' The lines beside his eyes are deep now crinkled like his humour at something awful.

'It's easy for the likes of you to laugh. Some women are desperate.'

'And you do them a good turn?'

I'm suddenly unsure of where this all is headed. He didn't strike me as a religious nut, despite him meeting Molly at Mass.

'A good turn, indeed, a handsomely paid one?'

'There's hardly any coming these days. With me here and all…I'm not as respectable.'

He laughs again and takes out a cigar. 'Respectable, eh?' He fumbles to find his matches. 'So, you want to go upmarket?'

'Yes.'

'You want to get the bastards out of rich bitches?'

'I used to be a midwife. I know my stuff. I like number thirty-four, but think I could be better. Make things better for myself and Molly.'

'Do you now? Molly mightn't want to go with you.'

'Molly is family.'

'You whore out your family?' he sneers, finding the matches from inside his pocket. 'You're some doll, eh?'

'Molly chooses…'

'Leave it with me. I'll see what I can do.' He nods up at Tiny, and they go to leave. Suddenly, he turns and touches my cheek with his unlit cigar. 'I might find other ways we could do business. Whore like you with brains and ambition? Who knows what we could do together.'

He laughs again stepping outside, the big fellow glancing up and down the street, that thick neck owl-like, checking for danger. I can see why people want to kill the fucker.

Chapter 4

'That Professor doesn't love me,' Molly mentions at breakfast. She's hunched over her porridge but not eating much.

Tess giggles, her features not pretty at all.

I throw her a look of steel, while comforting Molly with, 'No. He only loves himself, Molly darlin'…'

'None of them want tae marry.'

Molly plays with her hair, and Tess giggles again. The head is thumping on me as usual, and Molly looks too sad at this hour of the morning.

'I'm not married…now,' I say.

''Cause no one is asking ya,' Molly says with a pout on her lips.

Tess really laughs, and I fling the dishcloth at her.

'One man did once. Mick Moran was his name. God bless him. The other fecker wasn't a choice, I'll grant you that. But being married isn't all sunshine, Molly.'

'I wanta be married.'

'They'll not want your Fionn,' Tess chirps in. 'Men only want their own children.'

Molly looks at me intently.

'Like lions, they don't want another lion's cubs,' Tess adds. 'Irish men want virgins.'

'Like Our Lady?'

Tess laughs again in her ugly way and shuffles on her chair, looking at me to help the nonsense.

'Irish mothers want good girls for their sons. You'd want a nice quiet girl for Fionn.'

'I want Fionn for myself.'

'Exactly.' Tess shrugs and eats her porridge.

'Men think we're bad,' I say, rubbing my forehead.

'Why do they want us, then?' She pokes me as if it will make my answers better. 'Why do they tell me Molly is their favourite?'

Tess sighs. 'They want us. But don't want us.'

'Professor says he needs me.'

'He needs you for a quick poke, Molly. He doesn't *need* you forever. He doesn't need to marry you.' It sounds harsh the way Tess explains it all, and yet, there's no other way to say it.

'But…' Molly looks into her tea. 'I am good.'

'You are good, darlin', yes. It's them that are bad. Christ, at this hour of the morning, it's all very confusing.' I try to make light of it but know Molly is all in a whirl about something.

'All is bad.' The mug in her hand gets a clunk onto the table. It's the way Molly has of summing everything up very well in such a few words that gets under my skin every time.

'Yes. All is shit.'

'But you said you'd make it all better?'

This is directed at me. I had told her that. She is right.

Tess gets there before me and says, 'She lied to you. Nothing ever gets better.'

Molly rises to her feet, up off her chair in one movement. It topples over.

'I didn't lie, Tess.' I swipe at Tess-the-bitch with the tea towel, but Molly is gone out of the room before I can say much else.

'They all want Molly,' Tess grunts. 'Professor, the soldier, the sailors. Jesus, if a candlestick maker arrived, he'd want her too. The rest of us need a chance.'

There's a lump in my throat. I know how she feels. Although I don't want to be ridden for money, it would be nice if a man asked for me once in a while. If one wanted me, for being me. It's odd how us women get. Don't want to be objects, but then object when we aren't looked at like an ornament on display.

'Sure, I'm on the shelf at this stage,' I mutter, and Tess doesn't disagree. I could really slap her. I'm not that old in the grand scheme of life. I've lived a fair bit, that's all. 'There's a big difference between being old and living life well,' I say to the wall more than Tess.

She's an odd-looking creature, with a hooked nose and funny eyes, her spectacles thick, if she wears them, and she has bad breath sometimes. I'm not overly surprised Molly gets more asking for her.

The other girls are all too sporadic in their trade. Some come and go, depending on the prick they think will find them a better life.

I took a knife to one of them whore-stealers a few months back and cut his ear good and proper. Since then, none of the local scum have come back, but Tess also said, 'Professor had a word, no doubt. In case they steal Molly.'

Tess washes her bowl and spoon, humming to herself. She's stayed longer than most, and I wonder sometimes about her large family in Carlow.

'Did you get any letters recently?' I ask.

'Bitch,' she spits. 'Don't you take the post in most mornings off the floor? You know they don't want to know about me.'

'Jesus. Sorry for asking.'

The face of her mellows slightly. 'Sorry. Just I heard ya say to the Professor you're thinking of moving.'

'Course I'd take you, Tess,' I lie. I would rather have a girl with good eyesight and better teeth. 'Sure, you are like the furniture.'

'Are you taking the old furniture? There's nothing much in this place.'

I don't answer her but slip on up the hall, thinking of how awfully perceptive she can be for an uneducated, country whore.

Chapter 5

There is a commotion and naked girls on the landing. I can hear male voices, and in the whiskey haze, there's a few swinging cocks.

'They're fighting,' one of the girl's shouts. 'For fuck sake. Drunk, they are. Do something, Peggy.'

I go back into my room and rummage around half asleep for the hunting rifle I bought at a big estate auction in Kildare. It is cold to the touch, and my fingers curl around it. I poke it into the landing mayhem.

A male voice shouts, 'She's got a gun.'

'If you don't shut up, I'll use it. There's to be no men here overnight. Shut the fuck up, or get out.'

I peer into the half-light. There before me are three men, mostly naked, and Tess, another lassie called Mary, and my Molly looking all flushed.

'She was in the tub again, Peggy. Getting her boyo to carry up buckets of our hot water – them on the range for the morning.'

Molly does look damp and clean, and there's a blond fella with a bucket and him in his underwear.

'Get back to your beds, the lot of ye,' I holler and cock the rifle higher. 'There should be no men here at this time of night.'

Most disappear, and I close my eyes to stay in my half sleep and turn to go back to bed.

'It isn't even loaded,' taunts one of the males.

I turn back, and he's visible in the light from the street. I aim the rifle again. Unsure of whether it is even capable of firing, I pull the trigger and take a splinter out of the floorboard not far from his bare foot.

'Now,' I scream, but his arse is away before I can even finish the word.

'Mad bitch.'

The leap of him makes me grin and wakens me totally. I know the neighbours will alert the sergeant's men, and I'll have explaining to do but my joy at his fear is fun.

Sergeant Joe Bushnell is less amused in the morning.

'A rifle?' he asks me for the third time.

'Family heirloom. Didn't know it would even fire. Went off by accident.'

'Have you registered a firearm?' he asks, trying to be stern. 'Let me see it. You know you cannot have an uncertified weapon here. We're always looking for those with guns and holding guns for the IRA.'

'IRA, me arse – I don't have time for politics.'

'They don't have much time for it either.'

'Don't be giving out. Sure, we need something for protection.'

The vulnerable woman act usually works on Sergeant Bushnell.

'Get me this weapon and don't be firing it again. Do you hear me now?'

'It's probably all out of bullets. I'm keeping it, though. You're not taking it. Cost me a good few pounds, did that rifle.'

'I thought it was an heirloom?'

I'm away up the stairs kicking myself for not lying well enough.

He turns the old weapon over and over in his large hands and takes a good long look at it. 'Old all right, Peggy. But it's still loaded. I'm taking out the bullets.'

'Sure, what good is it without them?' I ask, but wish to heavens he'd hurry up. No man will want to see a lawman in our kitchen.

'Anything else to tell me?' he asks, handing it back and placing the bullets on the table to roll about.

'Not a thing, no.'

'Professor bothering ye at all?'

'Who?'

'Arrah now, Peggy.'

'No. He's good to number thirty-four.'

'Is he now?'

'Would you be jealous, Sergeant?'

'Course not.' He pulls at this jacket and makes the buttons all stand in a neater row. 'If you could tell me anything, the law would be grateful.'

'I may be many things…but a snitch is not one of them.' I'm angry at him. Very cross, indeed. 'Now, I've work to be doing.' I point to the front door.

'It's me who should be cross, Peggy. Me, who helps keep things all quiet at the station for number thirty-four. Don't be dragging attention here again now. Do you hear me?'

'I hear you.' I start making my way down the hall to get rid of him, the bullets in my fist and him not looking for them anyhow.

Tess appears when he's away. 'He has a soft spot for you, Peggy.'

'Stop it now. We know each other a long time is all.'

'I thought you weren't old?'

With the rifle on the table, I'm nearly tempted to use it on her. I lift it and stomp up the stairs like a child.

The door gets a pounding as I pass it, and I need to prop the rifle beside it to open the latch. There, like a drowned rat, is the young buck who comes to see Molly most days and looks like the fella on the landing last night.

'Is she in?'

'She's busy.' Tess passes the door with clean sheets.

'How come you're all wet?'

He snorts and tries but fails to get past me.

'We told you, she's busy.'

He isn't very old. Blond-haired and blue-eyed so he seems about sixteen but possibly is in his twenties.

'How come you're so wet?'

'I fell in the canal.' He pulls at his shirt to move it out from his muscles. He's a labourer; he has concrete caked on his shoes.

'You need to go home and get cleaned up, then.' I close the door on him.

He pounds again on it like a madman, hollering and shouting up at the windows for Molly. The sergeant not being long away, and the neighbours scared following the gunshots, I open the door with a flourish.

'Fuck off home, young fella.'

He looks stunned.

'I'll ban you from coming to see her at all, if there's any more of your nonsense.'

'Is it true she sees the Professor?' His eyes fill with tears, and I wonder if his own father shouldn't give him a talking to about the ways of the world.

'Who told you that?'

'Some big buck with no teeth threw me into the canal and told me that Molly was taken.'

'Molly is owned by nobody. Not you. Not the Professor. So get home with yourself now.'

'I love her,' he whispers, coming up the steps again closer to me so no one can hear of his love.

'You're young. Lots to learn. Molly needs someone to look about her. Care for her. Are you ready for all that?'

He nods, the hair wet and dripping now onto his face.

'She's a whore, young fella. Not a pure girl to take home to your ma.'

'Don't call her that.' He wipes his nose with the back of his hand.

'The Professor gave you a warning.'

'Molly's mine.' Those blue eyes are brimming over now. Those eyes are too much for me to watch. Crying folk always get to me.

'Fuck off home and leave us be for now.' I slam the door.

'He makes me tingle,' Molly says when I ask about him.

'Tingle?' I peel the spuds and hand her another knife.

'Nice.' She peels one whole potato before she adds, 'He wants to marry me.'

My heart sinks. As much as I want Molly to be happy, this is the worst time for her to find a fiancé. With the Professor liking her and maybe lifting us up in the world, she can't think of leaving me now.

'Has he means to keep you? Does he work?'

Those red curls nod, and she doesn't look at me.

'Did you meet his friends or family yet?'

A shake of those curls and I get relief. Once Molly is known to them, things might change.

'And Fionn? Does he want him?'

Those blue eyes bore a hole through me. 'Course.'

The rest of the pot of spuds are on to boil before I chance to say anything else. 'The Professor likes you.'

'He'll not marry me.'

'But he likes you, and he is a dangerous man to make angry.'

I know she's listening even though she is taking the knives and forks from the drawer and the plates down from the dresser. 'Did you tell him about this young fella?'

She shakes her head. Molly usually says little unless asked, and the Professor knows something because the young fellow has had a dip in the canal.

'The Professor is jealous.' I take her hand. 'Men get angry when jealous. People say he does terrible things to those who make him angry.'

She unbuttons her blouse and turns around. There on her back are two great big long slashes. I reach out, but she winces.

'Did the Professor do this?' I turn her round and ask her again, 'Did he do this?'

Her eyes flit all over the place.

'What happened?' I lift the box from the dresser with the iodine and dab it on despite her protests. 'What happened, darlin'?'

'He doesn't love me.'

'Did you ask him about love?'

Her shoulders droop forward. 'Yes.'

I dab the gash that looks the angriest. It doesn't look like the skin will break or bleed. 'But you don't love him?'

34

'I might if he'd marry me.'

My stomach feels sick. It's the way all women go, myself included. Marriage being the success we strive for. Whether it is a good marriage or a bad one, we're better off stuck to a man with a ring around our finger to prove we've achieved in life. Molly's no different and is using all she can to fulfil the only ambition she knows.

'He did this because you asked if he loved you?'

'Yes.'

'So, you won't ask him again?'

'No.'

'Good girl.' I pull up her blouse and turn her around to do up her buttons. 'You've got me. I'll always look after you.'

'Better, you said.' She pulls away from me.

'Yes, but it takes time. Time to make enough to move us out of here.' I'm also thinking it will take time for the Professor to find us a place and for me to tackle him again about bettering our situation. 'Molly, you cannot fall out of favour with the Professor or we're stuck and in trouble too.'

She starts to hum her lullaby.

'He's a powerful man. If anyone can get us out of here to something better, it's him. And you can make it happen.'

She stops humming.

'He'll not marry me.'

'No. But he likes you. He got angry, that's all. He will want you in a nicer place. Just leave the asking to me.'

She nods. 'Fionn too. He'll like him too?'

'Yes.' I know she means can we have Fionn live with us, but now isn't the time for the truth in its entirety.

'Tess?'

'And Tess.'

She seems brighter suddenly. Like the clouds have parted, and she can see the sun. Her face loosens, and she almost smiles. 'But let me do the talking. You don't want the Professor to hit you again.'

I get a jab of guilt. Strong and long, it sits in my belly. I see myself whored out to a brute, thinking if I said and did the right things, he'd love me. Until now, I was thinking only of the wrong Molly did by asking silly questions. But she was right to ask about her future and wonder why she was made do what he wanted for nothing much in return. I do this to her, and I should know better. But what can I do right now? We need to work together on things. I will think things through, while she keeps him happy. We'll get to a happier place, if I work us as a team. It'll happen soon, I'll make sure of it.

'He was bad to hit you,' I whisper. 'It was wrong.'

'I won't see him again?' Those blue eyes look so hopeful. 'You make it better.'

'If we're to get him to take us somewhere nice, then you need to keep him sweet on you.'

Her eyes fill with tears, like the boyo's on the doorstep.

'And you need to get rid of that young fella, too, that keeps calling.'

The tears fall, and she doesn't hide them or mop them up. She stares into the distance, and I feel so bad at what I am asking of her.

'No,' she says. 'No.'

That's all she says. I know she's keeping her options open. Whether she's consciously thinking it or just aware that any one man who might marry her is better than the life she has now.

'OK, Molly…but the Professor might get rid of him if you don't.'

She shrugs.

'Let me do the thinking and the talking.'

She nods and starts to hum. None of her dinner is eaten, and she sits in a daze making my heart sore.

Her distant behaviour lasts even when we are in the parlour that I rent out sometimes. It can hold a small bed as well as our chairs and a wireless. But sometimes, in the late evenings, we all sit together and get lost in the musical programme on the wireless.

Tess is plaiting Molly's hair so it will have even more bounce and curl in the morning. Molly is on the floor in front of her like a little girl. It is nice to see her relaxed and looked after. Even if she's ignoring me.

'How are things now?' I sit into the best high-backed chair that I know has seen more action than most beds.

'We're chatting about how the married ones don't care if their wives like "it."'

I can see Him home from the pub humping onto me and telling me, 'Don't look at me and spread them legs.'

'I like doing it,' Molly says.

'We know you do. But you can't like it *all* the time?' Tess says.

Molly shakes her head and ruins that particular skein of hair in Tess's hands.

'I hate some of them,' Tess snorts, 'but, sure, that's life. There's only a few that'll want to see you're all right. Most don't care.'

I am thinking of the soldier and his kissing. He was unique all right.

'Like that soldier fella. He's a *lover.*' Tess swoons all comical, and Molly giggles. Tess holds Molly's hair tighter and pulls her head back and says, 'Like you don't know, ya wagon. Stealing him from me.'

Molly shakes her head again.

'Don't lie. He said he was seen ta, and he was askin' for you. Like all of them that are any good. They all want Miss Molly.'

Molly doesn't speak but picks at her nails. The song on the radio makes me sing along. '*Mona Lisa…men have loved you.*'

The arguing better not start in earnest. I don't fancy admitting it was me that had him in the kitchen for free. Tess finishes the braid, and it looks all neat.

'You could be a hairdresser, and you're a good cook.'

'Make more money at this. Quiet these days, though, eh? Professor might be scaring them off. Or the sergeant calling.'

'Nothing we can do about either.'

'Suppose not.'

'I'm gonna get Fionn soon,' Molly says to us both like it is special news she has kept hidden.

Tess throws her eyes to heaven. 'There's no talking to the likes of you.'

'I make things better myself.'

There's a confidence to her I haven't seen before. An innocent confidence that she can better herself, all by herself. As if us women can do much to drag ourselves out of the gutter.

'All by yourself?' Tess asks.

'Tired of waiting.'

'Aren't we all,' Tess replies. 'Fed up of fucking.'

'What are you going to do?' I ask Molly. 'The Professor won't be too happy if you flit off on him, and I don't fancy dealing with him if that happens.'

Molly's beautiful face scrunches up, and she picks her nails some more. 'He isn't my problem.'

It's the way she says it. She's so brave. Like a new wave of strength has caught her into it and is bashing us off the shore of common sense, just because it can.

'Aren't you all cocksure?' Tess rolls her eyes. 'If he gets pissed off, he's all of our problem.'

Molly shrugs, and my gut clenches. She's up to something, and yet, I can't blame her. I know she won't have thought things through to the end, though, and whatever is in her head is not possible in the real world.

'Think or talk to us before you do anything.'

She shakes her head. 'My life.'

'Peggy hasn't been good to you or nothing?' Tess says.

Molly bites at the corner of her ring finger's nail.

'I care about you, Molly. More than anyone.' I gulp at the truth of it. 'I worry about you. Look out for you.'

'You use me,' she says and gets up off the floor in front of Tess. 'You,' she points at me, 'use me.'

It's only a few words, and boy, do they hurt. They hit me between the eyes and sting like a nettle.

'She ain't that stupid,' Tess says, changing the radio station and filling the room with static noise.

Chapter 6

Dublin city breezes in through the open windows and doors. With the saucepans and sheets all washed, the May sunshine eases my hangover and makes all seem better. I got myself and the girls a few beers, and we're out in the sunshine, slurping from mugs amongst the sheets in case the neighbours see us. My greasy hair is all tied up in a scarf, I feel so cool and content. Billie Holiday croons from upstairs. Molly's favourite song is on, and she is squawking, '*Summertime and the living is easy.*'

We all smirk as she roars on and comes dancing around the back scullery; a flimsy floral summer dress stuck to her between her shoulders, and she's shaking those red curls as she moves to the rhythm.

'*Your daddy's rich and your ma is good lookin'.*'

The concrete steps are warm. My hands love the feel of the heat from the usually cold stone. I'm so glad to see Molly happy for a change. It lifts everything in me to see her in this form.

Molly puts the song on again, and we all laugh. She is one reason I couldn't escape. I know she won't leave her Fionn in Cavan. She talks non-stop about 'when I'm rich.'

I've hidden her stash. She has shown off her money before and lost it. There is still not enough to make any great difference to her situation.

Tess comes back outside, muttering, 'That young fella is back.'

She means the drowned canal rat who is going to spoil things for us all. I can sense it, like a fortune teller looking into a crystal ball. I can hear the shit-stirrer in the kitchen as I let the sun warm my face.

'He'll marry me,' Molly said this morning again, and I know she thinks, *I'll get Fionn.*

I'm tired of telling her that won't happen. But the music is gone now, and I can sense that Molly has stopped dancing.

Tess asks, 'Were you ever in love, Peggy?'

Usually, I'm guarded, but today, I'm tired of my mask, so I say, 'I can see myself all those years ago when Mick Moran walked into my life. He wanted to marry me. I should have let him.'

They sit looking at me so I go on. 'I wonder where he is now. The newspapers were in full swing about my fall from grace. But fair play to him, he did visit me… I imagine he breathed a sigh of relief when I told him to forget all about me.'

'Why?'

'I was in prison, for one thing, and I never wanted to marry again. Married women can't work. But how I loved the breath off Mick. It tickled my neck and all the way down to me arse. A fine man, he was. I let him call on me for a long while before I gave in to them dimples of his. I waited patiently on his invitations to the pictures or a dance on a Saturday. I loved his Mammy's healing roast on a Sunday, and the rest of his family were grand. It was so normal. For once, Peggy Bowden was living the life of a normal girl. I was so happy…'

Out of nowhere, we hear Molly scream. Loud and long, it curls out into the back yard. We all jump. There's another holler. It isn't a noise humans usually make. It's a loud, unnatural noise that echoes out and around the house.

When I step into the kitchen, there's blood on the kitchen floor. The girls start their drama of gasping and shrieking. I warn them, 'Stay quiet and outside until I call ye.'

Molly is huddled under the table, swaying a little.

'Molly?' I hiss. 'What's happened?'

I stick my head under the table but cannot work out where exactly the blood starts and ends. It is pooled in a few places and is under the table as well. There's no sign of her new boyo. It seems to be Molly's blood.

I shut the kitchen windows to the world and ask, 'Molly, what's happened? Where is he?' There is no answer until I ask quite a few times.

'Gone.'

'Is it you that's bleeding?'

She shakes her head. 'No.' But I've known her to plop out a baby on the kitchen floor and be surprised as to what it was.

'You sure?'

'Stabbed him.'

I need to kneel in the biggest pool of blood. 'Where is he now?'

She shrugs and attempts to push her hair out of the way, smearing a bloodstained hand across her cheek. The wretchedness of her almost makes me cry.

'Come out of there. Let me see you. I'm worried.' I try to pull her arm a little, but she knocks my hand off her. 'Is he definitely away?' I'm fearful that a half-dead man might still harm us both.

'Yes. Gone. Won't marry me. Doesn't want Fionn.' Her blue eyes have a glazed look that I haven't seen before. She looks away from me. What I presume is the knife clatters on to the tiles. Her legs move up so she can cuddle them.

'Who needs a man, Molly? Sure, you have me and the girls.' I'm sitting fully in the mess, waiting for a knock on the door or for the boyo to appear with the sergeant or a wound that is fatal. There is a lot of blood for such little noise.

Molly ignores me and rocks to and fro and starts her lullaby.

'Please come out. Tell me what happened. Please?'

Her ignoring me is terrible. I'm always the one who can reach her, get her to comply. 'Molly,' I say over and over in various tones until my patience starts to go. 'I'm going to have to clear up this mess. You silly girl.' I try to sound motherly, but she just sings even louder.

Myself and the other lassies clear the evidence off the floor, and she scrambles over into the corner near the range when I poke her out with the mop. She looks unhurt herself, and the girls make eyes at me as we watch the red water swirls in the enamel kitchen sink.

My hands have started a nervous shake. Even with a swig of brandy from the bottle, they don't stop. Molly hasn't been this violent before. There's always been a taste of her oddness, but nothing that drew blood or continued this long.

'Do ya think she killed him?' one girl asks.

'Wouldn't think so, or someone would be calling.'

'She needs to be taken away.'

'You'll go before she does,' I say.

I hope that my Molly comes back to me soon. The door gets a serious rapping. I hold my breath as the girls go to answer it. Staying in hallway, I listen. It's only a man looking for a poke. A sigh of relief leaves me. Back in the kitchen, Molly is making tea. Her skirt tails and all down her left side is messed with red splodges. I pull on a clean dress that I had drying above the range and stand with my hands shaking on my hips.

'Talk to me.'

The silence is filled with the boiling kettle.

'We'll be all right. Just you wait and see.'

The knife is in the sink and looks clean. Her back is to me at the range, and she seems unnervingly still and calm.

'We could put on some of your music?' The outside evening looks like rain now. She shrugs, and I long to wrap her into my arms.

'Do you think you hurt him bad?' I will need to protect her if Sergeant Bushnell comes with his boys. 'Did you hurt men before?' This stabbing carry-on might have been why she was inside the cells with me. Her silence is deafening, and the teapot clatters and makes a huge noise to my sensitive ears. 'You cannot do that again. Do you hear me? You cannot use a knife like that. They'll take you away. Take you from me.'

The back of her shrugs again, and she fixes her hair.

'I need you here. I need you to stay with me,' I continue like an ignored itch. 'I need you with me, Molly.'

She swings around, and in that instant, I don't know her. Those blue eyes are wide and wild. That once beautiful mouth all contorted as she laughs at me. 'I don't need to stay with you. I hate you.'

The words lash me as hard as the rain on the pane. Her odd smile ends that clear and careful sentence. I feel stabbed too. Beyond her outside, a sheet has taken off in a gust of wind and is tangled in the barbed wire on top of the wall. It's drenched, torn and tangled, and I'm helpless to stop it.

I haven't slept well. The nightmares are bad, and Molly doesn't come in to ease them. She barely talks or looks at me since the stabbing. Days have passed, and they seem the same to me. She just hisses like a cat at me if I ask her anything at all.

No guards have come yet, but I'm shaken. Surely to God I am. I've even muttered a few prayers. It's too eerily quiet, and I'm unnerved by everything. Thankfully, the Professor hasn't called either, but every time there's a knock on the door, my heart spins in my chest. The whiskey isn't helping. I know that. But with my mother before me, rocking in her chair, and the thoughts of the gaol – it is all too much when I close my eyes at night.

If it isn't my mother, He appears and thumps me around the cowshed, or bends me over in the byre while Molly laughs along, drumming her spoon off the milk buckets.

The clock in the kitchen says two o'clock. It's only early afternoon, yet my head needs a pillow to rest my weariness. When I pass the front door, the knock on it startles me. I don't really want to open it, but I must. I also think of the money we need, so I open it anyway. The noise from the street streams in, and there's a figure on the doorstep.

'I'm looking for Peggy.' The big lady has a shopping basket and a large string sack full of groceries.

'Yes?' I say, uncertain of what she's after.

'Come from the doctor's.' She nods downwards. Her hair looks clean, although she's not wearing a scarf or hat. But her face looks like it needs a good scrub. It is then I notice the dirty marks are wrinkles with pigment changes in her skin due to the sun. Pregnant women get those skin changes sometimes, so I stand aside and let her in.

'I'm looking to be relieved of something.' She puts down the bag and basket in the hall, and I see she has a mound of a belly. 'Not as far gone as I look. But our own woman tried to rid me of it, and then, I heard of you. I canna have another, missus. It'd kill me.' She grabs my arm, and I sense she's desperate all right.

'You got a man?' I ask.

'He's none the wiser, don't you fret. Has seven others to fend for and to keep him occupied. Seven sons. So, my man won't be none the wiser. Has enough to do. As far as he's concerned, I'm out in Dublin to stay with my mother for the night and do some fancier shopping.'

I move off along the corridor towards my medicines room, saying, 'There's magic in the seventh son of seven sons.'

'The youngest has the healing hands all right. But sure, no man could cure me of this problem.' She follows me, looking around her. 'Even St Brigid herself couldn't rid me of this complaint. I have the money. Me mother said I need you to sort things. He shakes his trousers at me, and I'm caught.' She sighs loudly.

My hands tremble as I turn the lock which sometimes sticks. Today, it squeaks a little but opens easily. From when we step into the medicines room, I feel cold. This large woman undresses, unconcerned that I'm quiet. She talks on about her children and the upcoming marriage of one of her many cousins.

'This will be all done for, then, and I might get to dance without wetting myself.'

I do what I always do. Her money lies there at the head of the bed. I know it's all there. I take it, but leave some of it back as I sense she has need of better shoes. From what I can glimpse of hers, they're looking very pinched on her swollen feet and are not very new at all.

'I know this is the right thing for us all,' I hear her say, and I shake more than usual. The whiskey, my mother and that blonde bitch are before me as I use the syringe to suck up the vile stuff to help this woman. 'Does it hurt bad?' she asks. 'Never did this before.'

'Make sure you go straight to your mother's. The pains will come in a while. Stay until it's all away. You might need something for an infection after. Watch yourself. But your mother will look after you.'

'Me mother is the best woman. She has someone all sorted to look after the children. Said many do this, and it's my decision. I canna have another. It'd kill me.'

I kneel in front of her, and I push the plunger into the syringe and let the medicine flow in. She says something about her last baby. I get distracted. I pull back on the plunger.

There are faces before me, women that were desperate, babies I have brought breathing into this world, little hands on their mothers' breasts, eyes of girls relieved to be free of torment. They all are there. Coming and going as her loud voice carries on.

Then, the tone of her voice dips and trails off. I notice that the liquid is all gone from my syringe and probably has been for a while. I sit on my heels, looking at the empty tool for a few moments, and realise that the woman isn't talking anymore. There's not a sound from her. Nothing. She lies there motionless, her hands on her middle. A trickle of blood runs out from between her legs and into the towel she's lying on then seeps over onto the grey sheet. A calloused hand flops down onto the bed.

I stand to look down upon her and shake her slightly. The other hand lands on the mattress with a thud. Suddenly, a large sigh of air leaves her. It lingers around her, hovers there over her, like I do. There's nothing for me to do but stand there, frozen. Her skin turns grey like the sheet.

This half-naked woman before me is dead, and I must've killed her.

Chapter 7

There, on the bed, is a dead woman. How have I come to this?

My breath is quick, and my chest heavy. There's a depth to the dread in my soul. Even in my darkest days in the gaol, I never felt like this. There's an emptiness to her suddenly. She was here, then gone. I'm stuck to the spot gazing at the shell before me, lost in a fog. The tears come. They fall. I gulp and make a sort of a snort. I'm an animal, but somehow, I have killed my own kind. Few animals even do that for no reason. Sweet Jesus, I'm a murderer.

I want to put her clothes back on. What was her name? Such a nice soul, with no name and no pants. What kind of person am I? She needs to look more dignified. A panic rises in me – this poor woman needs her pants on. I'm weeping uncontrollably. My face is so wet, and my shoulders heave great shards of pity into my throat. What right have I to cry? It's not me who's dead.

The pants will be hard to put back on by myself. The angle of the body on the bed makes any movement precarious. She might fall off. Then what would I do? More blood trickles, and the aroma of faeces comes off her when I try to manoeuvre her. I can't… I'll just have to leave… 'Sweet Christ Almighty, save us.'

Dropping to a heap on the floor, I mutter, 'I'm so sorry. Dear God, I didn't mean… I don't know…oh fuck.'

This poor woman's corpse doesn't answer. I glimpse the ceiling, and the Hail Marys trip out between the tears.

I cannot even think. Everything seems as frozen as her lips. All is blue and grey like her skin. I need help to move her and help to hide my mistake. What happened? I'm not at all sure.

One minute, she was wittering on about weddings, and then, she stopped...dead. Stone, cold dead.

I leave her and click the key around in the lock and stand in the narrow hallway thinking on who will help me. Sergeant Bushnell is a big man and sympathetic, but I doubt his fondness would stretch to helping me dispose of a dead body.

There's no way I can explain to any authority what I was doing to her. I cannot go back inside again. It would surely kill me to be locked away again.

Where does someone dispose of a human? I cannot burn her. Jesus, I've killed a person. I can't think. Bury her? Where? I need a car. Who has a car? As I picture myself and Molly heaving the woman's dead weight onto the bus, I snigger with pure nervousness.

Snuffling up the snots dangling from my nose, I know I'm the worst person in the world at this moment in time. The back of my hand is wet with my sorrow and shame. The hands that killed someone tremble in fear and guilt. The pain in my chest is huge, and there's a vile taste in my mouth of a retching stomach. I raise my ear to hear the murmur of Molly humming a tune somewhere upstairs. Molly will help me. Even if she hates me, Molly will help, and she never talks – unless she has to.

'Molly?'

There's no reply. Every step on the stairs is like a trek up Mount Everest. Every step bringing me to the reality that I will have to admit to my Molly that I have killed a person. A real, live person who walked into my room and who now is a large, heavy female with no beating heart and no life, lying on that bed. A woman in a sorry mess, who will have a large family coming looking for her... I stop and swallow the vomit in my mouth.

Molly is in the bath, singing and washing herself as I enter. She ignores me.

I stand over the sink, the waves of my breakfast rising in my throat. 'I feel sick,' I admit and continue to be ignored. 'I need your help. Something awful has happened.'

She starts singing again. It's as if I've never even spoken.

'*Molly!*' I shout. The water splashes as she jumps in fright. Her singing stops. 'I need your help. I'm not sure why you hate me, but I need you to help me. I need to…'

There's a knock on the door of the bathroom. 'Peggy?'

'What, Tess?'

'Sergeant Bushnell's downstairs at the door. I've let him in. He wants to talk to ya.'

My heart skips a beat. The throbbing in my head seems as long as any marching drum. I lean into the sink and throw up all the remaining bits of my porridge into it. Molly resumes her washing and humming, swirling the facecloth round her breasts as I wash my face.

'Peggy?' Tess sounds frantic, knocking rapidly while whispering my name in earnest. 'He looks all official. He's got me worried.'

'I'm coming,' I shout at her. 'Tell him I'll be there in a minute.'

Molly washes on and ignores me looking at her. She says not a word as I close the door. The steps down the stairs are even more difficult to take, each one taking me nearer the sergeant and his questions.

How in the name of God am I going to look the law in the eye knowing what I've just done? How am I going to defend Molly and myself yet again? There's a drag on each step, and yet, I am at the bottom of the stairs and nearer my fate.

Sergeant Bushnell is a good man. He would never dream of me being as bad as I am. He doesn't bring me any children since I was caught before. Any time he comes to see me now, it's to ask some awkward questions and to look down his long nose at me. He's got a bit of power since he moved to the rank of sergeant, and like all men, the power has gone a little to his head. But he's a good man, if there is such a thing.

'He's in the kitchen,' Tess hisses at me when she comes up the hall, and then, she flies up the stairs.

I stagger past my locked medicines room, only briefly thinking of the body behind the door, and walk on down the narrow corridor to our small kitchen.

Sergeant Bushnell is standing looking around him as I enter, holding on to the door to steady my nerve and my heart.

'Peggy.' He smiles.

'Sergeant.'

'I've come about Molly.'

I walk gingerly to put the kettle on the range to do something, anything, other than look at those official eyes that could lock us up again.

'I need to speak with her.'

'What about?'

'Some young lad arrived into the station with his mother. She was hollering and screaming about how he was attacked by your Molly.'

The teapot needs a wipe. So, I give it a good rub, willing a genie to come out of it and rescue us all.

'She cut him up badly about the face, Peggy.'

I turn to look at him, genuinely shocked. 'What?'

'Apparently, it happened here.' He looks around.

'His face?'

The always ready kettle starts the rumble of a boil. It's then I see a large blood smudge on the kitchen dresser door in the sergeant's line of vision. My heart thumps loudly in my chest. I'm sure he can hear it. The bile from my stomach burns up my throat.

'Did you know about this slashing she did?' He takes my arm in his big hand, turning me to look at him again.

'Was he badly hurt?' I cannot meet those big blue eyes for long, and I move around in the hope he won't pin me down. He removes his cap and puts it on the table, moving around to sit down by the blood spatter.

'He has a good few stitches on his jaw and around his neck and a few marks on his middle too. Someone definitely cut him. His mother was all for coming over here.'

I pour the water into the teapot and swirl it. My stomach is doing the same. 'Well, that's something,' I say, not wanting to say anything at all. Willing this all to come to an end. The dead woman most probably stiffening in the next room, and all the while, me talking to the sergeant in circles about Molly's crime. 'I'm glad he's all right.'

'Someone attacked him, Peggy, and he says it was Molly. Where is she?'

I'm hoping against all hope that Molly's still in the tub and doesn't come dancing into the kitchen.

'Joe,' I chance his first name, 'you know I need to protect my Molly.'

'But who will protect people from her?' He's sitting in the chair with his back to the blood.

'The young boyo most probably promised her the stars and didn't deliver.' I think I add in three scoops of tea leaves. 'Molly doesn't say much. She hasn't been herself, all right, but I doubt she's a harm to anyone like that.'

'She has before. Stabbed at her own uncle and the priest that came to take her away. Cut them.'

I feared as much. I slump into the other chair not making the tea anymore. My eyes fill with tears. I want to confess everything to the sergeant and make it all go away. If I tell him, will it all just disappear? I open my mouth and look at him in earnest.

'You didn't know that?'

God, the gorgeous eyes on him. He leans forward.

'I didn't know she cut people.'

'Well, it's worse this time. Her second offence. This mother of his isn't taking it lightly, and I couldn't blame her. He's scarred for life.' I can hear him talk on about how he stopped the mother storming in here and how the young lad looked scared out of his wits and of how Molly would need to make a statement.

'Please stop this, Joe. Molly doesn't understand. This is ridiculous. The young fellow was probably in a brawl in the pub and cannot tell his ma. He's using Molly – he knows she cannot fight for herself. A boyo like him has promised to marry her. He's possibly got cold feet. This gets rid of all that. I won't have you annoying my Molly.'

'You didn't see or hear any of this?'

'No.'

'The young lad says you were all out in the back, cackling and laughing in the sun, but the windows and doors were all open.'

'Why didn't he wait or call for help?'

'He ran away.'

I rise to finish making the tea again, getting the strength from somewhere to keep upright and get my brain working. 'Why didn't he tell us if it happened here?' I ask, putting out mugs.

'Scared out of his wits, with his face hanging open?'

I say nothing at all and cannot move.

'He says she jumped on him when he fell to the floor and stabbed him in his middle. There was a large gash in his side. He says there was blood everywhere. I need to speak to Molly.'

'She knows nothing, and this will break her heart. She loves that bastard, and if she thinks he let her down like this, she might...'

'What would she do?' The voice of him is soft, and I can hear he knows the truth. 'She has to make a statement and talk to me. If she has nothing to hide, then we'll all be happy. Go get her now, Peggy, and this will all be over.'

There's nothing left in my arsenal of words. Nothing left in my heart that will give me the audacity needed to stand up to him.

The dead woman in the next room and us two back in prison are all I can think of. I've never felt so awful in my entire life. Everything is falling apart all over again, each deed and sentence tumbling in on itself. One little action from me and a few slashes from Molly and our world is abandoning us. It all seems so unfair, unjust and cruel. And yet, it is us who've brought all this upon ourselves. I cannot breathe with the pain of it, the weight squashing me into the abyss of hell. I'll roast for sure now. We are doomed. Even the inquest into His death and my trial the last time over selling the babies…nothing is as bad as this. The pulse in the side of my head is throbbing, and I'm fucking exhausted.

'I'm so tired, Joe.'

'I know. You're a good woman. Doing your best. Your own mother…' He stops.

He's right. A lawyer tried to use that in my defence before. But it's true. I couldn't mind Mammy, and the law-man said it affected me. Now, I suppose I try to mind Molly. I've let everyone down all my life, and I've let myself down at every turn.

'I'm not a good woman.'

He pours me a mug of tea while I stare at him and think if only I'd married a man like Joe. If only I'd taken up with Mick Moran all those years ago and not been an independent woman, I'd be all right now. I would've been cared for and been safe my whole adult life. I wouldn't be sitting in a hellhole with a dead woman in my house, prostitutes upstairs, a sergeant in my kitchen and a halfwit in my bath.

I start to laugh.

It comes up from my empty belly and shakes my whole body, tumbling out of me like a wave of nonsense. Joe looks at me oddly as I bang the table in fake glee at my ludicrous life. Tears fall and I hold my middle – every part of me is sore. Every part of my emotional innards exposed to him in this tiny kitchen, and he hasn't a clue about what's happening to me. I feel my mind leaving me as I chuckle to a stop and stare at the brown liquid in the chipped mug.

'I'm finished, Joe. There is nothing left of me.'

Chapter 8

There seems to be nothing for it but to get my Molly out of the bath. I need the sergeant out of the house. A dead woman lies up the hall, and until he speaks with Molly, I'm not going to have the peace to move that poor woman's body anywhere. We can both hear the gramophone start upstairs.

'Go and get her now,' Sergeant Bushnell says after a few slurps of his tea.

Past the medicines room and small hallway mirror, I go. Pounding up the stairs again takes every ounce of my strength. The door to the bathroom at the top of the stairs is locked now, and the music blares from inside. The other girls are somewhere about, I'm sure. But I dare not call them out, in case the sergeant questions them.

I knock as hard as I can on the bathroom door. 'Molly?'

Nothing. The music goes on, '*Hush little baby, don't you cry.*'

'Molly, open this door. I need the bathroom, and Sergeant Joe wants to speak with you.'

Nothing.

I thump very hard on the heavy door. '*Molly!*'

Nothing.

The sergeant is at the bottom of the stairs, looking up at me, his attractive face and kind eyes imploring me. I see him that night I took him upstairs when he needed me. I need him now, but know he will forget all I did that night to make him feel like a man again.

I shrug and move to come back downstairs. 'She cannot stay in there forever. Let's get more tea.'

He meets me halfway up the stairs and stands very close to me. 'Turn around. She needs to talk to me now. Or else we take her in. This fellow's mother will want answers, and trust me, she isn't someone to mess with.'

'Neither am I.' I lean into his chest and look up into his eyes. Rubbing my fingers over his mouth, I give him my most alluring look. 'We could spend some time…until she comes out.'

'Not now. That kind of stuff is beneath a woman like you.'

Although he doesn't look cross, he seems definite, and he moves me gently out of his way to ascend to the top of the stairs. He pounds on the door. It looks like cardboard under his large fist. 'Molly McCarthy! Open this door.'

Nothing.

I stay halfway down the stairs. I cannot bear to think of her naked and afraid. What can I do against the arm of the law that's battering to get in at her? My poor Molly is possibly shivering in the corner, rocking to and fro and hoping it can all be ignored. Humming and in her own world. I hope she'll stay there and not answer him at all. Then it's all her word against Tommy's. Surely there's no proof. My mind swirls like a river. Fast and frantic, the thoughts cascade together is a rapid torrent of worry.

'Molly!' the sergeant shouts.

The music stops and doesn't start again.

Sergeant Bushnell looks as if he's lost his patience. His eyes are bulging and his face red. 'Open this door. Now.'

No answer.

'Key?' he hollers at me. There is only one, and Molly has it.

'No other key.'

My heart is about to stop from the worry of all of this. I know it has skipped a few beats. I'm waiting for it to just cease pumping, like that poor creature downstairs. At least the other girls have had the sense to remain in their rooms, and there's no sign of any men. He raps on the door with both sets of knuckles. It sounds painful in every way.

'It's all right, Molly. You aren't in any trouble. Peggy is here, and we'll look after you.'

There comes no answer. I grab the bannister in despair, sinking downwards, praying with every breath that it'll all be over soon.

'I need to break this door in,' he says.

I don't answer him. He batters the door for a good while, yelling. I hug the wooden rails too tightly, picturing that lady's last gasp as the air left her. Joe stands back and charges at the door. His shoulder rams against it. With one kick of his giant foot, the whole area around the lock smashes. His foot kicks what is left of the panels of the door away from the frame. I cannot look. I hear the door disintegrate – the creak and groan of the destroyed wood. All the while, I stare down at my locked medicines room, wondering about all the secrets behind locked doors.

Then, he's above me, looking pale. 'Ring for a doctor. Ring the fucking station.' He shakes me. I stare at him. He runs back up the few steps to the shattered door. 'Now, Peggy.'

I am there fixed to the spot, my arms entangled in the bannister, unable to think, move or speak. I hear water sloshing in the bath, and the sergeant shouting about stopping the blood, the tear of fabric and him grunting.

Something has happened to my Molly. What has she done? I find myself standing in the remnants of the door. Before me is a mess of blood, Molly's severed wrists in pieces of towel that Joe is trying desperately to tie.

He sounds out of breath. 'Did you ring already?'

I stand there, mouth open, tears falling. My life is in shards. I stumble on the splinters of wood at my feet.

'Peggy?' Joe shouts at me.

I look at him. Everything seems far away. He's wrapping Molly in a towel to cover her beautiful skin. Her red hair soaked and trailing in the watery blood on the floor. He tries to lift her from the bath, but the slippery floor and her skin don't help him. Slowly and carefully, Molly gets draped onto a tiny towel on the driest part of the lino.

'Why is there always blood on my floors?'

'Cradle her in your arms, then. I'll call for help. For the love of Christ, woman, don't just stand there!'

He marches towards me and pushes me further into the room to be near my Molly. I can hear his large shoes on the stairs, and I watch the water in the bath. She is lying there, half draped in a small towel and looking lifeless. My Molly looks unnatural, not human at all. Her mouth gapes slightly open, as if to smile or speak suddenly and come back to me. I kneel to see the bandaged hand touching the gramophone player that is still turning but has no music.

Her hair is soaking wet when I touch it with the tips of my fingers, and her face is so cold. My ear close to her mouth senses no breath, just emptiness. Like the woman downstairs – surely life doesn't drain away so quickly? Surely a death is a lingering, noisy thing? I clutch her hand.

Molly moans. It's the most welcome sound I've ever heard. I grasp her head to cradle on my lap, as Joe instructed. When I hold her, she moans loudly, and when I try to cover her with the towel, she attempts to do the same.

'Thank Christ, Molly. Thank Christ you're alive.' Tears blur the room and the returning sergeant. 'She's alive.'

'Good. I'll get a blanket. We'll keep her warm.' He looks at me for instructions. The nearest bedroom is my own and should be empty, but he's disappeared and returns with my own patchwork blanket and a sheet. His face is red and sweating.

The ad hoc bandages are seeping with blood, and as I lift her wrists, the screech of tearing sheets hurts my ears. I hum Molly's lullaby and see Tess in the doorway with her eyes wide in shock. I move my head to tell her to disappear. They all know to leave if there's trouble, so I just hope they all get a chance to escape before the police come asking question after question. The slight, scared Tess disappears, and I can hear naked footsteps on the floorboards.

Joe didn't let on to hear them leave. He works on at Molly, telling us, 'All is going to be well. Wait, you'll see.'

'You are a good man.' I touch his arm, and he smiles a crooked smile. 'Where is this fucking doctor?'

It seems like hours. Molly, although always pale, looks deathly white now. I hum away for something to do, but Molly doesn't join me and doesn't moan again.

'Maybe we should have taken her in the car?' he says as he looks at his wristwatch for the twentieth time. He's about to get to his feet, when we hear the door getting a battering.

'Thank Christ.'

The splayed arms of my dead creature downstairs flash before me. I should tell Joe about her, about my house of death. Tell him about it all. This is what God has led me to. To confess on my knees here and now – to save my Molly.

But there's an awful commotion, with the thumping of male feet on the stairs, shouting and moving Molly and whatnot. My mind won't work. The world is murky as the tears fall from me. When you care for someone so much, the fucking crying won't stop no matter how hard you try. They carry Molly out and down the stairs and out into the street where people have gathered to see the goings-on.

The door closes behind them all. The top step of the stairs takes my weight. The voices outside are loud, and the bang of the door startles me. Then there's nothing. All is still, so very quiet. I can see that woman's shopping sitting just to the left of the front door.

But I'm all alone with my bloodied bathroom, my tears and a dead body no one knows about.

Chapter 9

Number thirty-four and me is all that's left. I always told myself I'd be gone from here before I was that age on the door – but how do I leave this top step of the stairs? I'm in a daze – numb, uncertain of what to do next. The front door opens, and Sergeant Joe Bushnell looks up at me. I need to be in his arms and for him to tell me all will be right in the world again. But there's another pair of guard's boots with him. I recognise this bastard. He's a real thug, known for real violence and not doing things by the book.

'Peggy,' the brute grunts looking up the stairs at me.

'I want to go to Molly.' Off the step I get and descend the stairs.

'They'll not let you in,' Joe says kindly. 'I'll take you to her tomorrow.'

'Will you now?' this brute says.

I can't recall a name for him. I need them both out of the house, before they find out anything else. I tremble as I reach the bottom of the stairs.

'Have you anyone to call on?' Joe asks, disregarding the stares from his companion.

'Just go.'

'We know the truth now, anyway,' says the bastard with the thin moustache next to Joe. 'She's guilty of hurting that God-fearin' young fella.'

'God-fearing young fella me arse.' I spin around. '*No* man comes here for anythin' to do with God. He took advantage. If Molly cut him, he deserved it.'

'If?' The thug's bad breath is on my face. 'That whore did it, all right.'

'Let's go.' Joe pulls on his sleeve. 'Peggy doesn't know anything more.'

'If that witch lives, she'll go down for cutting that young fella.'

Joe pulls lightly on the brute's sleeve. I look away and listen for the click of the door.

The hallway floor has tiny spots of blood on it. I hadn't considered Molly dying after she moaned at me. But, of course, Molly had wanted to die, and Molly nearly always found a way to get what she wanted. If only she could have been a mother to Fionn, she would have been so happy. I should have figured out something. It's all too late now. Molly is lost to me, and she'll be as good as dead if they put her back in prison.

My hand is on the handle of medicines room. It shakes, and I don't want to turn the lock, so I walk on to the kitchen. Two lonely mugs and Joe's hat sit on the table. There is no one to rescue me.

That blonde girl from a few weeks back started all of this. The bad luck she brought with her into his house started all this badness. Bitch!

There's nothing for it but to unlock the medicines room. The mechanism catches as I turn the key, but it opens reluctantly. There she lies, just as I left her. A definite dead grey colour now. The poor creature looks unearthly. My own skin is peppered in goose pimples, and the hairs on my neck are sensitive to every little noise: the slip of my hand from the handle of the door, the tap of my heels on the floor, and the dust lingering in the sunlight dancing ahead of me.

Looking at her, she's at peace, having drifted off mid-sentence. But why? She's not old. She didn't seem sick. I'd been putting in the solution. All was fine. I'd pulled back on the syringe...

I fall to my knees by the bed in front of her like she is the grill in the confessional box. 'I pulled back on the syringe. I pushed air into you. Surely it wasn't that?'

I hear someone's presence in the house and lurch to slam the medicines room door closed. The key is not on the inside of the door. I ease the door open and glance up the hall. There's no one there. My hand stretches to get the key, but it flusters me when I try to get it out of the lock. Darting my eyes up the hallway again, there's no one that I can see, but I'm convinced there's someone in my home. There are no further noises, only a feeling that someone is in the house.

'Hello? Who's there?'

No one answers. All is still, like the dead corpse on the bed.

I bang the door closed and lock it with difficulty, leaning all my weight against the wood. I wait.

Footsteps? On the stairs? The rats, bats or pigeons way up in the house? Maybe. No. A groan leaves one of the floorboards. The house does that sometimes, telling off the world for allowing me to pollute the walls. There is a creak of another one, and all falls still. There is a sense of foreboding; an ill wind lingers over me. My panting sounds frantic.

I'm just afraid of everything now. What will the Professor do if he hears of Molly? There is no way I can move this body on my own. I could bury her in the back yard, if it wasn't all concrete slabs and in view of the neighbours' windows. Her mother knows she came here too.

There's a crumpling noise as I slide down to sit on the floor and look at the mess of my life. Men with pitchforks at my door, the looks of nuns from under their habits, the judge's gavel cracking down. I'm caught in cells again with the screams of faceless women. The guards' hands on my breasts, the squeeze and pressure and the stench off grimy uniforms.

I crawl over to peer up at the life I've taken. 'I'm sorry,' I lean up on the bed, 'I didn't mean for this…'

It's so pitiful. The sight of my dead husband, not dissimilar to her now. He was all crooked with no breath in him in the finish. She's more serene, and I didn't mean to make her heart stop, but she has the same pallor of nothingness.

My heart thumps loudly as I rest my face on my knees. I killed her. I did this. People will come looking for her soon. Her family knows where she is, not like others who steal away here and don't tell any of their own. My fears start to multiply. Folk unafraid of violence will descend on me, demanding to know where their loved one is.

I wonder has she gotten stiffer. Rising off the floor, I move her arms to sit across her chest. No, she is not much stiffer. The money near her on the bed gets added to the pile on the dresser. Ignoring the mess between her legs, I pull her dress over her and tuck it in at her sides to make her look less exposed. Her curls feel soft as I sit them out around her head on the bed. Those wrinkles she had are looking less deep, and the blotches gone. There's a gloss to her skin.

'What's your name?'

The silence is wretched.

"Click" goes the lock. I jump. Holding my breath, I stare at the handle. There is no turn. No sign of a living soul. My breath heaves out. In and out, in and out, I drag the air from around this nameless cocoon. Tears fall, and I cannot help it.

'Everyone good deserves a name. I will write a note. I'm going to have to go without seeing to you properly… Sally. I'll call you Sally, after my mother. I'll leave you in peace… Sally.'

Hard like ice, her forehead is under my palm. A Hail Mary is fitting and quick. The top drawer in the dresser has a paper and pen. Finger marks are left in the dust alongside the rectangles of valuable paper that used to bring me such pleasure.

I prop the scrawled, damp note on the dresser and stuff the money into the tin in the top drawer marked with Molly's name. Blotches of tears stain the note, despite me using my sleeve.

Sergeant Joe Bushnell,

I sit writing this letter afraid and worried. I must leave for good. No matter how bad things look, please believe me when I tell you that I didn't mean for any of this to happen.

But it was me who cut that young fellow up. He was bad to my Molly, and I left this poor woman in this state. Please make sure her mother knows she was in no pain and slipped off on me before I knew what happened. Somehow, for this woman's sake, try to keep why she was here her last secret. Please, Joe. This is not for me, but for her and her family. She was a good woman and doesn't deserve for her memory to be blackened. It's all my fault.

It was me who let her die.

If Molly survives, please make sure she is put somewhere safe and is not blamed for anything. I have left her money in the top drawer of this dresser. Please see that she gets it and gets to at least see her son Fionn. I'm not brave like Molly, so I'll run and hide where you'll never find me.

I'm sorry, Joe. I hope someday that God will forgive me.
Peggy Bowden

A quick wash and change of clothes makes me feel more alive, but I don't know the person looking at me from the mirror in my bedroom. I empty the dregs of the whiskey bottle into me. There is so little of any value in my life – an old Bible of my mother's and an address book with scribbles about America and places I might have to run to.

Despite all my wanting, all my greed, all my trying, there is nothing that is of any importance around me. Nobody to say goodbye to, and nothing to leave behind. The girls will not return until they know all is better, and that's not going to happen any time soon. I tidy around my room and leave the newest navy strapped shoes on the floor by the bed. A bag doesn't take long to pack, and the stash of cash is stuffed into various places about my person and into a carpet bag and handbag.

The train timetable to Belfast slips into my purse. It will take me to a different country and from there, I will think about what I will do. I leave my medicines room and the house unlocked as I head out into the night air. There will be no trains to Belfast until the morning, but I cannot take a chance on dead Sally's family coming to find her tonight. Sergeant Joe will call in the morning to take me to see Molly, and although I hate leaving her, I know it's the best gift I can give her now. She doesn't need me anymore either, hating me for whatever reason that's come into her simple brain.

I march through the empty streets of Dublin, watching the rubbish blow about in the wind. It was all her fault. That... that blonde girl, her coming to me in her fancy shoes and hat. Swanning into my life, making me feel uncertain about my trade. It was her who made me hate myself and returned me to the past, weak and vulnerable. Reminded me of torture, so I slipped up, unsure of myself. What was she called? I didn't know her name either. No one decent has a name. Blonde Bitch will do.

The heavy clunk of the prison bars echoes in my ears, but the crisp night air is silent. There is an odd car, but no one in the streets. A cat slinks into the twilight, and the streetlights make my eyes hurt.

Lights out in prison was the scariest time. No one can tell you the fear you have when they take your freedom and turn out the light. They house you against your will and move you about like cattle. There was talk about a new women's prison, and although there wasn't that many of us, we could've done with more room all right.

'Women aren't supposed to be criminals,' our gaolers said. 'Dirty whores and killers, ya all are.'

Looking them in the eye wasn't a good idea and raising your head up to stand tall meant you got knocked or dragged down. Many of the women with me were bad bitches; some needed those bars to shield them from the world. Most were hardened by circumstance, mad because they were told they were, some like Molly were too beautiful to be allowed to tempt men and too fiery for the nuns.

In prison, you were a nobody, a nothing, a thing to forget. Meat to be molested in a dark corner by a bastard, if you weren't watching yourself. Sure, who had I to visit me in a prison? Some of my nurses came once or twice with an odd thing I could trade, but the shame was too great for most of them. The ones that did come had eyes full of pity. I looked a state, I know I did. Even without mirrors, the reflection in the full sinks were enough to scare myself. It was the days' labour that broke me.

'Untangling used ropes, like the used auld ropes ye are.'

Constant bad chat where I'd daydream of dancing in the ballrooms of Europe that I wanted to visit, speeding around in cars they never would even touch and kissing film stars that took me to dinner. I was always away in my dreams.

'Wanting is good, Peggy, but don't want too much,' Mother would say, rocking and knitting. 'Strong women in this day and age need to be more than schooling smart. Remember to be proud but clever, Peggy.'

I squat down in an alley and piss into the gutter. There isn't much clever or proud about me now. Stumbling on through the streets, I weep. A car passes, but I still let out long, hard squeals of self-pity. Then, I sob on for Molly and lastly for the poor lassie I've named Sally. The poor critter lying dead on a stranger's bed – all alone.

I'm so lost in my grief that I fail to notice a black car reversing back towards me.

'Peggy?' a familiar voice asks.

My face is caked in salty tears as I glance into the back of the car. 'Professor,' I manage. I'm glad to see him.

'What's wrong?'

I choke back the tears. 'It's Molly. She's in the hospital.'

'Get in, woman.'

I pull the handle and sit into the back seat placing the bag on my knee. The car moves off. I'm so full of emotion, I think I might piss the back seat, despite my emptied bladder. I don't look at his beady eyes or slicked hair but breathe in his cigars. I can tell without even looking we are heading back towards number thirty-four.

He hands me a large silky handkerchief and asks, 'What the hell is going on?'

'Molly killed a woman who came for a procedure and then tried to take her own life.'

I've said it before I think of it. The lies just spew out of me like an explosion. As wrong as it feels, when the lie is out, I can't take it back. I can't reverse in the stunned silence between us. He wouldn't like me lying about Molly.

On I go, like the bad bitch that I am. 'She slashed some young fella about the face too. My heart is broken for her. For myself. Sweet Saint Brigid, help us all.'

'Jesus.'

The back of Tiny looms, driving in the front, and we turn familiar corners that I said goodbye to only minutes ago, thinking I would never see them again.

'There's that dead body in the medicines room. I didn't know what to do.' I'm sobbing now, looking at the large shoulders ahead of me, thinking he could move Sally with one arm.

'Molly did a bad butchering job, then?'

Even a man like the Professor is shocked.

'She didn't know how to do it…but I wasn't there.'

The lightning I fear doesn't strike me down, and I hope against all hope that Molly will forgive me my lies. She's going down as it is, and the likes of the Professor won't tell the law, but he might be more inclined to help if it's Molly he's saving. It's a move I hope I don't regret.

'Fuck.' He puffs on the cigar.

'Police came about the stabbing she gave a young boyo and the body lying there in the other room and me not letting on.' I howl this at him like a banshee.

'So, the law doesn't know about the dead one?'

'Not yet.'

'Where's Molly?'

'They took her away. She slit her wrists.'

'Christ Almighty, Peggy.'

I snivel into the hanky, nodding like I'm the one aggrieved. 'I know.'

'She's gonna make it?' His voice sounds concerned, and the back of Tiny's head looks huge.

'I dunno.' I start to cry all over again and blow my nose. 'She's my Molly.' I mean it so much. There's such love for her in me. 'I don't know how I'll cope if she isn't alive.' The guilt is driving the tears out of me, and I slump in the seat. 'I decided that I'd take the blame and just run away. That was my plan.'

'We got word about something, but I'd no idea you were on the run.' He kind of chuckles, and I glance at him. 'I'll sort out that body. Take one problem off the cards for Molly.'

The sigh that leaves me mingles with his puffed-out smoke. 'Would you?'

'Sure, it's my stock-in-trade.' He pulls up his collar with pride at how he disposes of problems. I shudder despite the heat and the tension in the car. The night is stuffy and so is my heart and head.

'But she needs looking after well. She's a good woman.'

'Who is?'

'My Molly. I'm so tired.'

'Was the young fella she stabbed that idiot Tommy?'

'Blond and blue eyes? You threw him in the canal.'

'That's him. Bastard deserves all he got. Was warned off. If Molly hadn't hurt him, someone else would have.'

'We were in the backyard and came in to see all the blood. Sergeant Bushnell, of course, wanted answers, but Molly was in the tub, and…when he broke the door in…well…there was more blood. But this time it was Molly's…'

I cannot control the weeping that comes from me when it all sinks in. Everything and all the lies and truths I'm telling.

'Do you think she'll make it?' His thin fingers reach my hand. 'Molly is one of my favourites.'

It sticks in my throat, that statement: one of his favourites, as if she's a pair of shoes, a sweet cake or some object.

'I love Molly,' I say.

'Let me sort things.'

'I'll owe you something in return?' I know the answer before I even ask the question. Surely disposing of a dead body isn't cheap or easy.

'This needs to be done before it's light, and once Molly hears all is well, it'll help her get better.'

He sounds like a Good Samaritan as if taking away that poor woman's body is like throwing out the scraps.

'Molly was so sad – she thought someone might marry her.'

He chokes a little and coughs for a time. I look at him then, right into those hard eyes of his.

'You know I couldn't take on a girl like Molly.' His moustache moves nearer to me, and I smell the whiskey off him. His bony hand comes out and touches my teary cheek. 'I need a pretty, clever woman. Someone like you.'

'Please stop the car.' I grab Tiny's shoulder and try to get the car door open. I spew vomit out into the street. The silk handkerchief slips out and lies on the pile. It seeps the liquid into it and lies there looking at me. I heave again, and all my stomach empties out on top of it.

I wipe the remnants away from the corner of my mouth with the back of my hand, and I slink back into the seat, minus his handkerchief.

'Sorry. I think it's the smell of the cigar and all that has happened.'

Tiny hasn't even looked around, but moves the car on for a time. When I look up, I'm back where I started at number thirty-four, and the Professor is looking longing at me with his hand on my thigh.

'I stink of vomit,' I say as he cuddles me into him going up to the front door. 'I'm so ill with it all.' I pretend to heave again, but he seems unconcerned for his fancy shoes.

'You're an educated woman who's lived it all. You'd understand my world and be able to…Well, we'll talk about that later.'

The door is open, so it takes no time to show him the mess in the house. I grab the note as the Professor lets out a low whistle of surprise.

'Jesus, Mary, Joseph and the feckin' donkey, Peggy.' He surveys it all. 'I thought I could cause trouble.' He sniggers and lurches for me again, despite the corpse on the bed. The way he nuzzles my neck makes my stomach churn, but thankfully, Tiny appears with my rifle, all smiles. I head for the stairs, like they will provide sanctuary.

'Where did you get that?' the Professor asks the big fella.

'He can have it. Please deal with that poor woman while I clean up.'

'It's for Molly,' he says, and I know his stare is following me up the stairs. 'I look after all my favourite girls.'

I heave again, and although my stomach is empty, liquid lands into the sink. Afterwards, I mutter prayers and apologies to any saint or ghost who may put in a good word for me somewhere.

'We're away, Peggy,' his voice echoes up the stairs. 'Look after yourself. I'll call to see how my girls are soon.'

The silence in the house is eerie again, the creaks and groans of it mimicking my own as I roll on the bed in mental agony. I think this fear will drive me to do what Molly did. To think I was jealous of the attention Molly received from the likes of that vermin. To think I abandoned her to him. And now, I've made her indebted to the scum, and it's all my fault to start with.

I vomit into the sink yet again before I fall into the bed without cleaning up much at all.

Chapter 10

Joe Bushnell's face is before me when I waken. I jolt up, uncertain of where I am and what person I am.

'Poor pet,' he murmurs and holds my hand.

I sit upright and pull away from him, worried he's checked elsewhere in the house and found messes that maybe the Professor didn't take away at all.

'Poor Peggy,' he mutters again and moves further down the bed to give me room.

'You only know the half of it.'

His look is full of pity. 'I rang the Royal City Hospital. Molly's stable but still in danger.'

I groan and flop back to the pillows. 'Indeed, she's in danger,' says I, the bitch who has put her in more of it.

'How are you?' He rubs my leg under the covers. It feels nice to have a caring hand on me. I don't know when that last happened.

'Once she's out and I'm away from here, I'll be all right.'

'Where will you go?'

I shrug.

'There was money on the kitchen table downstairs. Quite a bit of money.'

'Money?'

'A hundred pounds or so. Where did the likes of you get that money? And why are you leaving it lying about?'

I gawp at him, uncertain of what he is talking about, and yet, he seems sure and he's a man who knows how to count notes. Our stash would never be anywhere for the Gardaí or anyone else to find. It must be some other money, but I can't figure out what he means. 'Money? A hundred pounds?'

He nods. 'There's a lot of men in a hundred pounds.' The disappointment almost drips off him. It pains me to see him disgusted at what I had to organise within these walls.

'I needed to make money somehow. Specially after prison.'

'Suppose.'

'Who'd give me a job, eh? My face all over the papers, disgraced twice before I was long in my twenties.'

'You shouldn't have been made to marry that Sligo bastard.'

'No. And I shouldn't have been in the gaol either.' I need the toilet and away from this conversation.

'A hundred pounds...' His hand reaches into his inside pocket, and he plops it out onto the bed.

'I didn't let men with me for that.' I'm quite proud that I was with very few men for money over the years. Never could literally lie to it. 'Took too much out of my soul.'

'Did I take something from your soul?' he asks me, and I remember how sweet he was the night he asked me to see if he was still a man.

'You were special.'

I'm being honest. He was kind and gentle, and was uncertain of the way he should have been with the likes of me.

'Here's my telephone number, if you want me for anything. If you need anything at all.' He looks at his nails, but then, his eyes meet mine. There's longing in his face. 'I always needed you.' His lips meet mine, and I jump back.

'I vomited last night.' I take off out of the bed. 'I'm sorry.'

My mind whirls like a spinning top. Just awake and suddenly, Sergeant Bushnell tells me he needs me. Years I've waited for men to notice Peggy Bowden, and suddenly, they're all flocking at once when I feel as sick as a whole hospital.

The tub is cold and not very full. Only a bucketful or two from the sink, and it is pinkish from Molly's blood, but I feel clean. Joe can just leave. I cannot deal with men today.

I dry the ends of my hair with a towel and look into my bedroom. There's no Joe. The money's sitting on the bed looking indeed like a hundred pounds. The Professor must have left it. There is no other explanation. There isn't the sound of Joe in the house, and no sign of the blood or faeces in the medicines room, just a slight stain on the mattress. The house is stuffy and in need of fresh air, but there's no tinge of death that I can tell. I put the woman's basket into the back scullery and put away her items into my own cupboards and try not to think of the children.

My kitchen is empty of life and the hallways too. Out the back is warm, but the washing line swings in a low breeze.

There's a timid knock to the front door, and I creak it open ever so slightly.

'Hullo.'

It's my soldier boy, looking so handsome I could melt into him.

'We're closed,' I mutter, hoping he can hear me as I close the door.

The timid knock comes again.

'We're closed.' I holler through the shut door.

'I'll come back.' I hear his footsteps move away, and my back hits the wood a few times, punishing me for not letting him in. It's a good while since I've seen him, and yet, he makes me flutter in my pants with just the thought of him over these past few weeks. Over a month it must be now, and so much has happened.

The fighting about it had ended up being something I want to forget. Molly being the brunt of the girls' jealously and my silence.

'She just shrugs and denies she had him,' Tess had screamed at me in the back yard.

'Keep your voice down. What's done is done. Move on. It was one poke.' I winced as I said it, knowing if I was paid by the likes of him, I'd want more and want to fight for him too. 'Men ain't worth fighting over; he'll be back.'

'Aye, and he'll want Miss Molly.'

'She can't help being liked.'

'Maybe we'll all have to be screaming about how good they are.'

Tess was mad as hell, but I didn't care. He had been kind of worth the wait and worth the hassle.

I regret not letting him in now, but there's enough going on in my stomach. It swirls and lurches like a rollercoaster. Nothing can stop it, especially not the sight of dried blood and the gone-off milk stuck in the milk bottle in the bowl of water in the scullery.

The telephone box across the road stinks of stale beer and damp cigarettes. The hospital won't tell me how Molly is.

'Are you family? I'm afraid I cannot give out any information about Miss McCarthy.'

I curse loudly, hanging up the telephone, banging it down a few times for good measure and cry about my lot. The house is empty, and none of the girls return, and I'm glad of that, despite the loneliness.

The knock on the door the next day comes as I'm trying to keep a cup of tea in my churning stomach. There's a letter on the mat as I go to answer the door. The knocking gets louder and more fevered. There before me is an old woman of about seventy and three little boys hanging on to one of her hands and the pockets in her coat.

'My daughter's gone missing,' her country accent tells me. 'She was to visit places. This was one of them.' Her eyes open wide, hoping I understand her meaning without saying much in front of the children. She takes one hand from a little snotty-nosed boy and delves into her coat. She hands me a photograph of my dead Sally.

I cannot look at the woman standing before me until I compose myself. I shuffle my feet and look at the photograph, squinting, taking my time.

'Her name is Dorothy McKenzie.'

'She didn't come here.' I tell myself that she never did.

'Dot was to visit with you and tell you of her problem.'

'I'd ask you inside, but this isn't a place for youngsters.'

'Nor for anybody.' Her voice cracks. I'm angry at her tone. It's judging and nasty, despite what her daughter came here for.

'I don't know her and she was never here,' I lie.

'Her family are worried sick. If she comes here – you make sure she comes home.'

'We miss her,' the youngest boy pipes up and sniffs the snot back up his nose.

'Sorry, I can't help you.' I look at the letter in my hand and close the door.

The old woman's hand stops the door from fully shutting. 'I'll be back,' she says.

The vomiting now makes me think I will die. It hurts every part of me. That poor woman and those half orphans making me ill. Everyone knows it is the mother who raises the children, and I took their mother. Lying whore that I am stole their only hope in life. The crying goes beyond the beyond. I'm wretched with worry, fear, guilt and just so very sick. So sick that I telephone the doctor. He's used to visiting number thirty-four.

'Old, but still in need of sin,' he purrs anytime he arrives with supplies for the girls. Tess usually obliges, but I'm hopeful that the sight of my pale face and the stench of vomit might cool his ardour.

'There's only one thing it can be if you haven't eaten in the last few days,' he says, moving the glasses off his nose. 'When did you last have your monthly?'

'There's no way in hell that I'm pregnant.'

'I bring supplies, but do you…'

'The soldier,' I gasp, seeing his head between my legs and then my arse on the kitchen table and him planting his seed in me.

'That's a good name for a baby's father,' the doc says, snapping his bag closed. 'We can take samples, but you're a midwife, Peggy. You can do your calculations.'

My head sinks into my hands.

'Despite all your own preaching to the girls and providing them with precautions, unlike all the other houses I know, you end up in the family way. Well, I never.'

'Oh, stop your yapping.'

'No use being cross with me.' He makes his way towards the top of the stairs. 'It's very quiet in here.'

'My girls are all away at the minute.'

'I was sorry to hear about Molly.'

'Yes.'

'She's my favourite.' His feet go down the stairs.

I count the days repeatedly over and over in my mind. 'I'm fuckin' up the duff.' I scream into the pillows on my bed, before I race to vomit into the toilet.

The dread of all the unwed mothers I've met enters me. It's all consuming, turns all I know upside down. All the silly plans I had turn inside out, and all the world laughs in my head at how stupid I've been. The sprinkling of happiness is smothered in the fear of the looks from the community that know I'm on my own with a baby. No matter where I run to, it will be the same. I might as well hang a sign around my neck: "Fucked, abandoned and a fool." I believed in the place between my legs to keep me safe. It never produced anything before. There's no friend to confide in and not one of my own to look about me.

Those seven boys are before me in my sleep, ready to murder my baby when it's heaved out. My mother ranting at me about my education and how I'd let myself down for a quick shag with a handsome stranger who thought I was a whore. I waken in a fever, and the sickness is unbearable, and I fall back into a bad slumber. I know, of course, I could end the pregnancy, but I can't do that either, can I? Is it right to want away from it? I survey my wardrobe of cheap or tattered clothes, and the house – would it be right to bring a baby here? Will I even be allowed to keep my own baby?

All babies need fathers. Respectable people have fathers. I never had one that I remember, so I do want one for my own baby. 'My own child.'

I call Joe Bushnell.

'I can't even hear how Molly is,' I say before Joe has finished saying his number.

'Peggy?'

'I'm sick as hell.'

'I'll call the hospital now and ring you back. If I miss you, ring me later.'

I give him the telephone box number and hang up, clinging to the telephone as if it's a life raft in an angry ocean.

Using his rank, he obviously gets told more than me, because when the telephone rings again, I hear, 'She's holding her own.'

I sigh and thank him over and over.

'You still sick?'

'Yes, I am miserable and sorry. I was stinkin' and didn't expect...'

'Do you want me to come over?'

'Please.'

What excuse might he give that wife of his? While waiting on him, I change the sheets on my bed, lock the medicines room, tidy around the house a bit, and wipe the last of the blood and the sick from the bathroom and the cupboard in the kitchen. The letter I threw on the table catches my eye, and I rip it open.

There's a solicitor's embossed fancy paper, and it says:

Please contact the above solicitors.

Mr Larry Sheeran, of 100 Merrion Square, Dublin wishes to get in touch with you. It is in relation to your late mother's estate.

Yours sincerely,

McDaid Solicitors

My mother had very little of anything, and what would a Larry Sheeran know anything about it? My head is swimming on me with the worry of everything. I shove the paper into my handbag and hope that the world could stop turning for just a little while.

Bleach fumes make me gag, but the place is more presentable now. The thoughts of a friendly face coming to see just me for a change gives a lift to the misery. Molly is holding her own, and I'm holding bread and black tea down.

It all comes around so nicely in my head as I think of being snuggled in Joe's arms and of our baby… when in through the back door comes Tiny carrying a large box and the Professor with a bottle of what looks like champagne in his hand.

'I hear Molly's on the mend.' The trilby hat gets thrown onto my kitchen table. Tiny smiles and his mouth looks healed but empty. 'Don't suppose you have glasses for this champagne?' the Professor asks as I stare at the box.

'You can't just swan in here –'

'Shut up your complaining, woman. Didn't we do you a good turn?'

'Did you leave money behind the last day?'

'You're pale as death.'

He sits, and Tiny grins on.

'Tiny did. For the rifle. He likes you.'

'What's in the box?'

'Present from the Big Lad.'

Tiny nods at it. His dark hair has grown more than the shorn look he had on that first day. His eyes are kind, I hadn't noticed that before.

'But, Tiny, it's an old rifle, and I don't deserve a present.'

'Didn't see what he left for the rifle, but if the man wants to be good to a woman… Don't spoil it. Open the fuckin' box. He's all excited.'

'I'm waiting on someone and…'

Tiny's head nods repeatedly towards the box, willing me to open it, his gummy smile huge, and his hands fidgeting with excitement at the buttons on his jacket.

'Who's calling on ya?'

'Sergeant Bushnell.'

'At this time?' His eyebrows rise.

'He was to get me news of Molly. He's known me years.'

'Does he get rid of problems for you?' The voice sounds jealous, but I keep my eyes on the box.

'Not like you do.' I ignore the stare of him and the beating drum in my head. 'He's a soft touch, is Joe.'

'We could use that in the future.'

I don't ask what future he's thinking of, but I've a feeling it's a great deal different to the one I had been planning three minutes ago.

'Open the box and put this poor bugger out of his misery.'

Tiny comes over to help me. He moves the lid of the cardboard back so I can look inside. From the most ordinary cardboard box, I pull a blood-red hat, with a glorious red feather in it, and the height of it is ready for the races in the Curragh.

I'm beaming at the Big Lad. 'How could he know that I would pick this very hat for myself?'

'I dunno,' the Professor says, 'but he wouldn't take the hat box as it would give away what was inside. Spent ages in the warehouse finding one to fit it and has pestered me to come here. Thirty-four. Thirty-four.' The way he imitates the Big Lad saying the number makes me giggle.

Tiny speaks, and his tone is low and foreign. 'Peggy. Thirty-four.' He motions for me to put it on, and I cannot help but do as he wants. His big hands twirl me around and round, and I keep twirling round the kitchen, loving the feel of the expensive hat.

'Gorgeous.' The Professor grins under his thin moustache. 'And the hat isn't bad either.'

I take off the hat and instantly come back to the real world. I reach up to kiss the Big Lad's cheek and whisper, 'Thank you' in his surprisingly small ear.

'Spent a fortune on you, he has, Peggy. He might need more than a peck on the cheek.'

'I'm no whore.'

'Oh, yes, that's right… You're respectable.'

'I've made a great deal of myself, when you think of where I started.' I sound braver than I feel.

His eyes look around the small kitchen, and the side of his mouth twitches in amusement. 'A long way, eh?'

'Please sit, Tiny,' I say, pointing to a chair; he hasn't taken his eyes off me or the hat in my hand. I place the hat back in the box and thank him again and smile. His respectful gaze is so mellow. 'Tiny seems too nice to be with you.'

'You should see what he does to those he doesn't like,' the Professor says, holding the champagne bottle and picking at the thread holding the cork. 'Boys call him the Butcher. I told him you're a butcher too. Think that's why he thinks well of you.'

That wink again. I move nearer the sink. 'I'm so sick these days.' I lean in over it, hoping now that I do vomit and chase them away.

'Trying to get out of talking about what you owe me? That woman will never be found. There'll be no trace of that body. That's not easy to do, Peggy-weggy. So, we need to talk payment.'

'Seventy pounds, OK?'

The plonk of the heavy unopened bottle on the table seems so loud. 'Seventy pounds?' he shouts. 'Have you that amount to spare?'

'That's all I'm giving you.'

'But sure, that's a grand amount.' The mouth on him is all twisted into a grin. 'Where did the likes of you get seventy pounds?'

'He gave it to me.' I point at the Big Lad.

The Professor wheels around on his pointed shoes and glares at the Big Lad who is fixing the lid on the box.

'Tiny moved her for you, and now, you pay him with his own money?'

I shrug and look out the kitchen window.

'So, you screw the man twice. And him not gettin' a proper screw at all?'

'I'll be good to Tiny, don't you fret.'

'How much did he leave you?'

Tiny looks uncertain, and when the Professor rubs his fingers together and points at me, Tiny seems to get his meaning.

'One hundred pounds, for Peggy.'

The Professor shakes his head. 'Soft touch, he is.'

None of us are sure why a man like the Big Lad would give me money, never mind a cold hundred pounds.

The Professor wheels around on me. 'So, why not give us the whole hundred pounds?'

'Because I need money to get a dress to go with the hat.'

The weasel laughs and doubles over in the chair, and Tiny looks all confused at us both.

'You're some doll.' The tears are tripping out of him. 'Taking advantage of everyone and looking angelic to boot. Honest to Christ, the head on you there now. Looking all innocent. It wouldn't surprise me if you play every man like a fiddle.'

'Is that a deal, then?' I hold out my hand for him to shake it.

He spits on his palm and stands to take my hand in his.

'I won't lie with you,' I tell him.

He shrugs. 'You might have no choice.'

He spits again on his hand and pumps our hands up and down and watches my chest jiggle. 'Deal,' he says. 'We'll speak no more about it now, and we'll give Tiny back some of his money for a job he did himself. You're some operator, Peggy. Come here, you.' He heaves me into him and wraps his arms around me tightly and smacks his thin horrid lips up against mine. His tongue penetrates my shocked lips and swirls into my mouth. I squirm like an eel and hear the front door getting a knock.

'Jesus.' I break free from his hold. 'I'm part of no deal. Fuck off me.'

'All right, Miss High and Mighty.' He lifts the bottle and nods to Tiny to get up. 'We'll be back for his money. Go let your sergeant in, and we'll all stay stum about the bodies around thirty-four.'

Both of them are gone, leaving the box with the red hat in it on the table. Another knock comes to the door. Louder this time.

Chapter 11

'Joe,' I say, pleased as anything to see a good man at my front door. 'Come in.'

He acts like he's on official business, but his clothes are his own; a woollen jumper with triangular patterns on it and a shirt collar that matches a blue in the jumper and a pair of navy trousers that look tidy and brown shoes with laces.

'You look so different.' I use it as an excuse to take in all of him. His dark brown hair is all brushed and sitting to one side like a schoolboy's. He is handsome in an ordinary kind of way. My heart and head thump on, and I'm glad when he puts the kettle on in the kitchen like he's used to doing it. I sit down.

'What's in the box?' he asks.

'Nothing much.'

I jump up to put the box into the back scullery and hope I can just forget all the bad things in my head.

'Still sick?'

'Much better.'

'It was all a bit much.'

'Yes.'

The kettle whistles.

'There's not much to eat. No milk. I've been in such a state.'

'Course you have.'

'Did your wife not mind you leaving at this time?' I look at the clock that tells me it's after eight o'clock.

'She's used to the hours. And, sure, I'm back for my hat…' He pauses and looks at me. 'But she's left me, you know. Few months back. Took off with my boy, to her mother's people in Cork.'

'Arrah, no.'

'It's been a long time coming.' He sighs and sits with the mug warming his hands. 'We all know it was no marriage.'

'Still.' I blow on the hot tea.

'None of the girls show up?'

'No.' There's a silence. 'Thanks for turning a blind eye to all that. But I think I need a change. Perhaps all this happened to get me and Molly straightened out.'

His lips curve upwards, and his eyes sparkle at me. 'What's the plan?'

'There isn't one…yet.'

'I'm asking for a transfer down the country somewhere quiet.'

My heart falls from my chest all the way to my toes. 'You can't.' I stop myself getting tearful. 'You can't leave Dublin.'

'There's a few things at work, and Dublin's getting too rough. I need a nice cushy job until I retire. Somewhere where there is little to bother a guard. You know?'

A single tear falls.

'It's a long way off yet.'

He either hasn't seen my tear or ignores it. I wipe it away and try to think of something to say that isn't begging him to take me as his wife so my baby doesn't need to be gotten rid of or isn't a bastard.

'You all right?'

'Tired.'

'Molly will be grand, you know, but they may want her committed somewhere.'

'What?' I remember to breathe.

'Well, with the stabbing and her problems.' He points to his head. 'She's a danger to herself and others. She'll probably be sent away for…'

'Sent where? How long?'

'Depends. But it's for her own good.'

'Own good, me hole.'

'You need a life too. You cannot be responsible for a girl like that.'

'Like what?'

'You know, she's hard managed. She needs to be with her own kind.'

'I'm her own—'

'Aren't you looking for a change? A new life?'

'That I am.'

'I could get you work maybe in an office or somewhere.'

'Respectable work?'

'Yes, like a lassie like you should have.'

'Lassie?'

He blushes. 'You're not an auld one yet.' His wink is ten hundred miles away from the Professor's.

'Would you save me, Joe Bushnell?' The blush goes deeper. 'Would you be my knight in shining armour?'

'Stop your teasing, Peggy Bowden.'

'You're a good man.'

'Come to the pictures with me tomorrow night?'

'Pictures?'

'Like normal folk,' he whispers over the table at me. 'Go out for the night?'

It's been years since I was in a cinema or out with a man for a night. I'm shocked and speechless.

'Well?' His face is eager for an answer. My conscience telling me I should explain my predicament.

'I'm not the woman you think I am.'

His leaves his mug and moves his chair over to sit right next to me. We are perched together right beside the very corner where the soldier sat my naked arse. Joe takes my hand in his. 'I'm not the man you think I am, either. Is anyone how we think they are?'

I shake my head and wonder if he's right. Is everyone hiding the type of secrets I've hidden all my life?

'Come to the pictures. We'll take it from there.' He sounds confident in our future, and it is great to feel some of it.

'Right. Tomorrow night.'

'I'll come get you here. Say seven?'

'Will I cook us some dinner first?'

'Do you cook?' His voice is high. 'Really?'

'I make a good stew.'

'Right, so. I'll be here for six.' He gets up to leave me, and I don't want to wait to be in his arms and safe and warm.

'That money, Peggy?' he asks in the hall when I hand him his hat.

'Wasn't mine. All sorted.' I pat his arm and kiss his cheek. The smell off him is fresh and clean like the man he is.

'Do you have all you need?'

I gaze into those blue eyes, hoping he might kiss me. I might feel normal and wanted. 'Almost. But let me know what they're doing with Molly. If I can do anything at all for her. I don't want her going away again.'

'She'll get treatment and be in the right place.' He opens the door to leave me with his lies. We all know there are no good places for lassies like Molly. I picture her in a jacket, tied and bound, as they inject her with things to keep her quiet like they did to Mammy. Joe's lips brush off mine, and he's away, waving from a few feet down the street.

Chapter 12

'There's not enough there for all of your girls,' the owner of Foley's pub and shop says with a knowing look. 'Tess normally does the shopping.'

'Did you not hear about Molly?' I ask, knowing if the grapevine hasn't got it around by now, there's something amiss.

'Terrible business. And there's that missing woman too.'

I nearly drop the milk bottle I'm holding.

'Her people have been swarming over the place, asking questions, saying she was to be around here to see some doctor.' Mr Foley gives change to a boy and looks on at me. 'Sure, we all know the only good doctor about these streets is yourself.'

'Her mother came to me, all right, but I never saw the poor woman.' The shake in my knees must be noticeable.

'I told them if ever there was a kind woman in the world, it was you. And if she was with you, she was in the safest of hands.' He blesses himself and reaches under the counter. 'Cigarettes for Molly, no charge.'

The Woodbines sit on the counter, and his generosity pains me physically.

'They won't let me see her or tell me how she is.'

'After the Tommy slashing?'

'You know about him too?'

'Sure, his ma was screaming about it all over. No wonder the young lad wants away from home. Wagon of a woman, she is.'

'We've had a hard time of it.' I place my few bits of shopping up on the counter, unsure if I have everything but wanting away from the world.

'And the Professor? He's calling quite a bit?'

I look up the street. Number thirty-four is in view, but it's a good distance for spying.

'Bad piece of work that.' He leans in closer. 'Ya hear me now. Watch yourself, pet.'

'As long as Molly is all right.' I'm rooting for my money in my cleavage.

'With God's help.' He blesses himself yet again as if I am from the devil himself, or my life is cursed. 'And the sergeant looking about ye as well?'

I cannot believe that he knows about Joe, but sure he knows all the rest. 'He's a good man.'

There's no reply, and he stops placing my groceries in the basket I gave him.

'Mind yourself. I'll say a prayer for Molly. I cannot believe though she did what she did. Christ, it was awful for ya. Are your other girls coming back?'

'I would've thought respectable people would be glad if I shut up shop?'

'Sure, pretty women are always good to have about. And there was never any bother from your place. Despite what people say.'

'Thanks.'

'*Are* you shutting down?' He looks delighted to have a snippet for the snug in the pub. 'There'll be a few sorry men about.'

His wife arrives in from the back of the shop and looks down her nose at me. I'd love to wear my fancy hat into his shop just to see the look on her.

'No plans as yet. But Peggy Bowden aims to move up in the world. That's all I'm saying.' I turn on my heel.

'Good for you, good for you.'

There are some good men in the world, even if they like to gossip like women. The day is fresh, and the sun is sneaking out from behind the clouds. The smelly fecker who collects the rent is at the doors, so I sit on the bench looking into the tiny green space where the young ones have made a bald patch in the grass until he moves on. His eyesight is poor, so I figure if I smoke

Molly's cigarettes and wait a while, he'll disappear like all the other problems in my life.

The Professor is foremost in my thoughts. Paying him seemed almost too easy. Life always has a nip in the tail. Would the likes of the Professor be able to swing something and get Molly out of wherever they sent her? Joe might take me to see her, help me talk sense into her about the future. I could make another deal with the devil and get Molly out – surely, I could? And somehow get her Fionn back?

In Dublin, as Peggy Bowden, would I be able to keep my own child? I've been ordered not to have children under my roof, according to my bad solicitor, but would that mean my own children too? I'd never thought to ask as I never expected any – ever.

But if I married? I would have a different name? Peggy Bushnell. Peg Bushnell. Sergeant's wives would be free from the suspicion of a past like mine. Maybe moving back to the sticks would be good for the likes of me? I'd need to lie with Joe, sooner rather than later. Being no fool, he could work out a few things, if I wasn't smart about it. Maybe I could tell him? Lean on him and trust him to love me anyway? The cigarettes are harsh, but they're helping me think. Molly tried being honest with that Tommy and look where we've all ended up.

Tricking a good man is just another nail in my coffin. But, sure, it isn't a lie if he wants it to be true. Moving out of Dublin removes me from the Professor. It ends the line of disasters and takes me away from the questions about that McKenzie woman they're all looking for. That letter pops into my head. Who is Larry Sheeran? Although that name does ring a bell from somewhere. Past caller at thirty-four? Someone I sold a child too? No. Mammy's estate? Sure, all Mammy had was me, a few sheep and cattle and the land. She didn't even have a nice wedding ring.

The air is nicer, there's no noise, no humping upstairs and no girls to watch. I'd be free to cook, clean and be a good wife from now on. Wouldn't that be nice? Course it would.

Kids come to kick a mucky ball over and back, and one little boy stands picking his nose watching the others. I touch my belly and wonder what the little creature in there is doing. What he or she may be like. Would they be tall and handsome like the soldier? Pretty like me?

People passing are looking at me with my basket, wondering why I'm sitting in the middle of the day staring into the future all by myself. Why does it matter so much what people think? Why couldn't I sit here until I became a statue? What would it matter to them or to anyone? Why do I care if I look odd? But I rise off the seat and put the Woodbine away into the space between the milk and the meat cuts from the butcher's.

Tiny's a butcher, eh? I don't think too hard about what he might have done to that poor woman. Or why he might have left me so much money and bought me the hat. Best not to dwell too much on things when I'm stressed enough as it is.

The smell of cooking in thirty-four reminds me of Mick Moran's mother's house on a Sunday when I was courting him. Life was good then. He'd swing me around the dance-halls, and we'd laugh together at the pictures and kiss passionately in the dark. I would have done anything for him and those dimples. I let it all slip away. Didn't want things quiet and nice for us. How stupid I am to dream of big things.

Tess or I cooked for the girls in thirty-four most days, but the smells got lost in my organising and working. Maybe it's my condition that makes me notice the whiffs and scents around me. A stew has a warmth to it. Perhaps it even makes this house smell like a home.

Joe's brought a bottle of sherry. I can see him from the window, coming up the street. It's in a paper bag shaped like a bottle. It's years since I had sherry, and my fanciest dress isn't fancy enough for it. Blue lace on the collar – I thought he might wear his fancy blue patterned jumper. The coat covering him is heavy for the summer, but he looks good enough in his plain trousers and dark jumper. He sees something across the green where the children play. The tree hides him for a time. Then, I see his head is in the window of a black car.

Tiny gets out and goes to the boot. He and Joe disappear behind it, and I squint to see if the Professor is inside the car. The lace curtain goes back into place so I can spy without being seen. But then, the car moves off, and Joe is marching on with no paper bag and his hands in his pockets.

'I dropped the sherry I had for you,' he says when I let him into number thirty-four. 'Got flustered.'

'See anyone you knew on the way?'

'No one better than yourself. You look nice.'

He isn't looking at me, though, so I twirl for him in the kitchen like I did with my expensive hat on.

'Something smells good. Stew, you said?'

'And spuds.'

'A woman that can cook, eh?'

'Any word of Molly?'

He doesn't answer me, but takes the beer I've given him.

'I'm going to go see her. I'll get past any matron.'

'No,' he says plainly and slugs from the bottle. His hand goes through his hair. 'She's been moved.'

'To where?'

'Don't spoil the evening now.'

'Joe?'

'I'm starving. Get the dinner on the table, woman.'

It's the way he orders it, as if I were a wife. I know he's just distracting me, but that annoys me too. 'Fuck you!'

He's shocked, sitting there.

'I'm her family.'

'You're not. That's the trouble. Her family have committed her for good, and that's an end to it.'

I smash the plate I've taken from the top of the range where it was warming. The noise of it frightens us both.

'Jesus!' He leaps back with the chair. I go to hold the sink and stare into the evening sun dipping over the barbed wire. I cannot speak to him.

'There's nothing any of us can do. Even the Professor's hands are tied on this one. I asked him if he could bribe someone somewhere to get her back to you. He thought he'd rough me up a bit and broke your sherry.'

The plate shards are crunching under my feet as I make my way to him. I put my arms round his waist and look up into his blue eyes. 'You did that?'

He moves the hair on my forehead and tucks it behind my right ear. 'I tried. For you.'

'The Professor is a shite.'

'He gets shit done, Peggy, and you wanted Molly...'

'Oh, Joe...'

'I can handle the Professor.'

Tears are falling, and I can't stop them. I place my head on his chest and listen to his good heart beating away all on its own. One kind hand of his is in my hair, and his body feels so warm and safe.

'You shouldn't have done...'

'He owes me a thing or two, does the Professor. Stop your worrying. I don't think he tried too hard, though. Said something about her being trouble for you and better off locked away.'

I say nothing but curl into him, not wanting him to tell me any more bad news.

'He was fond of her?'

Joe continues to caress my hair. It does feels nice, yet the conversation is terrible. Little does he know that the weasel has eyes for me now. The Professor might take more from me than most. Men like him don't just take, they invade, and I might not be able to stop him. If I was with Joe, he might be less inclined to bother me. Or would it entice him all the more? It makes me feel sick to think of him leering, touching and taking pieces of me when he pleases. My body is one thing. It's been stolen many times before, but I always had a future, and it was mine to change for the better. If the Professor sidles in, I will lose all that, and my money won't be my own at all. I'd be a prisoner again, a married woman without the respectability. The shudder that goes through me, makes me sink deeper into Joe. With him, at least I might be able to be a version of myself. I could stand tall and be a Peggy with pride. I would be somewhat free. Wouldn't I?

'Didn't the Professor like Molly?' he asks.

'Yeah.'

'Fickle fucker, he is. Said he has sights on other things now, and that Molly was a beast in a beautiful body. Said horrible things.'

'What things?'

'He's all talk. There's got to be a way to bring that fella down. We never can pin much on him.'

'You're not at work now.'

'No.' His hand moves to find my chin. He moves my head away from his chest so I can look at him. He wipes the wet away with his thumb and leans in until his lips touch mine.

It is like in the films, but, sure, there isn't a longing in me for him. It is like I'm kissing a relation. It feels wrong, but I know I need to make it worth his bother.

'Umm,' I murmur as if it's nicer than it is. His tongue is urgent and more passionate than I remember, and his beer bottle changes hands and gets put into the sink. 'The dinner,' I mutter as he fondles my breast, and I break from his mouth.

'Can't it wait?' He takes my hand and leads me to the door.

'Suppose.'

I watch his feet as he makes for the stairs. He knows where to go. I follow him like a little lamb. The steps that took all my energy when the days were hard, are the same steps so full of guilt, and they are even harder to climb now, when they should make me so happy.

I manage to smile at him as he sits me on the bed and stands back to take off his clothes. If I went to confession, would the priest forgive my horrid sins against Joe? But he's so trusting.

I stand to take off my clothes too. I slowly reveal myself to him in the light of the evening streaming through the net curtain. I place myself under the covers like a present, and he joins me. His flesh is close and then beside mine. He's warm like a hot water bottle, and as his nose comes level with mine, I close my eyes and let him do what he must.

He slides on top of me, and I open my legs. I close my eyes tighter than a nun's fist around a shilling and think of the soldier and the passion I should feel for this fine man. He grunts and pants near my ear, and I grab his back like I should. He's inside me, but I don't move much as his weight crushes me into the mattress, and really, there's no need to prolong anything. One last hump and he's over the finish line, and I've a father for my baby.

He kisses me lightly and murmurs, 'You're wonderful.'

I don't feel wonderful, but I lay there, hoping I'm looking content. 'The dinner. I've got to see if it's burnt.'

'It's all right to lie a while with me, you know.'

'Not while the dinner is spoiling it's not.' I kiss him quickly on the mouth and jump from the bed like a young one in love. 'There'll be more of that nonsense, Joe Bushnell, but there'll need to be a dinner first.'

His laugh is pleasant, and he turns over in the bed as if he will doze a minute.

'Get your trousers on. You're taking me out, remember?'

'What happened to more of the nonsense you mentioned?'

'You cannot be ready for more of that yet?' I put on my dress and bend to slip on my strappy sandals. 'The dinner will be on the table in five minutes, and then, you're taking me out.'

He's happy. I can tell by the way he sits up in the bed. 'Right so.'

From the washbasin in the bathroom, I take a facecloth and swirl it around to freshen me up. I walk down the stairs quicker than usual. I've solved both our loneliness and filled it with a love of sorts, and a baby to boot. A Joe Bushnell doesn't come along every day for a girl like me, and although he's married, his wife is long gone. These steps are bringing a better life for us all. I skip into the kitchen and get a new plate from the dresser and try to forget about Molly for the moment as I sweep up the broken one.

Just as I am about to call up the stairs that I've the dinner on the table, there's a knock to the door. I peek out the living room window and can see no one. I don't want to let the world into our time together. Then, someone turns the knob and walks right into my hallway.

It's the elderly lady from a few days ago, minus the children. She's standing looking around the hall, fixing her hat to make sure it doesn't move. Then, she looks to her right and sees me with the net curtain in my fist and the guilt of the world in my head.

'Hello again,' she says, coming towards me, leaving the outside door ajar. 'I'm calling looking for Dot McKenzie, my daughter?'

'I remember. I was just about to have my dinner.'

'Don't you care about a missing woman? A mother of seven children?'

I need her gone, and fast. That's all that I can think of. Out the door. Out the door. 'Of course I do. I just meant…'

'The neighbours here say you're good, despite this place…'

'I don't know many of them.' I walk towards her.

She looks like thunder might, if it had a face. 'Most around here have been kind. Out to help us look and search.' She bores through me with her eyes, and the guilt heaps on again as she goes on. 'I've heard ya had your own troubles.'

'Yes.' I know it's odd not to invite her in, but with Joe upstairs, I just want her gone. Out the door. Out the door.

'No one else will come here. Police even scared of ya.' She looks me up and down like I'm a bold child. 'Some Professor and his son, warning us to take our people home. They don't like a commotion on their patch.'

I look up the stairs. There's no sign of Joe, but he must've heard her in the hall – I've left the bedroom door open.

'They say the word is there's no point looking no more.' She looks strong, rather than grieving, and it's a long time since I feared another woman. 'Is there a point in looking, Peggy? Is there any point in looking for my precious girl?'

'Your family must do all they can.'

She knows my name – well, of course she does, but I don't know hers. She moves silently towards me and takes my arm in her gloved hand. 'Woman to woman, here and now. I've money, if that's what it takes. But you and I know Dot came here and what she came here for. She'd never leave that daft husband of hers or her weans. Much as I didn't want to see her in a mess of life, Dot was happy. Happy 'til she came here.'

The old woman is looking at me. I know her anger is stuck to me, even though I'm staring at my tiles finding bits of dirt from the street.

'She never came here.' I pull my arm away.

'There's nowhere else she had to go. The grocer up there remembers filling her bags with her groceries, and he thought he saw her reach the door here. It took a bit of persuading to get that out of him.'

'I never saw her.'

'Swear it on the Holy Bible. Swear it on your own mother's life.' She's so close to me in every way. I'm flushed and panicking.

'I swear.'

'Someone here opened this door to my Dot. Someone here opened this door and let her in, and she was never seen again.'

Joe must be listening, or he'd have come down looking to be fed by now, and my nerves are shot to bejesus. All I can think of is getting her out the door. Out the door.

'Mrs…'

'I'm Dorothy McKenzie's mother. Mother to the best daughter in the world, the grandmother to a squad of kiddies. Mother-in-law to an ass of a man who's drunk all of his savings dry, crying about the woman who never came out this door again.' She's starting to shout. 'The police and the gangsters of Dublin might look after *you*, but who looked after my Dot? Where is she? Where is my baby girl?'

I just look at the tiles and move to get past her to get the door open fully. 'Please go.'

'Someday, you'll understand. I curse those who know where she is and won't give us peace.'

Out the door…out the door she goes, and I close it with the most welcome clunk on the lock, my heart leaping like a frog and my throat on fire with the burning rising from a stomach in turmoil. I hold my belly and think of the stress on the child. On my child, on my baby girl? My head rests on the wood, and I breathe, seeing my belly like Molly's swollen in the gaol where they've sent me for Dot's murder and them wrenching my baby girl from my arms. That woman cursed me.

'Peggy?' I turn to face Joe in his shirtsleeves and bare feet at the bottom of the stairs, his face full of concern.

'The dinner…'

I move towards the kitchen. On past the medicines room that housed this nightmare and into the kitchen where the dinner looks lukewarm on the table.

'I heard that woman. I didn't come out – she was at the station…'

I fill two glasses with milk.

'She's lost her daughter.'

I want to confess to him. But would a moral man like Joe ever understand what happened and what I did?

'Molly killed her, didn't she? It's all right. I saw that woman's shopping in the hall. I remember it now. The world and his mother know that Molly did her in. That's what happened. It was one of the reasons there wasn't much fuss. Molly was in custody anyway. We all know she did it.'

'Don't, Joe…' I pray I know the right thing to say now. 'Don't ask me.'

'We'll say no more about it.' He takes his fork and knife in his hand like nothing has changed. And, yes, the madness is still spinning around in me.

'Molly's too sick for this world. She should've been put away long ago. We all know that and only for your kindness looking after her…'

'Kindness? I used her.'

'She liked the whoring.' He munches on a carrot. 'What else could a lassie like her do? She couldn't work anywhere else. Where would have her?'

The kitchen is in a blur as he goes on.

'Her family should have looked about her. Looked after her when she got out. But, sure, she accused that uncle of all sorts and cut him up, and well, they finally did the right thing and put her where she belongs.'

'Where's that?'

'I don't know. They took her back down the country.'

'Where?' There's quite a few places she could be.

'I dunno.'

'I need to see her.'

'Even the Professor couldn't find out where.'

I think of the woman who's just been here. Molly is like a daughter to me. As odd as that sounds, even to me, Molly has been someone I loved like I imagine it would be for a mother. She has been taken from me, and I don't know where she is either. An eye for an eye.

'Eat your dinner, love. Put all this behind ya. Molly did bad things, and she can't hurt you anymore.'

The sound of him eating is irritating.

'I can't hurt her anymore either.' I rise and think of the whiskey in the cupboard. The stuff that is vile, but it might pinch the pain away a bit.

'If only we knew what happened to the body,' Joe says between bites. 'Give the family something to bury.'

I swig from the bottle.

'The Professor helped her, did he?'

One crack of the whiskey bottle on the head and I could stop his questions. I am so tired of it all, of him, of all my lies. 'I don't know.'

'That mother is some woman, though, eh? As brave as a lioness.'

I take another slug.

'I'm beginning to think that women are vicious, you know. But there's no end to a mother's love. This meat is tender and as tasty. Can I have yours?' He reaches over, and most of mine is gone before I can reply. 'We'll find the body soon enough, and her family will have peace. We'll tell them it was a madwoman, and that she's been put away, and that'll be that. Now eat something.'

He turns around, and I see a totally different man than the man I had in my head. This man isn't the Joe Bushnell that I wished into life. He's a watered-down version of the movie-star man of the law I had in my daydreams. The Joe who would save me from the world isn't there at all.

'Whiskey? Drink never solves nothing. Stop that now, woman. Come eat.'

I put the cap back on and raise the bottle over my head. One good whack, that's all I'd need. One good thwack would do it, but I lower the bottle and place it back into the cupboard.

We don't go out. There's no mention of it from him, and I'm too tired anyhow. We sit listening to the wireless. Me with my head in the crook of his arm and him snoozing, with his feet up, and the socks he put on smelling a good bit. The snores of him during the night would wake the dead, and I mentally count my stash, planning that the Professor might take another seventy pounds to throw Joe away somewhere.

The kissing of him in the morning smells like stale cabbage. The feel of him looking for his way with me again, making me drift away to dance with Mick in the Gresham.

I gave in to Joe, so he is certain about the baby later. Days ago, I'd have wanted this so badly. I would've thought it the best idea and greatest privilege to be under a man like Joe, but now, I feel I'm more trapped than he will be and I hate the person I've become.

Peggy Bowden is a liar, a murderer, a gangster, a butcher and a whore.

'I think I could love you, Peggy Bowden,' he murmurs into my ear when he's done.

'I think I could love you, Joe Bushnell,' I hear my mouth saying, when all I feel is hate for him and myself.

Chapter 13

Number thirty-four is all I've really known since prison, and in a way, it has become another prison of my own making. I rarely leave the walls, and if I do, it is to go to Foley's shop, the butcher's and back. I only realised this morning that it's weeks since I went further.

'Want more, but don't want too much.'

My mother is before me as I check out my belly in the mirror. It is still flat. My guts howl for food, and I think I'd like soup. Mammy always made great soup. My hands are pruned in the sink, doing my washing, the water milky with soap.

'Potato and leek with a dash of cream,' I ask the clothes as I hang them over the clothesline. 'Like Mammy made.'

I'm not sure how I know Mammy's people were not the same as those around us. It was the way she was thought of, until she went a little mad. The ladies in Mass always treated her differently, and the priest even seemed a little wary of her. We were dirt poor, but had more than we should have had. I got new shoes every Christmas that fitted me, and I got sweets more than most. My life wasn't too bad, until she took a turn in her brain. She had loved the very breath of my father.

Although I don't remember him, I was told that he was in the war. Why they went away to fronts far away is still unclear to me. There was no call or popular thought for those who fought for the British Crown. Perhaps that's why they treated us the way they did. Like outcasts, like something they didn't understand fully or want to be involved much with.

He'd been tall, had Daddy. At least he was to me in my dreams. His photo did not give much away, except that he was handsome and could tie a nice knot on his tie, his hair all to one side, looking thick and healthy.

'Why must war eat good men?'

Mammy's address book and Bible are at the bottom of the bag I was running away with. My washing is on the line and blowing in the breeze. Thirty pounds sits on the table, and my wonderings about the past and the present lay like a book of sorts before me.

'My family is different to most,' Mammy said when I asked why we didn't know them. 'They didn't like your father.'

'Why don't they come see us now he's dead?'

Only a child could have kept asking.

'Don't burn bridges, Peggy. Never burn your bridges,' she said. I know now what she meant and wonder if I inherited her knack for trouble too.

The address book is scribbled on with her nice and terrible handwriting. The nice, from the days when she was lucid and knew things. The terrible, possibly from the days when she was lost. Why I want to decipher my family now, after all this time, I don't know. The house is so quiet I can hear my mind whirring and my heart longing to keep up.

There's many addresses in Sligo. Some I recognise, many I don't. Then, I see the word Daddy and an address in Dublin. It is the same address on the solicitor's letter for Larry Sheeran. Was Mammy a Sheeran from Dublin?

I don't hear anyone in the back yard until the door opens, and the Professor and a younger man are inside. Compared to the old-fashioned style of the Professor in his Crombie coat and thin moustache and trilby hat, this young fella looks like a dandy. He looks for all world like the Teddy Boys they all talk about.

'So, this is the famous Peggy Bowden?' the Teddy Boy sneers.

'Peggy is here less than two years. Kept very quiet premises, but she'll have no bother letting us take over her business from now on,' the Professor says to him. They both sit at my table, and there's no sign of Tiny. I fold the thirty pounds and put the bundle into my front, but they've seen it and are looking over at Mammy's address book.

'My business is finished.'

'You'll do as you're told.' The younger boyo spits when he talks. His brown hair is all lacquered and womanly in the curling it does, and his fancy suit is all dapper green and clean.

'This is the eldest son, Anthony.' The pride in the Professor is clear as a bell.

I stare at his eldest spawn, but he doesn't look away from me, intimidating me with his dark eyes bulging with badness. A shiver runs down my spine.

'Pretty Peggy is a good business woman,' the Professor says, grinning and tapping his matches on the table.

'Whether she is or she isn't, she's going to do as she's told.'

'Get out.' I get up from my chair angry as hell at the tone of this bulky teenager.

'Anthony here knows a thing or two about business.'

'Been to school, has he? Out that door now.' I point to the back door.

'You're brave…for a whore.' His hand goes to his hair to make sure it's in place. 'A whore that's alone…' He lets that sink in and doesn't take his eyes off me. All the time they're telling me he's the devil himself, and I've to sit down.

'I've seen the likes of you before.'

'No. You haven't. Da here thinks women need looking after. Has his favourites. To me, you're cattle.'

The years of abuse from the man who took me and my farm spring up from the heather, reincarnated to me now looking at this fellow. I shiver again and hold my elbows, crossing my arms to protect myself from the evilness he's spreading into the room.

'And cattle need managed. I can find the girls, and you can do the managing here for me.'

There is no dealing with this, no haggling, no debate. He means it will happen. Those hard features and his lips tighten when he talks, and his hand points at me. 'Whores need putting in their place. Sit down.'

The Professor smiles on with the pride only a father like him could have. I don't sit but think seriously about it.

'Sit the fuck down!' He thumps the table and makes it jump as well as me. He points again to the chair.

'Sergeant Bushnell will be here any…'

His voice goes all low and whispering as he points again at the chair. 'Sit the fuck down.'

I sit.

'You've been ignored for long enough. Taking us for fools and playing at having whores. This house can house many more girls and can rake in the money.'

'I'm getting a respectable job…'

The Professor laughs, and Anthony just stares.

'I don't think you heard me. You're going to house more girls here, and we're going to make a bundle.'

'The guards won't take kindly…'

'You leave them to us.' The Professor winks and a disgust crawls over my skin.

'Your other girls are looking to come back, but we've them housed elsewhere.'

Poor Tess and the others are under his thumb. 'What do I get out of this?'

'A percentage of the takings. Ten percent, say.' He tosses his head like he's thrown me a bone.

'If it was ninety, I might think about it.'

'Twenty?'

'I'm going straight. I don't need this.' My head throbs, my sickness so near the surface, and I want them out the door almost as much as I wanted that old woman out yesterday. 'Sergeant Bushnell is going…'

'Gonna wha'? Rescue you from this squalor?'

'I'm going to get a job and…'

'From who? Who'd vouch for you?'

'The sergeant.'

'His wife will love that.' Tony's eyes squint and his nose goes up. 'She's quite the catch. Daughter to that tough county councillor fella.'

'His wife left months ago. Went to Cork or somewhere…'

The Professor shakes his head at me. He seems certain the way he moves his hands to mirror his head. His finger goes up and moves over and back. 'No. She's not away. No. No. No.'

'Course she is. Sure, he said…'

'And you believe him, because he's a lawman?'

I believe them. The reality is sinking in like their words. 'I don't like your proposition.'

'That's a big word.' Anthony gets to his feet and drags me up from my chair. He holds my arm tightly yanking me into him and bringing his mouth close to my face. 'You're not listening. This is a direct order. No option, missus. Not one.'

'Peggy is educated. A trained midwife. She hasn't much morals. She kills babies in their mothers' bellies,' I hear the Professor say.

'I can smell the badness off ya.'

'I can smell it off you too.'

His fingers dig deeply into my arm. 'We'll have some girls here in a few days, and no doubt we'll drum up some of that other business. No bother.'

He lets go of my arm and beckons to his father to leave. With his hand on the back door, he looks back. 'Tell the rest of the neighbourhood. I'm in charge around here from now on.'

They're gone as silently as they came. The whiskey bottle helps none of the shivering I'm doing, and there's a flutter in my belly that I cannot get stopped. I'm sick again, but it's becoming so normal now I'm starting to get used to it.

Running away seems like a good plan but somehow, like the last time, I doubt I'd get far without the Professor knowing. I'm trapped like a rat. Trapped like the rat that I am.

I look around Mountjoy Square and think of how grand it must have been in the past. These gorgeous tall buildings housing people with ambition and respectability.

'Want more, Peggy, but don't want too much.'

The cigarette smoke makes nice rings from my mouth, and I know my stupidity isn't far from Molly's. I dreamed of a man loving me and placing a ring on my finger. Even when I didn't fully want it or him. But, like Molly, I was lied to or tricked into believing a secure future.

But then, I lied too. I lied quite a bit.

Two ladies pass chatting as they cycle on with their fur-trimmed collars and their hats modern and new. I'm so jealous of their freedom. How free it must be away from the house, talking to another about anything at all. I haven't a friend in the world. Now that Molly's gone and Joe's a bastard like the rest. There's a 'hullo' from the scrap man, and his horse ambles on. Although not free, a horse's life looks good to me today.

'Going somewhere, Peggy?' he shouts, looking back. 'I can give ya a lift, if you jump on the back?'

I trot a little to catch up. 'Thanks,' I holler.

The cart slows down, and I heave myself up on the lip at the back. I think I'll sit on for a time and let the world pass me by. The cars and the bustle die down at this time of the evening. Women with prams, men swaying into and away from the public houses, older ladies in scarves chattering together. The movement of the cart is like a rocking chair, or a crib, lulling me into a secure place where the worries melt into the smoke of my cigarette and blow away.

We turn into streets, and I sit on, and when he stops, I just smile and say, 'Going a bit further.' It's the getting away from Mountjoy and all its shite that brings me joy. When Molly and I had found number thirty-four in Mountjoy Square after leaving Mountjoy gaol, we'd considered it a good omen. Now, I'm not so sure. My mother's address book is in my mind, and the word "Daddy" scrawled across a page. *100 Merrion Square, Dublin.*

The pub on the corner looks like a lively place. I don't frequent pubs, although I've seen women go in alone, but I linger by the bus stop and look up at the house with the nice round number. Some women mill passed. I stop one to ask, 'Are the Sheerans still living here?'

The old one whispers, 'We are just passing. Back from the bingo. But, yeah, them Sheerans live there. Back from America a few months back.'

'The lights are on. They must be home.'

'They all say that the old fella is dying. The whole place is in uproar that he'd start the whole thing up again. But they say at the bingo that the bad lads are willing to let him die on Irish soil.' She blesses herself, but she's worried in her tone and concerned when she asks, 'What do you want the Sheerans for?'

'And the old man is called Larry?'

'Don't you know who you're dealing with at all, girl?'

I shrug.

'Them are the big people that travelled to Hell's Kitchen.'

'Hell's Kitchen?'

'New York, love. Have you been locked away or something?'

'I lived over about Ranelagh for years.'

'Ranelagh, eh?' she mocks me and looks me up and down. 'You look familiar to me. Would I know you?'

'Doubt it.'

'Pretty one like you might've been in the magazines or the paper?'

They're smelling gossip or some titbit of information.

'No. I'm Molly. Molly McCarthy. I just saw this address written down and wondered was it around here.'

'Where are you living now?'

'I must get on.'

I start my escape. But with that the front door opens across the street and out comes a lady in a nurse's uniform. One of the women near me says, 'Ask her how he's keeping.'

My feet totter over the street, and before the nurse gets onto her bicycle, I say, 'Excuse me?'

'Yes?' She is matronly.

'I need to know if Larry Sheeran... I'm enquiring how he's keeping?'

'The man is dying.'

'I'm enquiring for a family member.'

'His family are all in America.' She hops a leg over her bicycle.

'Please? I got a letter saying to contact him about my mother, his daughter...'

'Are you saying you are family?' She's a cold fish.

'I would like to know how he is.'

She glances over the street at my bunch of helpers, gawping in our direction and whispering feverishly to each other. I hope they cannot hear my conversation. The nurse's stern look doesn't bother me, but I don't know what else to add, and the rain has started.

'Call again, and we might get you to see the man himself. This is not the kind of thing to discuss in the street.'

'Indeed,' I say in my poshest voice. 'Tomorrow?'

The bitch is away up the street like a squirt of piss.

'Well? What did she say?' the woman over the street shouts.

I turn to walk away from them up the side of the street I'm on. I ignore them.

'Well?' she shouts again.

'He's not dead,' I shout back and walk as quickly as my legs will allow and turn back in the direction of Mountjoy Square. The lift of the cart was great for the feet but the pounding of them now on the footpath helps me to think, the cigarette pulling the thoughts forward while the cylindrical paper under my eyes and nose goes backwards.

'They're different to us, Peggy. Your grandparents are not good people,' Mammy had said when I asked. 'They don't like your Daddy.'

As I didn't know my father, this was never a helpful memory. Yet, Mother owned the land or at least had bought it.

'Cast a spell on him, she did,' Father Lavelle had said in my protests about the land being mine. 'No luck could come of it.

Poor Bowden fell for her good and proper. But a leopard doesn't change its spots.'

'I'm a blow-in, and with your Daddy gone, they've no reason to fully accept the likes of us,' Mammy had said. 'We'll cope just grand.' But she'd rung her hands like a mangle.

Perhaps what the locals felt for my mother wasn't respect – the looks when we went to the village. The whispers at the post office when she asked for stamps, and she explained to me, 'These will go all the way across the ocean to America.' I'm sure, too, she'd mentioned New York. Wherever her madness came from, it was possibly due to worry. Maybe Mammy wasn't cut out to survive all alone where no one wanted her. Here I am all alone, too, with no one in my corner.

Despite my mother's kind nature and her weekly trips to the altar rails, Father Lavelle had said, 'Good, honest man, your father was. With no family to guide him. An only child and his parents taken with the consumption. He wouldn't heed my advice. Said women change. Huh! Change indeed. They go mad.'

Mammy was strong, but I felt the world broke her. I touch my belly and promise, 'I'll keep my mind and fight for a better life for both of us.'

It's a good walk home in the mizzling rain, but the streets are quiet, and the night mild enough. An odd car slows down to see if I'm for sale, but no one bothers my thoughts.

'Peggy has a will of iron,' Joe Bushnell had said at my trial. 'Anything Peggy does, she does to help people. She sold babies, as has been proven, but Peggy thought she was doing good by the mothers and children. I know it's against the law of the land, but I want it on the record that at no time did Peggy Bowden hurt anyone.'

The lawyer had been tough and asked, 'Do you condone her behaviour?'

I'd been afraid for Joe then. We both knew he had brought me children that I had often abandoned out on the side of the road to Naas. Although he never told me, he knew that some of the children came from my Ranelagh maternity home. I think he also knew that I helped women not to give birth as well. Had he a soft spot for me then? Or did he just believe what we did was for the best? I never mentioned his name when the hard questioning came. Maybe there's a respect in him for me since then.

'As a member of the police force in this country, do you condone her behaviour?' the judge repeated.

Joe stood tall in the dock and said, 'I see many criminals every day, Your Honour, and Peggy Bowden is no criminal. She may have done wrong by the law, but she didn't do much wrong by helping them babies get good homes. That's all I'm saying.'

There had been an uproar in the court, and I knew Joe was putting his career in jeopardy that day. I did appreciate it. I knew what he was trying to do for me. I suppose I still do. Of course, it didn't work.

Evil Midwife Sells Babies, the headlines had read, and I'd laughed out loud when the local priest had testified against me.

'She never would come to Mass, and I knew for some time now that families from the country had come to Dublin to buy babies from her. It was a matter of proving it. Ireland's a small place, and country priests contacted me about where these babies might be coming from.'

The bastard had failed to mention they were sold by the convent he visited, too, and the Mother and Babies home up the road as well. But the clever nuns sent those children mostly to America or elsewhere where no priests or public asked questions. I was the church's competition, and they wanted rid of me, plain and simple. It was about money and power – as most things are. One woman couldn't take on to be so bold as to be successful and enjoy it as well.

I loved being well-dressed and well thought of. I lived the highlife and took my Mick Moran and his lovely dimples to fancy restaurants where he felt uncomfortable and I felt like a queen. It was the grandest time of my life. Champagne and cocktails, when other women washed clothes and ironed in the evenings when their children had stopped screaming and were in their beds.

Father Lavelle gave evidence, too, stating, 'In that maternity hospital, she preaches contraception. She drove her poor mother mad, and there was an inquest into her husband's broken neck and bashed in skull in Sligo.'

The objections were no good as the murmurs around the court were unstoppable. The image of me was very bleak. Even I was rocked about my past when it was laid before me like an ugly carpet. And sure, once the priests had condemned me in the courts, I was lost.

What a time the papers would have with me now. What would the likes of that priest preach from the pulpit next Sunday? Scaring the women of Ireland about what happens when they decide to go against them.

'To stop the conception of a child is a sin. To get money from others' misery is a sin,' the bastard said to me as he offered me confession after testifying against me. 'You must repent your ways, Peggy, or burn for eternity in the fires of hell.'

I'd been hard that day. Very frigging tired but as hard as nails, too, while I looked at the locked door of my cell. 'When will the likes of you repent? You and them nuns put me in here – *you* repent.'

'The guards should have locked you up long ago,' he spat at me in anger. 'The Mother Superior has been lenient with you for too long. You've gotten too big for your boots.'

'And, sure, men don't like women to know their own minds. Men like you will see that we lose it, get it taken away or that it will be buried in a locked room.'

'You should hide in shame for your crimes.'

'I'll be hidden. But I'm not ashamed.'

I'd been deeply ashamed and hurt, of course, just like I am now. All that I had worked for – gone. My qualification as a midwife was stripped from me not long after that. My maternity home was sold to pay my legal fees, and my freedom and fun stopped by those who would lock my door every day.

Unaware of the demon that's inside me, a few people pass by me now in happy chatter. What would they say if they knew? Will Joe truly love the likes of me? Could I really love the likes of Joe?

Mick Moran, too, comes into my mind. He'd been definite in his want to marry me until I'd been arrested all those years ago. The headlines then probably killed his own mother – a clean-living woman who'd told the whole locality that Mick was marrying a woman with a qualification and business in Dublin.

Mick had come to visit me in prison. God love him, he was as pale as snow, and with trembling hands, he'd sat across from me.

'Is your mother all right?'

There'd been no answer from him.

'There's no need to marry me now, Mick.'

I placed the ring near him on the table. I pushed the newspapers he'd brought me back at him. 'Go and live your life with a good woman and forget you ever knew me.'

The tears on his cheek got wiped away quickly before anyone else could see them. 'Why? Why didn't you just knuckle down and be my wife? This is what notions get you.'

Poor Mick now is probably still labouring away. With his intelligence, he could've been anything he wanted, and I knew the way he read Hemingway that he didn't always want to lump a hammer and dig holes in the earth. Mick understood people.

'Fools want things they can't have. Poor Peggy.'

Never would he speak ill of his own father, who had drained every penny to bet or drink. Mick loved the church and always prayed passing the chapels or holy sites. What would Mick think of the latest folly of Peggy Bowden? Murder and stabbings, abortions and killings would make him tut with disgust for sure. As I turn the corner and cross the street, there's a determination in my bones. Poor Peggy will be poor Peggy no more.

Joe's car is outside number thirty-four. The anger in me raises the sick feelings. The gossip mill must be having a fun time of it around here these days. Between gangsters and married policemen calling, I'll be a great source of amusement. There are a good few fag butts outside his car window, so he's been here a while. It is almost dark, so it must be around ten. In the summer, the day clings on like it doesn't want to leave.

'Where were you?' He's out of the car before I get a chance to even say hello.

'So, I hear your wife is still in Dublin.' I get out my key, waiting on his excuses.

'She came home suddenly. Says she's back for a while until we sort out what we'll do.'

'Where does that leave me?' I cannot tell his reaction well, despite the street light.

'You?'

'Yes. Me. Where does that leave me?'

'Can't I come in?'

'Go home to your wife, Joe. I'm so tired.'

He holds my arm and pinches it like that Anthony boyo did. 'I've been here for ages. Like an ass.'

'Joe. You're married. Go home.'

'She doesn't care about me. Some solicitor told her not to move out of the house. That's all. Told her I should leave. Shit, Peggy, I'm willing to overlook your past, for Christ's sakes.' His hand hurts me now.

'I'm tired. Upset. Let me go.'

He does as I ask. 'Let me in, and we can talk about it.' He follows me to the door. 'It's not as if you have any time for marriage.'

'But I like the truth.' I totally surprise myself with my audacity.

'Nothing has changed. I'm married, yes, but you're still –'

'I'm still what?'

'You're still my woman.' He tries to smile, but I know he thinks of me as his whore.

'The Professor called. I need away from here. But I cannot move in with you now. I need a good job. You promised to help me.'

'Is that all you want me for? You just want me for that?'

'You promised me…' I know I sound like Molly now. I hear her pleading with men to take her away from this very door, and the anger she must've felt surfaces in me. 'Like that young boy promised Molly.'

'It's not just that simple.'

'It was that simple when you wanted a poke at me.'

Someone passes on a bicycle and grunts a greeting.

'Jesus, Peggy. Where's this all coming from?' Joe tries to get my keys. 'This is no place for this conversation.'

'You're not the man I thought you were. The Professor will be back, and I'll be running his whorehouse. Do you think that's what I want?'

'He won't get away with that.'

'He can do what he likes. That son of his is worse, and he's in charge now. I need to be gone from here.'

We stand looking at each other in the gloom.

'It's not that easy, Peggy. Not that simple. I can't…'

'Goodnight, Joe.'

I turn the key in the door and close him out on the doorstep. To get shit done quickly, I'm going to have to get tough. That's all there is to it.

Chapter 14

I'm across the road from the Merrion Street address at the bus stop early as birds and worms. I have vomited into the hedge behind me already. There's no way this baby is going to let me forget it exists. I had thought during the night of using the concoction in my medicines room. But instead, my heart leapt with joy at the thought of a little hand grasping mine. So that was that.

The street is quiet. Much like it was last night —only a few flashy cars and two ladies with big wheels on their prams. A few boys on bicycles take a good look at me. The brisk walk took the cobwebs off. There's no one of any significance visible about this house.

Do I march up and knock or ring their fancy bell and announce that I think I'm his grandchild? The photograph album is small, but contains some proof of my relationship to Mammy. I've also got the Bible with her handwriting in it and an address book with American places at the back. He must know about me, if the letter is any clue. Other than that, I hope there's a family resemblance, and he can tell from the way I walk or talk that I'm a Sheeran. There must be money in them, too, if they can trip over and back to America and live here in this nice spot? But Hell's Kitchen isn't the nicest sounding of places. So maybe I'm grasping at straws. But beggars cannot be choosers, and maybe Mammy has guided me here for a reason. I know I won't know much standing where I am but I stand, staring up at the tall house like it's the answer to something. But what?

There's no bicycle propped against the railing, so I presume there's no nurse.

The back entrance should be easy to find, but I doubt I should snoop until I've introduced myself. I see the postman on his rounds and hear his whistling. The bus has passed a while back, and I didn't get on, so it is time for me to take the plunge, one way or another.

The door is surrounded by fancy plaster and carvings with glass inlaid like a half moon above the newly painted red door. There's a heavy metal scraper for boots by the entrance, too, at the top of the seven steps. I've counted them and clung to the iron railings thinking that shiny knocker is getting closer, and do I want to lift it at all? The brass gleams and the knob could show my face in it. This is the way number thirty-four should look. Beautiful and cared for, with one of those new-fangled doorbell buttons off to one side at eye level.

I press it, and there's a clang and another clang. Like a bell ringing inside, but the tone is loud, so it can be heard all over the three storeys and into the basement below the level of the street. A very young girl in a white apron and silly little maid's hat opens the door and says in a Dublin accent, 'What?'

She's neither a good maid nor a good girl. I've summed her up in two seconds, and she seems to do the same to me, as she says, 'We don't need nuthin' if you're sellin'.'

'I'm here to see Mr Larry Sheeran.'

The tail of her skirt is somehow caught in her tights as she turns around and marches off. I move inside to follow her. The hallway is bright, and the hall-stand holds the largest fern in Dublin. The grandfather clock is tall and in charge of the black-and-white tiles. The sparkle off everything tells me the housekeeper is diligent, and our march leads to a drawing room or fancy parlour to the right of the main door. Paintings galore hang over the walls. A large desk and two chairs are in front of a net curtained window. There's a small, elderly gentleman at the desk, and although frail looking, he doesn't seem to be near dying.

'This one wants to see you,' the so-called maid announces.

'Thank you, Martha.'

His glasses get propped up on his bald head. 'Yes?'

He sits up straighter, looking me up and down, from my best navy shoes that are hurting my feet to my matching hat that has a trim of lace on it. My dress and jacket are itching me, but it could be the nerves, so I smile and say, 'I'm looking for Mr Larry Sheeran.'

'Yes.' The voice is impatient with a slight waver. 'Did the men let you past?'

'I didn't see any men…'

'Not to worry. What can I do for you?'

'I don't know where to begin…'

'At the beginning. Please sit.' A shaking finger points to the padded antique chair in front of his desk.

My feet sink into the expensive rug as I do as I'm told. I haul out the chair as elegantly as I can. I sit on the hard seat.

'What can I do for you?' His accent is Irish but not thick Dublin and isn't from down the country. It sounds like some of the ones who came to Ranclagh to my midwifery hospital.

'I'm sorry to bother you. I believe you haven't been well.' I've my fanciest voice on to impress him.

His cheeks wrinkle as he smiles and removes his glasses altogether.

I delve into my handbag and produce the address book first. 'To start at the beginning, I got –' I stop, uncertain of what to tell him now. I try, 'Could I ask you if you have children?'

He doesn't look angry, but he doesn't help me to continue. The silence is short but painful.

'My name is Peggy Bowden. Perhaps you've heard of me?'

His nose moves upwards, and he squints in thought. He raises his eyebrows, questioning me as to why a man like him should have heard about me.

'My mother is Sally Bowden.'

His hands drop to the desk slowly. Holding his glasses in the tip of his fingers, he uses both hands to place the spectacles on the desk. But still, he says nothing. The air in the room closes in on me. I hope I don't vomit until I'm finished.

'I got a letter from some solicitors asking me to contact them about my mother's estate. But my mother also wrote this address in her address book.'

'Why didn't you contact the solicitors as they asked?' He doesn't sound angry.

'Lawmen always want money. I figured I'd come direct.'

He nods. 'And they put my name and address on this letter?'

'Yes, they did.'

'They were not supposed to.'

'I never knew Mammy was from Dublin or had family here. Is that why you contacted me?' I open the book so that I cannot see his reaction. I'm so fearful he'll scream at me to leave.

'How is Sally?'

Why was I not prepared for this question?

'Sally Bowden…your daughter?'

He nods and in a hoarse voice, little more than a whisper he says, 'Yes. How is she?'

'I'm your grandchild?'

Those handsome eyes widen, and he reaches again for his glasses to put them on. It takes a few seconds to position them with a worsened tremor, but I wait until he gets a good look of me.

'Of course, you are. You have Sally's nose and mouth. Your hair is the wrong colour, but I suspect that's not natural. You've her height and figure. I'm delighted to meet you, Peggy.' His hand stretches out, and I rise off my chair to meet it. The skin is soft and cold as ice, but the handshake seems warm.

'I hoped that you'd think I was like her.' I'm shaking with emotion but wanting to show him my confidence.

'Do ya both want tea?' the maid shouts from the hallway. I jump a little as her voice is so shrill, and I didn't hear her coming.

'Martha, for goodness sake, come into the room and ask us nicely. Yes, both of us would like a pot of tea.'

I don't look around at all and watch as he scratches his bald patch and fixes the grey wisps back into the sides beside his small ears. He's like a jockey in size. Small in comparison to most men but proportioned and although old, I feel that Mammy would think he is a "fine man" still.

'That maid is an acquaintance's child. She's a little rough round the edges, but she's coming along.'

I smile and swallow back my usual sickness and pull on my lace collar.

'Sally left when we started our bookmakers. She didn't approve. Then, she married. We lost touch. Sally's mother passed away, and well…a family is glued together by the womenfolk. I was busy and considered no news was good news.'

He pauses to take a handkerchief from his pocket. He cleans his spectacles as he goes on. 'America became my home, and well, you get lost in life and in a place like New York.'

'Yes,' I say, not certain at all what New York must be like.

'We got an odd letter from Sally through my sister, and of course we sent her funds now and again, which, thankfully, she accepted. But she said very little in her few letters, and then, they stopped. And my sister passed away. No one would give us any information. I've made a few enquiries, but I couldn't find anything much from Sligo. No one wished to help, but I've had people looking since I've come back. That's how you've found me.'

'I had just found your address, and then, the letter brought me here.'

'Could Sally not come?'

My voice breaks as I start to speak, so I say, 'No, she couldn't come.' He waits, so I have to tell him. 'She's gone to be with your wife and sister.'

His head falls into his hands. He clasps his bald head hard as if in pain and smothers what sounds like a sob.

'I'm sorry,' is all I manage to say as a tear leaves the corner of my own sad eye.

'When did Sally die?' He wipes his face with the handkerchief.

He uses that word which I cannot use about Mammy. 'Five years ago now.'

'How?'

I don't know how to tell him but out it comes. 'They say she fell down the stairs.'

'They?'

My mouth goes very dry. 'The people in the asylum in Ballinasloe. She was taken far enough away, so that it wasn't easy for me to get to her. As a young girl, I couldn't drive.'

'Young girl?' His voice sounds angry now. 'So, she was in that place a while, then?'

'I was sixteen when they took her.'

'Dear Lord. Poor Sally.' His face is muffled into the hanky.

'I was forced to marry a brute who took our farm. But he fell and broke his neck.' I take a breath and swallow a bad mouthful that appears from my belly. 'And I sold up and trained as a midwife.'

'Good for you.' He wipes away at his face with the handkerchief.

'I need to tell you more.' I'm not sure how much a man like him can take, but I'm a roll.

'Please, go on,' he says, moving his hand.

'It isn't good.' I stop to breathe. 'You were probably in America when I was…when I was sent to prison. I'm ashamed of it now, but I thought what I was doing was for the best and for the babies to get a better life. No one cared that I meant well, and they took all that I had again.' It's a ramble of confessions. I stop, but he's not looking disgusted.

'The solicitor did mention something like this. How long for?'

'Five years. I got let out for being good. I'm not as bad as it sounds.' I look at the floor and say, 'I tried to want things, but as Mammy said, I wanted too much.'

'I taught her that. Why did they put Sally away?'

'She lost herself. Went mad, they said. She would forget things, spend weeks in her bed. Have times when she would wander the roads in her nightgown and take to wailing non-stop. That kind of thing. I needed her, but they took her.'

'Why did no one contact us?' He shakes his head and seems to realise something. 'I always put off checking on her. Thought it a bother and she'd not want to know us. I respected her for wanting to be a moral person.'

'I never knew about Mammy's past.' I pause to think. 'A moral person? What do you mean?'

'She was ashamed of us.'

I look around, uncertain of how Mammy could be ashamed of this gentleman and a place like this.

'What did you do since prison?'

Although I've prepared a lie, I say, 'I ran a whorehouse until recently.'

Oddly, he just smiles, and the maid appears with the tea at possibly the best or most awkward time. She slaps down the tray and says at me, 'You can pour it.' Off she stalks with her skirt back to its full length.

'A brothel?' the old man asks when she's out of earshot.

'Of sorts. I've always wanted to be respectable, but it's not always easy when you've got a criminal record. All of Dublin knew my name from the papers, and well, I needed to survive.'

He pulls the tray closer and starts to pour the tea himself. There's a slight shake now and china rattles, and the tea looks strong.

'I disgust you, I'm sure...'

'No.'

'I'm sure I'm not...'

'You survived. You're strong.'

No one has ever said that to me before. I'm speechless.

He hands me a cup and saucer. 'I can tell you haven't heard much about us either. Our lives flashed through the newspapers too. But you were possibly in prison.'

'Newspapers? You?'

'Milk?' He holds up a willow-patterned china jug.

'Please.'

'Sally never liked my business. She always had strong views about right and wrong. It seems that you take after me, rather than your mother.'

I stare at him. Nothing makes much sense, and the milk in the tea is making me even more nauseous.

'You really don't know who we are?'

'No.'

'I suppose you could say I controlled most of the criminal activities in the city, for the best part of twenty years, until we left.'

My cup shudders back into the saucer. I'm numb.

'I've been doing well in New York. I think even your mother would be proud. I own legitimate businesses now.'

He looks so full of life, smiling a little, and his eyes on fire with a pride I wish I could be part of. 'It sounds like you've got Sheeran blood in you.' He sips at his tea. 'Not easy for a woman on her own to do what you've done. Your mother would be...'

'Proud? Really?' I cast my head down.

'That depends on how you look at things. Did I think you were bad to run a brothel?'

'No.'

'Who cares what people think? We all do things to survive.' The sips he takes of the tea are small but frequent.

'I never knew...' I peer around the room.

'I came home, telling them I was dying.'

'Aren't you?'

'Aren't we all?'

I laugh. For the first time in a long while, I laugh for quite a while.

He chuckles a little, too, and when we stop, he adds, 'We kept the house and rented it. But they're getting too old for such a big place, and I decided it was time to settle old scores and win some battles before I look at the lid of a box for eternity. The young upstarts see no harm in letting an old man return home to die.'

'So, you had to leave?'

'I felt I was too big to topple, but the rats took me down, and I left a sinking ship. I hear now from my ambassadors that Dublin needs a man like me. I'm back, but I think they're waiting for my coffin to go into the ground.'

'Is it not dangerous to pretend and be here?'

'Men like them presume I am on my last legs. So, I have an advantage.'

'Have you other family?'

'No.' He stops to look at me, really take me in. He adds, 'I have you.'

I need to put my cup down. My handbag has an old hanky; it's not clean, but I snuffle into it.

'I cannot get up easily or I'd comfort you.'

'I'm not alone anymore.'

'Don't cry. You're better than that.'

I believe him.

Chapter 15

The fire the cook makes in the grate is roaring up the chimney, and the nurse has helped Larry change into a robe fit for a king over striped pyjamas. He's shown me all over the house. I've met his bodyguards who'd been snoozing in the kitchen by the big range. I've seen the reception rooms and two upstairs privies with running water and pristine enamel white baths. Huge spacious high ceiling spaces with large beds draped in thick patchwork quilts and eider-downs. There are many bedrooms in pretty colours and patterns in contrast to the long, dark corridors with paintings that show hunting scenes and battleships. There's room for a large family, but despite the nice things and the time of year, it is empty and cold.

In the parlour, we play poker and twenty-five, which Mammy taught me. We have a delicious midday meal of scrambled eggs and brown bread. But he doesn't talk much of the past. Perhaps it's vulgar or inappropriate when we're getting on so well. I have only been sick once, and I go out to smell the late roses in the garden while he speaks to his doctor.

Now, the nurse tucks in a rug around his knees and ignores me as she says her farewell.

'You're staying here tonight?' he asks. 'We've agreed that, yes?'

'Thank you.'

'Call me Larry. Where do you live, is it far?'

'Mountjoy Square. Number thirty-four.'

He crinkles his nose. 'You mentioned you're no longer in business.'

'Something happened.'

'Oh?'

I'm not sure even Larry Sheeran would condone what else I do, so I say, 'Do you know someone called the Professor?'

'Evil man.'

'He's all of that.'

'Is he in charge of Mountjoy and Gardiner Street and that area still?'

'His son is taking over. Anthony.'

'The city's all cut up to hoodlums like him. What Dublin needs is one family in charge. Someone who can bargain with the Fenians and the Gardaí, and pool all the small fish into one pond and blow them all out of the water. Dublin needs a shark.' He grins and points towards the decanters on an antique sideboard with bevelled ends. 'Whiskey?'

'He wants to own me too,' I admit, listening to the whiskey slide into the glass. I hand it to Larry, and his hand touches off mine.

'I doubt you'd stand for that.'

I sit without a drink.

'No whiskey? Maybe you'd like something else?'

'I'm trying to cut back. But it is the most pleasant-smelling whiskey in the world.'

'This Anthony...?'

'He's new. Only out of short trousers. Vicious, though. Says he's taking over. He aims to take over number thirty-four. If only they knew we were related.'

'We need to decide on your future before they know too much.'

My head rests on his lovely, soft, high-backed chair. The type of chair I've dreamed about. Covered in green silk and sinking with my weight on it. 'My future?'

'Yes. That man wasn't my doctor. He confirmed everything you said. You've been very truthful, Peggy. I like that. We found out a great deal.'

'What?' He thought I might be lying, but I lie back into the green silk when I recall I'm usually one of the biggest liars in Ireland.

'You are Sally's daughter. You were a midwife. Imprisoned. Live in Mountjoy Square, blah de blah. But tell me this – who is Molly McCarthy? And the local police sergeant is on your payroll?'

'Joe? He's not on my payroll. Molly's a girl I met in prison. She's a halfwit. They took her from me and put her away somewhere.'

'Away?'

'Because she slashed a boy who refused to marry her. He found out that she has a son she pays to have looked after in Cavan.'

'Is her son still in Cavan?'

'Sent a postal order off for his keep on my way here.'

'Where is Molly?'

I sit forward in my chair. 'Could you find out?'

'I can ask.' He doesn't look all that keen to find out that information. 'She was committed?'

'Yes.'

'They're fond of committing women in Ireland. Those places don't give out information easily.' He pauses. 'So, you've nothing to return to Sligo for?'

'Nothing at all.'

'You're a straightforward woman. What you see is what you get.'

I think I'm far from that, but sure men think what they like.

'Will you stay here for a few days and get some colour back in those pretty cheeks?' He smiles, and I think of Mammy. It is like something she'd say to me.

'I'd like that.'

'We could discuss things.' His reading glasses topple off his knees. I rise to get them, and on my hunkers, I look up into those blue eyes and wonder how he intends to take over all the badness in Dublin from his chair.

'You don't think I'm the great man I say that I am?' He sips his whiskey, and the crystal sparkles at me in the light of the fire. 'You don't trust me when I say I can be the shark of Dublin?'

I don't want to insult him, but I don't want to lie anymore. I smile and hope he'll let me go to bed soon.

'You don't trust people. Yet, you trusted me to tell me the truth from the start. Why?'

'There's no point in lying. Nothing gets hidden in Ireland for long. It is too small a place. You would hear I was in prison. Half of Ireland knows about Peggy Bowden, the monster who sold babies. It wouldn't take anyone long to find out about me.'

The fire is bright, and the whiskey smells good, even from my distance. I feel so weak and tired. I rub my belly instinctively, hoping the child is all right, despite the stress I'm under.

'We'll need to tell each other many things.'

I don't want to talk to him anymore. I close my eyes and let the fire crackle and hiss for a time, and I drift away. Mammy smiles and holds my hand. She sings and opens her Bible, taking her hand away from me.

'Why did Mammy not stay, though? She could have been so comfortable here.'

It's his turn to close his eyes, and the glass leans on the rug on his knees. 'All in good time. All in good time. It's late. Would you like to go on to bed?'

'Yes.' I rise a little off the chair and the fire warms my cheeks.

'The nurse will come back shortly. I swear she knows how long it takes me to drink one whiskey and gets here before I try to get myself another.'

'Thank you for letting me stay here.' I look down on this man who is so new to me. There's only a little of Mammy about him. I wish she'd look at me from his face, but she doesn't. Those eyes are hard, and there's a nothingness between us, despite all my wanting. I long for his embrace, an acknowledgement of more than words that we've a history and a future together. Nothing comes to bind us, blood is all there is, and I hope I find the piece of him which makes him family. Am I like him? Do I want to be? I'm not sure how to be myself. I'm not even sure who Peggy is.

'Goodnight,' I whisper.

'Goodnight. All will be grand.'

'Grand.'

'I don't rise too early, so don't make a racket.' His voice sounds harsh.

The bannister on the stairs is smooth as silk under my palm, and the steps don't make any noise. Everything gleams like it should. It all looks like a hotel I wish I could have afforded even in my wealthier days. Number thirty-four seems far away, yet I walked here. I walked over this morning in my best shoes and dress to fall into a new life. Could all this be happening?

The bed takes my naked body like a hug takes a person, folding its blankets and sheets over me like the arms of an angel might take a tired soul into heaven. The pillow sinks me into it, and my eyes are closed before I think of making them shut. The comfort and sheer safety is like a cough syrup on a sore throat, the sigh from me huge. Mammy laughs in my mind.

'Tell me what I need to know, Mammy. I feel safe here. Is this where you want me to be?'

Chapter 16

I waken during the night, uncertain of where I am. I sit up, and in the faint light coming through the curtain, I can see the old heavy furniture: the large wardrobe that goes almost to the cornice and the dressing table with its huge mirror; the edges of the bed seem miles away from my toes and sides. I snuggle into the blankets and am safe from the world. It's like I'm awake in a wonderful dream that's all too much to handle.

Molly pops up from behind the large chaise longue in the drawing room that's suddenly appeared in my room. She's giggling, humming and rubbing the cushion up her dress. She isn't real and is fuzzy in the darkness.

'I've come to take your baba.' Her teeth are rotten when she grins at me. 'You took Fionn.'

I'm explaining, but she's not listening. I'm holding on to my own stomach as if the world was inside and I had to hide it from her.

'You took all them babies out,' she screams at me.

'All those babies were not for this world. There was nothing I could do.'

'Evil witch. It was the money you wanted. Don't pretend you were saving anyone. User and abuser, that's you.'

I'm there on the nice carpet, and I vomit onto it. Hurting in every place. Between my legs is all wet with blood, and the words are ringing in my ears.

'You made me a whore!'

'I didn't, Molly. I didn't.'

'Your whoring got ya rightly caught.' A long finger points to my middle which swells hard before me. The bleeding is gone and the vomit too. Molly looks calmer, and her teeth are white.

'You let me take the blame for everything. Taking the soldier off Tess, killing the woman, slashing Tommy. You know if you'd made things better, this wouldn't have happened.'

'You aren't my Molly,' I accuse the thing before me. 'You talk too good for my Molly.'

Her teeth turn black again and are covered in a slime. 'I'm no halfwit. I know many a thing.'

'You know I care for you. You know I do, Molly.'

'You care for no one other than Peggy Bowden. You took the soldier, the Professor and my freedom. *Bitch*!'

I'm shouting at her as she leaves me. 'I didn't mean to. *Molly…*'

The sweat is lashing off me when I waken. I'm stuck to the gorgeous sheets, panting and full of regret and guilt.

'I'm sorry,' I sob, and the pillow listens and comforts me. 'I tried. I really did.'

The morning comes through the break in the curtain. The basin in the room has running water. It's nice to wash and not hurry. There are no others banging on the door to wash their bits and bobs.

My clothes seem drab in the room as I pull the heavy drapes and move the net curtains behind them to look out onto the small, front garden and the street beyond the wall and path. The world is still moving, and yet, all is different looking. The sky is a clear blue, and the street clean. The people quickly passing are either on foot or on bicycles, and the cars are beeping in greeting rather than in anger. There's no sign of any children swinging on lamp posts, and the people look more comfortable in their clothes. They take tall and confident strides. The men with their briefcases or hats to hold, the women with their little hats all jolly and nodding at the menfolk. There's no cursing here, no jumping on the scrap wagon or shouting at the children and banging on the doors of a whorehouse. It is only a short walk away but worlds apart.

Can a man like Larry Sheeran take over all of Dublin again? Could Peggy Sheeran be one of those women in the Gresham that the waitresses almost curtsy before? Peggy Sheeran, the unwed harlot. Peggy from a whorehouse who can still keep going.

'They don't like it when people get too successful,' Mammy said, rocking in her chair. 'They say America loves the ones with ambition. The streets are paved with gold.'

'Really?'

I wanted America then and there.

'Paved with ways to make the world better. Paved with ways of making yourself better. They say you can be anything you want in America. But, sure, we couldn't go there.' Her knitting was moving at a queer pace.

'Why can't we be anything we want here?'

'The Irish don't like people who are too big for their boots.'

'I don't have any boots.'

No one would wear boots in Merrion Square.

I've no idea of the time, but there's no sign of the postman or milkman. The coal man is doing his rounds. I close the net curtain and sit on the bed. Joe Bushnell and the soldier, the Professor and Tiny…

'Men.' I fling the door open and stride down the hall, thumping down the stairs and stopping dead at the bottom.

'Tiny?'

There before me is the Big Lad, his cap in his hands and his smile wide when he sees me.

'Hello.' Like Molly in my dreams, he sounds unlike himself.

Maid Martha is at his heel suddenly. 'Yer wanted.' She pokes the Big Lad's sleeve and points to the study I met Larry in yesterday. Martha doesn't even acknowledge me and shouts, 'Breakfast is in the dining room for them that wants it.'

Tiny stares on as I make my way to the bottom of the stairs. My mind is whirring as to what I will or won't say. It looks like our news is out if Tiny is here. He'll say where he's seen me.

'I'm hoping you'll get to wear your hat?' Tiny says in perfect English, as nice as you like.

I curse before I can stop myself.

His gummy smile is totally different looking in this house. He has shaved and looks less rough in general. His clothes are still tattered in places, and there's dust on his trouser legs, but there's an intelligence in his face I haven't noticed before.

'I'm here to see your grandfather.' His bulky frame moves, and he disappears into the office and closes the door without turning around.

'Breakfast.' Martha's voice echoes up the corridor, and I can tell by her tone she's not in good spirits this morning. There's all sorts on the sideboard she points at.

'Tea?' she grunts.

'Please,' but she's away before I can say anything else.

I take a plate and spoon scrambled eggs, bacon and toast onto the plate. There's all fancy silver on the table. Jam in dishes with spoons that are too small to bother about, only they look so pretty. A large silver bowl with a whole pound of butter in it and a jug made of heavy crystal. The sugar is in lumps. The Big Lad knows Larry. He made a full sentence. He knows Larry is my grandfather, so the Professor will know too. But Tiny doesn't talk to the Professor. My stomach clenches, and although worried, I don't feel ill.

I'm almost finished wolfing down the eggs when Martha parades into the room.

'We all know who ya are,' she says as she slaps down the silver teapot.

'Do you now?' I've dealt with the likes of Martha all my life. Raised in the gutter and in need of looking down on someone else.

'Yes.' She stands with a hand on her hip.

'Since when do you know anything at all about me?'

'Since the men in the kitchen heard all about ya. Whore and seller of good folks' babies.'

'Good folk who don't want those babies. And those babies getting a good home – is that what you mean?' I don't look at the trollop.

'And men humping in your house at all hours of the day and night.'

'If there were no men, there would be no need for the likes of me. On yer bike, Martha, and don't be putting me off my breakfast.'

'A great man like Larry Sheeran doesn't need the likes of you turning up.'

'Watch your step, Martha.'

'Sure, the whole of Dublin knows that your halfwit Molly McCarthy killed that poor creature from down the country. We all knows it. And that poor creature up to see a doctor because she was sick and lost.'

I don't answer her and bite into the bacon which is hard and cold.

'Pick off the weak. That's what the likes of you do.'

'Martha. Fuck off.'

She stares as if I slapped her. Two hands on those thin hips now. 'Mr Sheeran always looks after his own, Ma says,' she stops, gulping in air, 'but I canna believe you're anything to that man in there.' She points back to the study and is a deep pink with rage.

'Who's that man that's in there now with Mr Sheeran?'

'I dunno,' she stammers, clearly uncertain why I'm not bothered by her insults. 'Do ya not hear me?'

'You're not very bright, are you?'

She gawps at me, her mouth open and her little maid's hat all tilted in her despair.

'If I'm family to Mr Sheeran, is it a good idea to insult me when I'm at my breakfast?'

There's a whitening of those cheeks. 'The lads in the kitchen are none too happy...'

'So, they sent you to tell me what's what?'

Martha nods and closes her mouth.

'Fuck off now, Martha.'

She makes a childish noise and turns on her heel.

'And never speak to me like that again.'

It reminds me of the junior nurses in Ranelagh. Them all cocksure of themselves in the big smoke of Dublin. They thought themselves big women with a career ahead of them. It always unnerved them if I was quiet and calm. Posher princesses found it hard to believe that a woman like me could educate and better herself. But I did it and made sure they knew I was proud of where I came from. A woman to be feared tumbles sooner or later, and it's women who help topple other women, as much as we try to solely blame the men. So, the young ones needed to know I would take no nonsense from the start and there were no chinks in my armour.

'You're scary,' one trainee had told me when I caught her snoozing in one of the side wards. 'I don't think you will forget this, and something will bite me later.'

Poor Martha might get bitten later, all right, if she takes me on again. Just like she needs to look down on someone, I need to feel bigger sometimes. I might need to walk on someone else sometime.

'Molly?' I whisper to the toast. Perhaps that's why I needed Molly around. Always I was thinking I was better than her. But then Molly had her way to make herself everyone's favourite. Molly had her own way of being the better woman. I'm not going to let Martha or Molly make me feel worse about things. I did and do what I can with what I'm given.

Chapter 17

The china cup in my palm is cold, and there's no end to my thinking until Larry's jockey's build is before me. His walking stick is holding some of his weight, and he's scratching his bald head below where he has perched his glasses.

'Good morning.' He sounds rested and in good humour. 'Did you get breakfast? Is Martha doing her duty?' He throws a paper onto the table and heaves out a heavy chair and sits. There's no sign of dying on this man.

'Martha has a big mouth.' I wonder how fond he is of his acquaintance and of moaning Martha. His chuckle reminds me of Mammy. 'I've had a lovely sleep and breakfast. Thank you.'

'So, it wasn't you I heard shouting in the middle of the night?' he asks while reaching for a small bell I mistook for a little jug earlier. It tinkles when he shakes it. A pleasant noise, until Martha appears.

'Yeah?'

'Martha, we would like more of everything please.'

'Everything?' She sounds crosser than anyone should be to their employer. 'Sir, us in the kitchen are not best pleased…'

'Martha,' he snaps. She's out of the room in a flash. 'Honestly, she would try the patience of a saint.' His glasses flop down on his nose expertly all by themselves with a flick of his head. Even they do as they are told.

'Tiny was here,' I say.

'Yes, our Big Lad. He has a soft spot for you.'

I cannot help but smile proudly. '*Our* Big Lad?' I ask.

'Yes.'

'He speaks English.'

'Of course.' The old man looks amused now, those eyes of his twinkling. 'He never said he couldn't. The Professor presumed he was Russian.'

'He works for you?'

'For a long time now. I needed someone inside operations here. To see if it was worthwhile coming home.'

'Did he know about me being your grandchild?'

'He got a pleasant surprise.'

'I got a shock.'

Larry smiles broadly.

'So, he won't tell the Professor where I am?'

'Definitely not. But he says your Sergeant Bushnell has been beaten rather badly.'

'Joe?'

'Something about snooping too much, even though he's been paid to be quiet. Asking for that missing woman's body to be found, so he can get respect for everyone. Including himself, no doubt.'

I feel sick. 'Is he badly hurt?'

'In hospital. All stations on high alert now, after an assault on one of their own. Anthony has been lifted, thanks to some eye witnesses being brave enough to speak out. That'll get him out of our hair for a while and annoy him further.'

'Eye witnesses?'

'People who like their tickets to America that will come through their morning letter box.'

'I hope Joe will be all right.'

'Don't we all. He's got work to do.'

'Work?'

'Joe Bushnell and most of the Gardaí in Dublin know what's good for them. One person like me in charge keeps all the other minions in check. I police things and make them look good.'

'Good?'

'Crime figures go down, and we give them lads who want a record.'

'Want to go to prison? I can't think of anything worse.'

'Some boys need the credentials and the training prison offers.'

'We just got raped in the gaol.'

The clock on the mantle isn't loud, but I can hear it click and tick.

'There's to be no more feeling sorry for yourself now. That's the kind of thing Sally would say.'

Him mentioning my Mammy and meaning she was a moaner doesn't bode well. My mouth hangs open.

'You were caught at something. Put inside. Punishment isn't easy, but you won't get caught again now, will you?'

Martha stomps in with a tray and clatters out new food stuffs and there's an aroma of coffee. My stomach churns like a butter maker.

'It didn't give them the right –'

'You had no rights. Have none still. But I thought you were strong.'

Martha sniggers and starts taking away all the used china and cutlery and leave the room.

'Please don't talk like that in front of Martha.'

'She's only a servant.'

'Exactly.'

'Is this the hard Peggy, then?' He smirks and puts two lumps of sugar in his cup.

'I'm hard as I have to be.'

'You also lied to me. You're an abortionist.'

I open my mouth to defend myself, but, really, there isn't any defence.

'What if you were caught at that?'

I look at the carpet. Its pattern is pleasant, but my shame isn't. 'Women needed –'

'No more of that.'

I'm angry he should think of ordering me about.

'Did this Molly kill that missing woman?'

I stare downwards.

'Aren't you going to say anything?'

'I killed her.' Somehow, I think this will make me seem hard rather than weak and stupid like I feel.

'And you paid the Professor for getting rid of her? This poor creature the whole of Ireland is looking for?'

'Yes.'

'I thought you were a clever lass.'

'I am. I survived, and I…'

'… have given the Professor something on you.' His eyebrow rises, and he seems disgusted at this.

'I told him Molly did it.'

He stares at me, and I stare back. Like all the other men in my life, he has changed quickly into a strange, judging creature, who sees me as worthless. The snippets of a kindly grandfather well and truly missing today.

'You let a sick woman take the blame?'

I shrug.

Did he smirk just then? Was it a wrinkled grin?

'There's more to me than you think.' My fist is tight, and my nails dig into my palm. 'Do you want me here, or not?'

He doesn't answer me but flicks open a newspaper. I want to throw something at this old man.

'I suppose you weren't given much opportunity. With no father and a mad mother and a halfwit hanging around.'

This cuts me deeply. 'Sally…was your daughter.'

'But she's gone now.' The tears he shed yesterday are obviously forgotten.

'You cried for her yesterday.'

'And that's an end to the self-pity. You should try it.'

'You aren't my father, and I don't have to listen to –'

'The truth?' His voice goes high, and I rise a little off the chair I'm on. 'I'm angry. Your word is your bond. You didn't tell me about the –'

'Women needed me.'

He grunts.

'I'm sure you've done much worse.' I accuse him with my voice and body, but he doesn't answer me. I cannot see his face well as he lifts the paper. We both remain silent for a good few seconds. He lowers the papers and is quiet, staring at the toast he hasn't buttered.

'Even I don't kill mothers, who are the backbone of the country, the salt of the earth. Mothers are sacred. I'm not much for religion, but even to me, a woman who is a mother is precious.'

'I didn't mean to,' I whisper, feeling Martha is lurking, and I don't trust her in the slightest. I look around, but all is still, and there's no sign of her. Then, I say, 'My mother wasn't all that precious to you. I did the best I could for everyone. My girls, the women who came to me, Molly, my mother – all the women I have ever met. I might be harsh, but I did my feckin' best. Which is more than you did for my poor mother. She died alone, thinking no one cared at all.'

He is quiet.

'That woman came to me. She was happy in her decision. She didn't die alone or in pain. She slipped away on me. I felt so bad, but what could I do? I could hardly call the police when she and I were committing a crime and a mortal sin.'

His glasses come off, and he pinches his nose.

'I'm a good woman. I've made mistakes, but I'm good, like my mother. In my heart, I'm good. You're no saint or scholar. You didn't get to be a big-time man without secrets. I just had people who could tell you mine – that's the difference. Women aren't supposed to be anything much, and if we are, someone takes us down a peg or two just for fun. Fate or God or some asshole destroys us.'

'Asshole?'

'Yes, asshole. I escaped from the torture of a beast. I educated myself. I took on the feckin' Catholic church. I've been inside. I've been raped by men over and over. I ran a brothel in the heart of Dublin with gangsters wanting a piece of me. Everyone wanting a piece of me, and I've done well. But no one got a piece of Peggy. I won't let you take me over either and make me small. Maybe this is why Sally left.'

I know my cheeks are blazing. My neck is tight, and I'm all tense and shaking now. He sips his coffee and nods.

'And while we're on the subject of mothers, I'm up the duff as well. So, there you go, your granddaughter is in the family way. You have an unwed whore for a granddaughter. I came here yesterday all ashamed and pitiful, but I'm better than that woman. I was all sorry for what she was, in comparison to you. I'm Peggy, and she's a damn fine woman.' I'm thumping on my own chest, full of anger. 'I'm damn fine the way I am. If I'm going to be a mother, am I precious to you too?'

I look at him, and his eyes are milky. Is that understanding in his eyes? Old wrinkles harbouring the night's sleep and merging with something I cannot place. He's so quiet.

'Don't you dare lecture me on morals.' I flop back into the chair, and he brings his two hands together, and they clap slowly at first and then over and over. The noise is strange and unnerving. His expression is unusual and odd to me. If it's mockery, it sounds too clear. If it's pride, it sounds too slow. I don't know what to make of him, but he stops, and I wait for him to speak. He puts on his spectacles again and looks ahead, but not at me.

'Sally left because she felt I was evil. Perhaps she was right. Your grandmother was always quiet and did what was necessary to be a wife. Sally always challenged me. She challenged my thinking. Questioned the very things I couldn't answer. Just like you.'

My breathing is quick, and there's a flutter in my tummy.

'I never told Sally things. It wasn't something fathers did here. America showed me the importance of family. The Italians all know how to be strong together. I learned a great deal about myself. We all just do our best.'

My hand shakes, so I grip the chair. 'I don't like when people judge me.'

'Neither do I.' He cracks a smile, and his wrinkles move. 'Tiny told me you had guts. He was right.'

'He bought me a red hat. I like him. You probably want me out. I need to go.'

'Go where? Back to Mountjoy Square? You shouldn't go back there.'

'But my things?'

'New life. New things. New beginnings.'

I'm not sure what's happening at all. I want away from him, yet I've nowhere to go. He's family, and if I'm not here with him, I'm alone. Where do I want to be?

'New children too,' he adds.

'I want this baby.' I sense I need to make it clear.

'Who's the father?'

'Does it matter?'

'Every child needs a father.'

'I didn't have one.'

He doesn't say anything, but the silence makes his point.

'So, does he know about the child?'

I shake my head. 'There's no need.'

'You'll make this child a bastard?'

'They'll have a father. Like mine. He'll be a figment of their imagination. A man in a photograph.'

'Surely you understand that things need to be respectable, for the child's sake?'

'Isn't it all a bit late for respectability?'

'To start again, you'll need to be married.'

'I don't need a man…'

'Yes. You do.'

'Mammy and I…'

'Your mother knew she had to marry a man to make you respectable. But he wasn't your father.'

I stop breathing. My heart skips two beats at least, and I choke on my own saliva.

Chapter 18

His voice seems far away, but we haven't moved. The breakfast things are still before us, and my life is in a mess on the tidy table.

'Sally left for Sligo. We weren't sure why at first, but word came through that she was pregnant. It was a shock to say the least. It was one thing we never thought we'd have to worry about with Sally. She was at the church almost every day, and there was no –'

'She married some man because of me?'

'They say she loved that Bowden fellow. And that he was good to her. Took her on, even though he knew all about her. But he can't have known her long. And then, he up and died.' He makes an almost mocking chuckle. 'Sally never had any luck. We sent her money for whatever she wanted, and they say she seemed happy.'

'They?'

'Your grandmother and my sister said she was happy. But then, of course – the war happened.'

'Yes.'

'I thought he was Daddy.'

'He was in every sense that mattered.'

'Who then was my...?'

'I've no idea. You see the damage it does...' He starts and stops. 'You need to at least think about a father for this baby. There must be some man who'd do? Even Sally found someone.'

In my heart, there's no one. The soldier fills me with lust, but as a mere boy himself who seeks out whores, he's not exactly prime father material. Joe is almost dead in a hospital and would bore me into an early grave. Any man I know is a married cad or a lousy blaggard. There isn't much hope for the baby. Joe Bushnell is the best of a very sorry-looking bunch.

'What had you planned to do to provide for this child?'

'A friend promised to help me find a respectable job.'

'That being what, exactly?'

'Secretary, something in regular work.'

'I see.'

'I know it's flimsy, but it's early days. I have time to get things sorted out all nice.'

'I need someone I can trust to help me start to run things properly here in Dublin.'

'Help run what?'

'The business.'

'I'm not sure…'

'I'll get rid of vermin like the Professor and a few other chaps who need a lesson.'

'Count me in.' There's nothing I would like more at that moment than to rid the world and my brain of the Professor and his son.

'It mightn't always be pleasant.'

'Is life ever that?'

'There are a few rules.'

I wait for him to continue.

'I'm in charge until they close the lid on my box. You never lie to me. You kill no more mothers or babies. You find a father for that child.'

I can tell he's thinking of all he can throw at me in one go.

'What do you say to that?' He sounds mellower.

'Count me in.'

'Shake on it?'

His freckled and bony hand stretches to meet mine, and when I shake it, I wonder if he cares at all. His grip is weak, and his eyes are hard to read as he says, 'Done.'

I draw my hand away, uncertain of everything.

Martha slinks in like a satisfied cat, and when she's clearing things onto the rickety trolley, I ask Larry, 'So where does Martha hail from then?'

'Martha?' Larry calls to her, although she's quite near. 'Tell Peggy here all about yourself.'

A grunt leaves her.

'How is that man Joe Bushnell that works with your father, Martha?' Larry winks at me then. 'Martha's father works with Sergeant Bushnell. I think you know him, Peggy? He was on the case of your Molly.'

I gulp back the hatred in my voice for that brute of a man. Known locally as the worst kind of pig. He is full of all sorts of trickery and hating most folk. Martha didn't lick her bad manners off the street. Her features are all scrunched up, but her head is tilted all proud and up high, thin shoulders back and her lank hair getting a fix. She mutters, 'Joe's in a bad way, I hear.'

'Martha knows how to hold her tongue,' Larry goes on. 'Don't you, Martha? And then, you and your father can take off to London, so you can be in those fancy West End shows, once we get all sorted.'

'West End shows?' I gawp at the specimen before me.

'I sing.' She fixes her skirt and apron, and I see Larry stifle a chuckle. 'I sing good, I do.' The trolley's wheels squeak, like I imagine she does, and I try to stop my laugh escaping, until I hear the wheel no longer.

'I thought you didn't want it known about me?'

'She wasn't to stay too long, and I didn't know you'd be here, but sure it has been decided you're a Sheeran, and so now, it doesn't matter who knows.'

'Is everyone in your pocket?'

'Mostly. We need now to get rid of the Professor and the other two main players in Dublin. There's a few politicians who need convincing.'

'How?'

'All in good time, Peggy. All in good time.'

'So how long will she be working here?'

'As long as it takes.'

'For...'

'For her to tell all she can to whoever she likes.' He rises and checks the hallway. It must be clear as he goes on, 'She's a mole that we need. Trickling out that you're here, and I'm not as bad as I make out. Tiny is taking care of the Professor today.'

'He's what?'

'You heard. We hit the others soon. Probably at the funeral.'

The breath leaves me and lingers in the room like the truth does. My grandfather kills people. As I watch the dust dance in the morning sunlight in through the elegant window, I cannot help but think of how alike we are, yet so different.

'You don't approve?' Larry is by the coffee pot again pouring the aroma into the room. 'You who...'

'I'm no one to judge.'

But in my mind, I have already judged him insane or at least a bad man. Mammy must have been petrified of what he could do. No wonder she was so scared constantly.

'How else are we Sheerans to make it back on top?' He grins at the lumps of sugar he's tossing into the cup. The rhythm of the stirring is irritating. 'You've killed before now, Peggy.'

My killing was different. My dalliances with death were not the same at all.

All was fine, until that Sligo one spoilt my notions. It was all fine for money, until she made it about saving women. It was all simple beforehand. Over the years, it was a crime I got paid for. Before the blonde bitch, it was me and the devil, but the area now is grey as fuck. Like Larry here, the deed I did was a means to an end, nothing more. But then, her blonde hair, that pretty face, her hand on my arm – the relief she showed me, it all became so much more. So much more vital, so right for her and me to do what we did. Larry now has that look about him. As if it is all for the greater good. But all I see is a murderer. That's how he probably sees me, and the confusion in me is wretched.

'I won't ask you to get your hands dirty. But you'll need to make unsavoury decisions someday.'

Some of the decisions I've made flash before me, and I laugh at how men think women incapable of messy choices.

'There's no going back now. The Sheerans are on the rise. We're going to think big.'

'But not too big?'

Mammy is smiling again in my mind, and her knitting is on her lap. The noise of the needles click-clacking.

'We're family.' He seems to be convincing himself as well as me.

'Can I call myself Sheeran from now on? Bowden isn't mine, and I hate all the other surnames I could or should have been. I want to be a Sheeran.'

'Of course, family.' He nods.

'Molly was family to me.'

'She's gone.' Larry sounds impatient.

'Yes.'

'You were more than good to her for long enough.'

I decide then I'm nothing like Larry. My conscience eats me, like it does to every woman I know. Try as I might, I can't feel fine with abandoning Molly. I find it hard to think it's all right to tread on the weak and move up for power. If I move up, I aim to take others with me.

'There's only so long family can hold on to the weakest member,' he says, looking directly at me.

I gulp back a mouthful of vomit. 'I'd like to find Molly.'

'No. We move forward in life. Not backwards.'

'Don't you care about anyone?'

'Why do you need to ask that?'

'I cannot place what kind of a man you are.'

The grandfather before me is possibly seventy-five, maybe more, and every time he speaks, he changes. Sometimes old and frail, almost loving, and other times strange and callous. Like now – he doesn't care about my confusion around him. He's not even listening to me.

'I'd still like to know where Molly is.'

'You'll have enough to do raising funds to keep your child and that bastard child of hers in Cavan. You don't think things through very well.'

'Speaking of funds. I need to…'

'Tiny will pick up anything of value from thirty-four, and your feathered red hat and all your belongings.'

'How did you know about my hat?'

'You told me.'

'I never mentioned feathers. Did Tiny speak of me?'

'Tiny didn't come here often. It was too risky. Martha's mouth, the nurses…'

'Your men in the kitchen?'

'They're trustworthy. American and bound by military training.'

'I like soldiers.'

'None of them are men for marrying. All have wives at home.'

Larry's on his shaky feet and heading for his office.

'I can get a soldier of my own,' I snap at his frail stooped back.

'Sweet Christ, could you not aim a bit bigger than that? Sally most definitely lingers in you. It'll take a while to lose such weaknesses.'

Mammy's crying in my mind shaking her head and looking to the floor like she used to in Mass. 'I wish I had been old enough to help Mammy.'

He stops and turns. 'Just like her, you are. Bemoaning the past and raking it into the now. You didn't and couldn't look after her. She was an adult. You were the child. You don't expect your baby to look after you, do you?'

'I can look after myself.'

'Is that so?' he mutters and is thankfully gone from my sight.

Chapter 19

It's a sad state of affairs when your day is to be completed by a man with no teeth bringing you your few measly belongings. The house smells of Ajax and carbolic soap. The comfort is apparent in every corner and hallway, but I'm like a criminal behind walls and net curtains.

'No. You mustn't go out,' the bodyguards shouted together, and they took to sitting at either door.

'I need air.'

'Open a window.'

They look identical in their grey suits and cropped hairstyles, one slightly greyer than the other. Both doing the bidding of a man who locks doors.

'Did Tiny come with my stuff?'

'No.'

The books on the shelves in the office or study aren't books at all, but old volumes of some law nonsense or poetry no normal person could read. The drawers everywhere are locked or full of boring regalia or empty like my heart. No photographs or pictures or real people. The garden is lashed with rain, and the rose heads are dropping.

My clothes are stiff with soap from the upstairs sink; I dried them in the airing cupboard I found – an annoyingly tidy space with the sheets all stacked like material in a shop.

'So, I'm a prisoner?' I muttered to Larry at breakfast on the third day of unbelievable boredom. He disappears for most of the day and with no chores. What am I to do? I'm supposed to enjoy this leisure, but all I do is wander the floors and think about every dilemma I raised up out of the darkness to heap upon myself.

'Staying indoors is for your own safety.'

'The Professor?'

'Gone.'

'Joe?'

'Who?'

'Sergeant Bushnell?'

'No idea.'

'Martha?'

'Sick, apparently. Doubt she'll be back, her father knows things are moving for the Sheerans.'

'The nurses?'

'No need to pretend now – is there?'

'Where are you going? You're in black…'

'A funeral.'

'The Professor's?'

'Yes. Are the questions over?'

'I'm bored. I'm used to doing…'

'All in good time, Peggy. All in good time.'

'I'm a prisoner.'

'It's for your own –'

'Yes. So, all of Dublin knows I'm a Sheeran?'

'All who matter do.'

'What's the word on the Professor? Where is Tiny?'

'The Professor is long gone. Tiny had to go away for a while. Questions to avoid.'

'My things?'

'In the back scullery. Did no one tell you?'

'Who would? There's no one here, bar those two yolks you are never without and that old cook who doesn't speak. Says I'm trouble.'

'How are you feeling?'

'Trapped.'

'I meant the baby?'

'Fine.' I rub my belly and think this baby is all that's fine about the world. Fine.

'You must be patient, Peggy. Like I am.'

I'm not sure what he's patient about.

'Things take time to sort. Then, all will be better.'

Molly's contemptuous look passes over me.

'At least you're comfortable here,' he continues as I see the Professor on top of my Molly in my memories. Him doing unspeakable ills to her, and me saying, 'Let me sort things. All will be better soon.'

'I'm very comfortable, but I should do something.'

'Would you like to shoot someone at this funeral, then?' Larry's glasses sit on his bald head as he eats his boiled egg.

'Are you seriously going to shoot someone in broad daylight?'

'I won't, obviously. All eyes will be on me. But daylight means a clean kill and sends out a message.'

'A message?' My mouth is so dry.

'The Sheerans are back, and they take care of business.'

For once, I wish I felt sick. People should feel sick about the killing of others. Perhaps it is survival of the fittest? They would kill Larry, if they got the chance. Fuck. They would kill me. It hits me like a bullet might. Right between my tired eyes.

'If they're dead, will their own not want revenge?'

'It takes time for them to regroup. By then, we'll be all established, and no one would dare.'

I stare at this meek-looking man. He doesn't look like a monster.

'You must stay here and be safe.' He points at me with his knife.

'I need to go out sometimes.'

'Back garden.'

'At least the rain has stopped. Yes. I'll go out and sit in the garden.'

'A lady of leisure, you are, Peggy.' His snort is annoying and lacking in respect.

'The cook says she would love to have my life now. When she does get a chance to speak, she mentions it a lot.'

'Aren't you delighted you can just sit here and be content? Not a care in the world. I'll look after you and the baby. You've realised that, I hope. I'm not used to dealing with a woman in the business. We might work together, once things get a bit more settled. Enjoy your freedom until then.'

I look around the dining room and think of the times in thirty-four when I pretended I was surrounded by such glamour.

'What kind of things will you need me to do?'

'All in good time. All in good time.'

Chapter 20

The butterflies are beautiful, freely fluttering showing off their fancy wings. Visiting flowers, they are. Working but looking fancy and pleased with the warmth. I've wanted to be worry-free all my life. My concerns are now for men I don't know, those who would kill me.

Joe and Molly enter my thoughts; I can see their disgust from here. As the perfume of the dying roses lingers and a bee buzzes, I see myself through their eyes. I am a corrupt Peggy, a user of people and part of a murderous family. Neither of them would want me now. Joe will have heard of my new-found family, and he'll say, 'Water always finds its own level.'

'Peggy will always work hard to get to the top,' Tess said.

What would ugly Tess think now? Will Anthony be killed too? What will become of my girls on the streets? As bad as a knocking shop is, there's safety in numbers. Even irritating Tess deserves safety. What would she think of me now in my fancy feathered hat in a well-kept garden? The lawn is so neat it looks trimmed with a scissors.

There's no option really but to be a Sheeran.

No cigarettes were in the back scullery and neither the cook nor the yolks who mind Larry would give me a drag of one.

'There's nothing nicer than the sun on your face,' Mammy said, as we were picking apples for the aristocracy up at the big house. I thought sitting in the big house's garden would feel so much nicer than sweating under the trees hauling boxes of fruit. Mammy decided it wasn't nicer. But here I sit now in the garden of a big enough dwelling, and I feel lost.

No one knocks on the door here; no one calls. There must be deliveries, but I never hear them or see them. The bodyguard yolks collect the post directly from the postman. It's all so enclosed that the path out the front seems the longest in the world, and the wall at the back is the highest in any fairy tale.

I can hear the traffic and the murmurings of life, but I'm dead to the world in this sunny garden. The bees and butterflies have more purpose and future. I'm envious of the colourful flowers all stuck in the one place but bowing and blustering about with visitors landing in and on them.

It has been less than a week. The hormones in my blood are raging and taking over any sense I have. I'd wanted the Professor to take me away from all of it. So, what's changed? I'm much better off with a man with means and ambition like my own, surely? Would I kill for my ambition?

'It's murder,' Tess said one Sunday evening. 'The priest says he knows the murdering that goes on here.'

'Murder indeed.' I wasn't expecting a moral lecture from the likes of Tess. 'A service that puts food on your table and makes your rent lower.'

She'd been quiet then, picking at her stew. 'It's more to you than money, Peggy?' Her eyes are wide, questioning. 'It's more than just that?'

'What else would it be for but to get us out of this shit hole?' I was angry at her questioning me in front of the others. Annoyed at her making me think about what I was. This was long before the blonde bitch came and changed me inside. A good while before that one came and made me her saviour. It's been happening since the world began. Women taking power of their own bodies and saying, 'No, I can't.'

'You believe it's right, then?' Tess had sniffed, but it was lost in her mug of tea. Her confidence was not as great as the church's.

'If men were in the family way, and they were scared or simply couldn't, what do you think they would do?'

Tess smiled up at me. 'There would be no stopping them.'

'Nothing stops a man from doing nothing!' Molly said.

'The doctors send women here.' Tess was thinking aloud.

'Exactly.'

Even then, in the safety of number thirty-four, I wasn't sure I was telling myself or them the truth.

'There's a reason for rules,' the worst officer in gaol would chant. 'And women who break them are the worst of all.'

Himself, the worst breaker of moral codes with his penis and hands.

Larry, too, can take a person's life and not blink, but he can scowl at my life. I feel shame all the time about the medicines room and all my dealings. But until recently, I could just push it all down into the pit of my soul. I was constantly telling myself it was for the money.

That dread and guilt is always here. I hold my stomach and think of the little life in there. All had been well until that blonde bitch stole the peace and quiet in my soul. It was to save myself. It was all wrong, but I was damned already, and the gains of it all were for me and Molly. When it became about others, my confidence abandoned me. It wrangled itself around the barbed wire like that sheet that blew away did on the clothesline. That tangled sheet blew away, but it didn't blow far enough to escape. I didn't escape far either, eh?

'Don't think of them. Just yourself,' a matron had told me long ago. 'They'll come and go. Protect yourself and work to improve your lot. Keep me happy, and your ambition will be rewarded.'

Larry seems the same as that matron. She'd been adamant that family planning was not something the nurses needed to know or discuss.

'The church and the menfolk don't like such chat. Remember what I said about rocking boats. Don't rock boats, especially if you're sitting in them.'

I know what rocking boats got me. Look at poor Mrs McKenzie and her boys. If I was a well-to-do lady, I could help the likes of that family in the future. Drag the boys into a life of crime perhaps after killing their mother – that would be helpful!? But maybe I could make amends somehow and use my standing for something better?

'Out of the frying pan into the fire,' Mick Moran joked about my knack for finding trouble. 'You've a heart of gold and nerves of steel, Peggy Bowden.'

'Bowden,' I said. 'Peggy Moran sounds grand.'

'That it does.' It's as if Mick is here beside me. But, sure, he isn't, and no man will want a bastard.

Names are funny things. I've always thought that. A woman changing hers to make her unsure of who she is and where she belongs. I haven't given too much thought to changing my name. The one name that might have been good for me is now lost. Where might Mick be now?

The stillness and my wanderings are interrupted by the noise of doors banging in the house.

Larry is all childlike when I go inside, hopping on one foot, singing, '*Ten bottles of beer on the wall…*'

The two yolks pour themselves a whiskey.

'It's all done. Boom! Boom!' Larry uses his walking stick like a toy gun. 'Oh, what screams and the sight of the chaos.' He laughs. There's an edge to the laughter that I haven't heard before. 'We've had a few to celebrate. The police are all over the place. They'd no idea what to do. If they'd been in the States…'

I steal a whiskey. It is powerful as it slips into my throat, burning me, paining me on the way down like the news. 'How many?' I ask.

'Them all and their minders. The Sheerans are back now! We sent out the ambassadors.'

'Ambassadors?'

'Members of the old group, all set up in their own quarter to look after Sheeran business. Take in the money and make us known again. It's all working grand, Peggy.'

'Looks like I came here just in time.'

'Taking you into the fold was quick, I'll grant you that. It helped speed things on.'

'How?'

'Count me in, you said. I knew my spies were right about you. All said you were in fear of being lawful.'

'Spies?'

He doesn't answer me.

'Didn't they call you the Butcher?' one of the yolks with him says. 'Even that sergeant called you that.'

'Did he now? And when did he tell you that?'

Larry waves his stick in the air. 'It's of no importance. All of Dublin is back in hand. We've to hit things right for weeks. And, Peggy, we need to show a united front. The women of Dublin need to know you're one of them.'

'I've a few rules myself.'

His laugh is fake again, lacking in emotion, stuck in the air like the smell of the whiskey. 'New clothes?' Larry asks, sitting into his favourite chair and grinning. 'Pick yourself this time. Not like that hat.' He points to the hat in my hand. 'I told Tiny you needed to be reminded of the finer things in life.'

'You sent the hat?'

'Of course. I knew you needed reminding of what money could buy. I needed to know if you were like me. Had a weakness for material comforts.'

The yolks have swigged down another whiskey and look at each other to leave. I'm there in my manky dress, the fancy hat drops to the floor like my open mouth.

'You knew I was there all the time?'

'After I came home, I found out.'

'But...'

'I needed to know if you were a woman to trust. I knew you could survive.'

'Bastard.'

'I think you'll find that's not my title but more your own or the name for that baby in your belly.'

I stare at him. Numb.

'You needed to be at rock bottom, and, sure, I didn't know how near to the knife edge you actually were.'

'I wasn't at the bottom...'

'You had nowhere and nobody.'

I touch my belly. He's right, of course, and on he goes.

'There's no point in playing holier than thou. You ran a brothel and did all sorts. You dealt with scum like the Professor and lay with God knows what?'

I'm standing there, looking down on him from a height. Seeing a man I barely know and thought I could love. 'It's all too much,' I stammer.

'Get over it, woman. We've to make many things happen now, and you worrying about whether I sent you a hat isn't going to matter one way or the other.'

'It matters. It's about trust.'

'But, my dear, you have no choice in the matter. I don't need you. But you need me.'

He gets off the chair very easily. The stumbling and trembling he did were obviously staged to win me over.

'It is simple, Peggy dear. I want you here as family, but I don't want to be persuading you every day of the morals of things. It's not as if your morals bothered you before. Make your choice, and let's get on to great things together. Or you could always go back to thirty-four...'

'I told you. Count me in.'

'That's a Sheeran.' He takes my hand and squeezes it.

I cannot smile, but I grimace a half one and turn to go upstairs.

'You can go out tomorrow and shop,' he says to my back. 'Make a splash in the best stores. Let all of Dublin talk about the new wave of Sheeran luck.'

'Yes.'

'Peggy, look at me.'

I turn back although halfway up the stairs.

'And get your hair styled nicely.'

I touch my head, and he does that laugh.

'You need to look like a lady now.'

He clips his stick off the black-and-white tiles and heads quickly to his study.

There I am, with the thoughts of shopping and all lying before me, and I've never felt more like a whore in all my life.

Chapter 21

There's no sign of anyone in the morning, even though it's early. The grandfather clock in the hall saying it is quarter past seven. I can smell the coffee from the dining room.

There is a newspaper lying on the table in the downstairs hallway.

Men Shot at Funeral, the headline reads, telling of the nation's shock at the murders in Glasnevin Cemetery. Two powerful and well-known men in Dublin blown away in broad daylight has stunned the entire nation. The article is very vague, with no names mentioned yet, until their families are informed. The two shooters were in masks and trench coats, and there was a regular blood bath in front of women and children.

The brutal beating of a Gardaí sergeant was mentioned further into the paper on page four, relaying the details from a previous report and saying the man is stable. The air of panic in Dublin almost seeps off the pages to greet me. As a city, Dublin sees little badness. The priests are privy to most of its mortal sins and rule with a rod of iron. Irish people are always worried about the neighbours' opinions of them, so worried they rarely do anything immoral. Their compass focuses on the looks they might get at Mass. The only murders are one-off crimes over land or an odd missing person who the fairy folk were blamed for taking.

There's other news in the sheets of thin paper, but nothing I can really concentrate on. Joe's wife is possibly holding his hand, waiting on him to waken, and Molly is somewhere dreadful with no one to hold her hand and make her feel safe. There's nowhere and no one for me neither.

The coffee goes cold in these china cups quick as a flash, and I don't fancy the scrambled eggs and smoked salmon on the sideboard. The envelope propped against the milk jug catches my eye: *For Peggy. Shopping.* Tearing it open, I find one hundred pounds, like the wad Tiny left for me last time, and a note saying, *Best shops, best clothes. Take the boys with you. Be careful. Larry.*

I touch my hair, thinking he didn't mention my hair again. The hallway has a chilly air as I shout for the yolks. 'Bill? Ben?' Neither man will tell me their real names, so there's a need to call them something. Although bad yolks don't ever need names.

There's a trench coat hanging on the coat stand in the hall, and the cook shuffles past me to take the breakfast things away.

'Where's Larry?'

'If Mr Sheeran wanted us to know his whereabouts, he would tell us.' Her greasy hair and ample backside turn themselves on me, and she's away into the dining room. The kitchen's full of the chat from the men, and there's two of them there chewing on something that looks like bacon. The place is covered in flour, and the smell of fresh bread makes my mouth water.

'I need to go to the shops,' I say, and neither acknowledge me.

'What time? They won't be open yet,' the greyer one says.

'Ten.'

'Yeah.'

The munching and chatting resumes, and I cannot see either of them taking a bullet for me. The thoughts of lumping them around with me into shops to pick women's clothes makes me want to scream.

I almost offer to help the cook to wash the dishes, but she snorts at me and mutters something like, 'No respect.' So, I go to wash my face again and look out into the street, to pretend I'm normal Peggy.

At ten o'clock, the car smells of something awful. Death maybe.

'Roll down your windows too,' I tell the heads of Bill and Ben from the back seat. 'It stinks in here.'

Both of them snigger like schoolboys, and the stares from passers-by at the big car do nothing for me. I thought being in a Bentley with nice leather seats would do wonders for the ego but no. Not one thing lifts me at all. The entire situation is dragging me lower.

The Dublin air rakes the smell of whatever has been in the car higher. I notice my stockings have a large hole. I take them off, rather than let the Dublin saleswomen think I'm some sort of tramp. The men pretend they don't watch me removing them, but I see them gawping in the mirror and twisting their eyes for a look, the buggers.

There's a determined step on me when they park the car that lands me near Grafton Street, and it doesn't take me long to start my shopping. I pick out underwear and stockings while the yolks blush like nothing normal in the corner of the shop.

Skirts and blouses, a day dress and an evening gown, three pairs of shoes, one sensible pair and two for dancing, a few nice scarves and a new coat with a fur collar. Of course, everything is in a bigger size than usual, and I can tell you that doesn't help the mood much either.

'In a bit of a strop are we, princess?' the dark-haired yolk asks me when I push some of the bags at him to carry.

'I'm in the family way. You need to carry these for me.'

The face on him then, looking at my stomach as if it houses monsters.

'And, no, I'm not married. And, yes, I was an eejit.'

'I'd no idea.' He takes all the bags and nods to the grey-haired fecker to open the shop door. 'Are you keeping okay?' he asks me when we're stepping it back to the car.

'I've been sick as a small hospital. But that's a good sign. I used to tell women that, anyhow. I'm not sure how good it is when your head's in the toilet most of the day.'

He grins. His accent isn't American as such. 'The wife was sick too. I felt sorry for her.'

The other brute nudges him as if he isn't to talk to the object they're minding. 'Keeping an eye out, are you?'

'No one knows Peggy yet. But after the big event, Mr Sheeran hopes to introduce her to the city, then we'll need to be more careful.'

'Big event?'

Both men say nothing but avoid the throngs of people. The two of them are pretending I haven't asked anything at all.

I try again. 'Big event?'

'You'll need a nice dress,' says my mellower dark-haired minder.

'Did Anthony get the chop too?' I ask, slowing him down with a little tug on his sleeve.

He nods, and we walk in tandem for a time as I take it in. 'Killed inside, he was. We've people everywhere.'

'Is Larry really in charge now?'

He nods again and says, 'He's been meeting some influential people last few days, and all is looking good.'

'I can hardly believe it.'

'You must.'

The second yolk is looking around trying to make us hurry, but I linger back in the crowds of shoppers and say, 'This big event?'

'I've said enough. Mr Sheeran likes to be the one in charge. Just enjoy the new life you…and your baby will have.'

'Yes.' I hold my stomach. 'Don't you miss your children?'

'No.'

We've almost reached the car where the heavy doors are lying open, and the other sullen minder is inside sitting. I go to open the boot.

'*No!*' my mellower companion shouts. 'We'll put all the bags in the back seat with you.'

'I'd like to drive past Mountjoy Square. I can show you the way.'

'No,' the bastard in the front seat says. 'We've work on. We're taking you back. That's all.'

I think about rebelling, but don't really have the energy. All looks the same in the city, and nothing looks out of place or unusual.

'Did you enjoy shopping?' the dark-haired minder asks me.

'I need names for you.'

'Names are not important,' the minder driving says.

'They are to me.' The sun is dipping in the afternoon sky, and I squint out at the world and wonder when I will see it again alone.

Chapter 22

Larry isn't at the evening meal. I meet the cook while exploring a bit. She grunts at me. 'Less of your snooping now, missy, and back to the sitting rooms and the main house.'

'Is Martha back?'

'No. Do you need food?'

'I want to go out.'

'Off with ya,' she snaps and points me back up the corridor.

The hall-stand has no hats and no coats on it, so I presume all the men are away. I try the front door, and it's locked. I check under the mat inside the door in the rectangular groove in the floor, and there's a key.

The lock takes the key and turns. I open the door like a prisoner from Mountjoy might have after years of imprisonment. There's an early autumnal crispness to the evening, and the street is quiet enough. I lock the door behind me and count the seven short footsteps to the path. Each one makes me afraid, as if I may be sucked into quicksand.

Nothing swallows me, and I'm at the gate. A woman on a bicycle rings her bell to warn me of her passing and smiles. The noise and the sight of a human smile is so pleasant.

Molly had been my focus when we were thrown out of the gaol. She was so fearful of open spaces for a while and crossing the street even caused her to shriek in fear. It soon left her, but I can understand now why she was that way. But now, all I need do is think of myself. It feels odd, like a limb is missing from me.

There's nowhere to go. No one to chatter to. I'm not lucky like the ladies walking.

'Nice evening,' one says and nods.

The footpath is hard and dry, the air smoky, but the smell of coal and peat are welcome. My legs are free to move, and my arms swing. I'm a few hundred yards into the joy of living again when the rain starts. With no warning out of a grey but not ominous sky, it falls. Large, bulbous wetting drops that drench my arms and shoulders after only a few seconds. I stand on the corner with nowhere to shelter. Nothing for it, but I have to run backwards to Merrion Square. It's all I can do.

The lashing rain strips me of my melting dreams of escape easily and effectively. The mat welcomes me back only minutes after I left, almost triumphantly accepting my wet shoes. The key goes under the mat after locking the door again.

Even the weather in Dublin is conspiring with Larry to keep me prisoner. The key is at least found and ready for duplication the next time I get an opportunity.

I sink into the bubbles in the bath upstairs and drift off in the steam. It is years since I could easily fill a tub with almost boiling water and linger in the suds. There is no one banging on the walls or doors, no carting of buckets from the range. All smells are clean and of lavender. There are perks all right to being in Merrion Square. Yet, the old life had its advantages. Doors I locked were mine. Doors I opened were mine to open. The streets I walked… I never walked far anyhow, I was prisoner, then, too.

Food and money aren't my responsibility now. The baby needs a good home. Here would be good for a baby. There is space and cleanliness to play. Larry might be a great grandfather. Great? Family?

The water bubbles up as I go under it, covering me in a protective layer of liquid. Like my baby, I'm submerged in warmth and safety. This is where Mammy wishes me to be for me to become a mother too.

'You were the greatest gift,' she'd say, brushing my hair. Although she never told me she loved me, I felt it through her eyes, her hands and her arms. Slowly, those precious pieces of her left. She almost weaned me from her, left me slowly and alone. I survived, and I will again.

'You're the greatest gift,' I tell my slightly swollen belly when I dry it and caress it in the long bathroom mirror.

Chapter 23

Larry looks frail and tired at dinner, but I don't let on.

'I got clothes. I aim to get my hair sorted tomorrow.'

'Good,' he mutters, looking at the newspaper. 'Not as much talk of the killings today.'

'Old news already.' I help myself to mashed potatoes. The meat is warm and the gravy tasty. The carrots are the way I like them mushed with butter and pepper.

'Eating for two?' The face on him now looks like a kindly grandfather.

I smile like a clean-living granddaughter might.

'There's to be a ball in the American Ambassador's Residence in the Phoenix Park. We're invited. It'll be an opportunity to show our strength. You must not leave my side.'

I'm already dreaming of dancing in such a place.

'Do you have suitable clothes?'

'When is it?'

'Friday evening.' He munches the meat but doesn't fill his fork again. 'We'll need to be a united front. You're a Sheeran now.'

'Aren't you glad to have me help you?'

He ignores me for a while then says, 'The Professor and that lot are gone. We control the city.' He says it like he bought me a bicycle or fancy hat.

'Am I in control?' I sip from the crystal glass. The water is very cold and stings my teeth.

'The Sheerans are back.'

'But I can't go out or…'

'There's a price for everything.'

I never have any choice in what I do.

'You can select your own minder, if you like,' he says.

I stare at him.

'Think about who you would have to watch over you in the future.'

Joe Bushnell is in my mind before I can blink.

'He'll be paid well, but you must earn money too. I'll be putting you in charge of various things soon enough.'

'What things?'

'All in good time.'

The merlot fills my glass as if by magic. I need alcohol to settle the pounding in me. The torture of it all is real now, the need to escape huge, and yet, there's a big longing to make something of myself. I can make something of myself here, can't I?

'Peggy Sheeran,' I say it out, and there before me, in my imagination, is the girl who left the farm in Sligo. I see myself all meek at the midwifery training, unsure of everything until I remembered what my Dora taught me about birthing. It wasn't that much different than calving, but they made it complicated with politics and relationships. Remembering who to impress, when and how, figuring out the things we should and could talk about, it all took learning, and I was a quick learner. Like now, I was petrified by the bigness of the world and the tasks ahead, but I did it. I became the lass in the Gresham dancing. I feared no one at all. The gaol ate that lass and tossed her into the pit of hell. There she is, in number thirty-four, starting again at the lowest form of womanhood and standing at the corner of Merrion Street, thinking of men who can make her better than she is. I spend my life lost waiting on Robin Hood to rescue me.

'Peggy Sheeran will rescue herself,' I tell the room, Larry and myself.

The voice on me crackles as I gulp back the tears. There's not much hope inside me for rescuing anyone. But, sure, there's naught else for it but to try.

Larry ignores my statements. Instead, he mentions a few bits and pieces about the empire in America. It's the type of boasting us Irish loathe.

'You'll love Hell's Kitchen.'

I'm back from the magical land of the fairies where Molly and I were dancing with singing bears. The wine or my mood just transports me away – far away from the realities surrounding me.

'Is your conscience bothering you?' he asks.

'No.'

'You're very quiet.'

'I just cannot believe I've got family, and that Mammy had kept it all to herself.'

'Sally never could come to terms with my way of doing things.'

'Your wife? What did she think?'

'She was called Peggy.'

'Was she?'

He nods but doesn't look sad. 'She enjoyed the finer things too.'

'Did she like your way of doing things?'

'She had no choice.'

'Did you love her?'

'She was a good wife.'

I'm about to ask what that meant when there's a loud rapping on the front door, and then, the doorbell shrills loud and long. It's so sudden and sharp, I jump. Then, the bell peels again for even longer. No one has been to the door, and the insistent thumping is scary, despite me having wished it to happen so often.

Ben and Bill emerge from the kitchen, and both attend to the opening of the front door. There's raised voices and the sound of a scuffle. I leap from my chair and retreat over beside Larry.

'The boys will deal with him,' he mutters, but he looks fearful for the first time.

The grey-haired yolk comes into the room, his face redder than usual, and his tie pulled to one side. 'Says he's here to see

Peggy. Won't take no for an answer. Brave buck, he is. Took a good thump off me and still won't go. We'll drag him out now.'

'Who is it?'

'Some young fella called Tommy.'

'Sweet Jesus.' I come out from around the table.

There, half sitting and half lying, is Molly's lover, his young face still scarred from where she cut him and the side of his mouth all bloodied from the thumping he's just taken.

'What in the name of…'

'Where's Molly?' he asks as if she never hurt him at all. The look of longing in him that only an eejit would miss.

'I've no idea where she is.'

'Don't lie to me,' he howls, rising off the floor gingerly enough, looking at the brutes and their bared fists. 'I need to see my Molly.'

'Your Molly got taken away because of that.' I point to his scar. 'That and your feckin 'mother.'

'I didn't want any trouble for her.'

'You promised her the sun, moon and stars, and look at where we all are now.'

He looks around the hallway, obviously thinking he did me a big favour. 'She's here? I know you'd never leave her. She knew you'd always look after her.'

I can feel a tear on my cheek. I wipe it away quickly before it's seen. 'How could I look after her when you squealed to the Gardaí? She got lifted and taken away somewhere, thanks to you.'

He looks so fearful, the critter. Like he'll cry. 'I didn't know they'd take her. Where is she?'

'I don't know, I tell you. They took her. She's gone.'

'Fuck,' he says, sinking into the slim chair in the hallway that usually takes an odd coat or hat. 'I thought she'd be back, and once I took care of Ma, we'd be all right again.'

'Nothing is all right.'

'They were saying she killed a woman from the country, but I didn't believe that at all.'

I gawp at him. Those blond locks of his make him almost childlike.

'Did she kill her because of me?' His blue eyes are on fire with worry and brimming with the tears of a man in despair.

'She's gone, and I cannot find out where,' I whisper, leaning down at him. All dry in the mouth, I am, and full of pity for him.

'Her son?' He searches his memory.

'Fionn.'

'Yeah.'

'He's where she left him.'

'I could've...' His hand rakes through the blondness of his hair.

'You didn't.'

'I could've looked after...'

'You didn't.'

Just like Joe, he arrives too late to be of any use to a woman.

'The Professor warned me off, but with him gone, and I heard you were here. I didn't believe Molly was gone. I thought it was safe now to come to get her.'

'Molly isn't safe, that's for sure,' I say cruelly. I'm so angry I don't notice who else is around us until Larry speaks.

'Get out of my house.' It's a simple request, not shouted or forceful, just said like he means it. 'Out, now.' His bony finger points at the door.

'Peggy?' Tommy begs with his features. They are all contorted, like he's in physical pain.

'You need to go, Tommy. I don't know where she is, and I'm no help to you now. None.'

'I'll tell the guards it wasn't her that hurt me.'

'Doesn't matter now. You're too late. I warned you.'

'Peggy, get this man out,' Larry says and taps away with his stick down the tiles. He nods to the brutes to follow him. 'There's no need for an explanation. That's your old life. Move on.' His voice is calm but firm.

Tommy looks so crestfallen, I feel like I will cry with him. He rises off the seat. 'I can't live without her…' Tommy mutters and makes his way towards the door. 'I can't.'

'It's all a bit late now, young fella.'

'I've left home. Told Ma I wanted Molly.'

'Oh.'

'Ma wasn't pleased.'

I open the door and lean on it, for my back and all my bones are sore as if I were flogged with the truth over and over.

'I miss our Molly.' He looks down on me. 'Best of luck to you, Peggy.'

The scar is not as deep as it might have been, but it's a reminder for evermore to him that he failed a woman he loved.

'If you find her, will you get word to me? Would they let her out?'

'If she cut you, Tommy, what might she do to others?'

'And, sure, she murdered that woman. I can't believe it.' Those blond curls of his shake and remind me of that blonde bitch who visited all those months ago. Another blond that changed the course of all our lives.

'Goodbye, Tommy.'

'Remember me, if you need any good men,' he says, scratching at his muscly arm. 'The word is the Sheerans are back and ready to take on men to work. I'm good with my fists, and with having fallen out with my Ma, I need…'

'Go home to your mother, Tommy.'

I close the door but hear him saying, 'Best of luck to you, Peggy.'

Chapter 24

There's no question the colour of my hair is more natural looking. I picked a darker dye which makes me more brunette than blonde. Tommy and that Blonde Bitch made me want to be less bleached. There's no goodness in me at all now. I got the hairdresser to change the look of me so I feel new.

The thickness of my hair is good for the styling she did. She showed me how to do the curls, and the ribbon sits well into the swish and the sway of the curves of my hair. I'm like a new woman.

'Peggy Sheeran,' I told the girl taking down my name for the next appointment. It didn't sound right, so I said it again. 'Peggy Sheeran.'

'All the women on our books come in regularly, and now, Mrs Sheeran, you'll be a regular.'

'You're a good saleswoman.' I smile at her, wondering does she know who or what I am. Ireland is a small place, and it won't take long.

'See you next Thursday.'

My coat is helped on. I hand over too much money, but I love the look on the yolks' faces when I go back to the car. They say little. However, I catch them winking at each other as I fix my skirt and sit into the car.

The fancy evening dress and the gloves I put on are nice together after I wash and powder myself. The red chiffon dress is not too red, and the white gloves make my arms look slimmer than I remember them. Red in Dublin, or anywhere in Ireland, makes a statement.

'Only a harlot wears red.' Father Lavelle's voice rings in my pierced ears – also a sign of true damnation. My shoes are high tonight, and the almost sheer stockings just visible under the tight hem around my calves.

Walking with my hips and legs constrained in fabric is unusual, and I practice, watching the creature before me in the mirror. She's a stranger, her mousey hair styled, her lips red and those high cheeks pink. The curve of an elegant neck and the arse on her big but pert enough. The swell of her bosom is bigger, and her belly curved when she rubs it, but she sure looks well. She knows she looks good. Damn good.

'Peggy?' the dark-haired yolk asks.

I've come into the kitchen to say I'm ready to go. I'm to meet Larry at the function, and I don't want to be late and make him angry. 'Is that who I am?' I smile at him and ignore the cook who snorts at me but doesn't compliment anyone.

'You look lovely. I'll get the car around.'

The cook does another snort, and just to piss her off, I twirl around the table a few times.

'Be careful of snorting at me,' I warn her, coming right up to her nose so she can see me good and proper. 'You're cooking isn't all that grand.'

Her cheeks flush, and she looks at the tiled floor. 'You're nothing but a whore,' she mutters under her breath.

I'm not sure what force of nature takes me back to her. Some sort of rage consumes me and launches me into her. My gloved fingers tangle in her greasy hair, and I haul her face downwards, slapping it into the table with a loud thud. One fluid movement is all it takes to smash her cheek into the edge of the wood. She barely has time to groan or scream. She slumps to her knees when I let go of the mop of hair.

'I'm sorry...' I start as her hands go to her head. 'I've never...'

The moan out of her tells me she's conscious, and there's no sign of blood. My hands are shaking and the ruffling of my dress moves me out of the kitchen and into the hall. My heart is beating fit to burst, and the guilt I feel from hurting her hurts me. I turn to go back in and see her sitting on her backside staring into space, her head intact but a red bump on her forehead and cheekbone. She doesn't speak, and neither do I. Her hand goes to heave herself off the floor and steady herself against the table that marked her.

When I see she is on her feet, I turn on my heel, and yet, fear makes me wait. What if she dies? Thumping someone's head off a table isn't exactly good for them. I hear the pots and pans move, and the noises are of life in the kitchen. I breathe deeply and hear my conscience telling me, 'She deserved that. She had it coming. All you want is to get along in life. Quietly get along and better yourself.'

Ben and Bill have the car running, and the noise of the engine drowns out the awfulness in my head. Never before, not even in the gaol, have I hurt another person like that. No matter how my beast of a husband tortured me, I never raised a hand to even protect myself. I didn't hurt any of the girls who could've done with a skelping, even though the want of it was close to the surface.

It never spilled out before. The shaking in my hands won't stop, but I don't cry as I don't want red eyes for the party. The wide swing in the road up to the big house is so grand. The lights take me a while to adjust to. The grandeur takes me even longer to take in. Yes, I'm entitled to see and be in this place. Course I am.

Larry is standing beside the elegant staircase. I can see he is stooped but not overtly frail. There's no sign of a minder, and his suit is dark and his dicky bow perfectly formed in a starched collar. Bill and Ben are on my heels, and all eyes are on me. I smile and greet people I don't know. There are whispers as I go towards Larry. He's like an oasis in the desert, and I'm the camel ambling through the perfumed air to get to him.

'Peggy.' He looks at his watch which he takes from his pocket. It is on a chain like the rest of his possessions.

'Grandfather.' It's my poshest voice.

'Some spot, isn't it? They've been refurbishing.'

I nod, noticing all eyes are still on us, and lots of people are openly muttering to each other while pointing in our direction.

'You look lovely.' His hand touches off mine, but he makes me twirl for him by pushing my elbow. 'Let everyone see the new Peggy Sheeran in red. Hard to miss you, clever girl.'

I'm more than uncomfortable. There's a little trickle of sweat making its way down my back, and my armpits are moist. Horribly so, my body telling me I don't belong, even if my brain thinks it should be here. The humidity doesn't bother others. The redness in my face is pounding now.

'Does my face match my dress?' I ask Larry, praying in some small way he's kind in his reply.

'You look grand. All is well.'

'Why are we here?'

'The ambassador has invited Americans, and most of New York knows Larry Sheeran.'

'I see.' I wipe my glove off my forehead and notice it is damp. I'm sweating like a racehorse.

'What am I to do?'

'Look pretty and new. I doubt any of your clients are here.'

'Bastard.'

'Less of that language, Lady Sheeran.'

'Did you get us a title and all? Do ladies and lords commit crimes now?'

'Larry,' someone shouts like they've seen a relation in a throng of strangers.

'This is my granddaughter, Peggy Sheeran,' Larry says as he shakes hands with a tall American. His hair is cut tightly and his eyes blue. Both are a long distance from my own and Larry's. His height is epic compared to the Irish surrounding him.

'Rod here plays basketball and is a great guy.' Larry smirks, and I know he's lying.

'Hello.' I hope I look virginal.

'I just love Irish women, you're just so demure and quiet.'

I see the cook's face hitting the table, and I know my eyes are no longer innocent.

'Larry, I need to talk to you…' Rod says.

'After.'

'Do you live in the States then, Rod?' I ask, but it's obvious where he is from.

'Yes, I'm over here on business.'

'I see.'

'I import and export.'

'I see.'

'Would you like a drink?'

'A brandy.' I touch my bump, asking inwardly for forgiveness. The heat doesn't seem as claustrophobic when I'm distracted. 'Yes, a brandy or a whiskey, please. Or anything at all.'

'One brandy coming up.'

'Don't get drunk,' Larry spits and then smiles at passing people. 'I need you with a clear head.'

'For what?'

'You'll see.'

The crowd move around like sheep. All bleating about their brilliance in business, the theatre, life in general, and although many have talked to me, I sense they can smell my past. It's the way their noses wrinkle when I say, 'No, not married. I work for myself. This and that, you know.'

One obnoxious woman in a fur stole decides she will be nosey. She won't take the patter that I've given others. 'Don't I know you?' she drawls.

'I doubt it.'

'I know your face.'

'Unless you were a visitor to my whorehouse, you don't know me.'

She laughs and looks me up and down. 'There's no reason to be rude.'

'I'm not being rude.'

'I do know you?' Her permed hair is tightly curled to her head, and she's wearing real pearls. 'I definitely know you for somewhere?'

'Or maybe it was from the time I was in prison?' It all just hops out of my mouth. 'I was all over the papers for selling babies.'

Her eyes with their terrible green eyeshadow go huge, and she walks away tutting loudly. Larry's deep in conversation with a man in an army uniform with a large moustache. Rod appears back beaming with two brandy glasses.

'Large queue.' He offers me the tulip glass.

'Thank you. I need this.'

'So, you're Larry's granddaughter?'

I let the brandy settle me.

'Would you like some canapés?' Rod asks. 'Food? There's some small bits on trays somewhere.'

'No, thank you. This dress is already stuck to me.'

'You look nice.' He winks, and I notice his eyes again.

'It's eyes like yours that got me into…'

'My eyes did what?' he says, but his wedding ring is hard to ignore. It sparkles at me as he drinks from his glass.

'Can I introduce you to…' Larry says, butting in between us.

I don't hear the boring old fart's name, or the names of the others as Larry points me in the direction of a great many people. I know I'm supposed to be making mental notes of who's who and what they do, but the heat again seems too much, and the smells from the brandy and the cheap perfume are stifling all together.

'Peggy?' The voice sounds familiar, and when I turn around, there is my soldier in his fancy uniform and his wonderful eyes all agog.

Larry has moved to sit in a chair, and he's not looking at me or holding my elbow, so I take in all of the man who gave me the child inside me and ask, 'What's your name?'

My darling soldier is blushing and him the one who showed no shame in kissing the hair between my legs in the kitchen in number thirty-four. 'Don't you remember me?' he asks.

'I remember you.' I doubt my smile is virginal now. I don't want him to forget the way he took me and made me want him every day since. 'I just don't know your name.'

He takes my hand, and I feel faint with the heat and the touch of him. His lips softly touch on the back of my glove. Through the fabric, my willingness to feel him is huge. The pressure of his fingers on my hand is light, but then, he holds my fingers harder. 'I haven't forgotten you, that's a certainty. I didn't know you'd be here.'

'Neither did I.' I watch his lips curl, and the dimples in his cheek dint inwards. Little holes that love could fall into, that's what they are. 'What do they call you?'

'I went to thirty-four again. But you've obviously moved up in the world.' He stands back and looks me up and down, smiling all the while. He's the best-looking man in the room, in Dublin, and he knows it. Somehow, I need to be nearer him.

'Don't move too far away.' I shift myself close to him. 'Yes, thirty-four is closed, but I am doing other things now.'

'Can you meet me?' he whispers right into my ear.

His breath sends a shiver thrill down to the arse clasped in my pants. A trickle of sweat follows the shiver. 'Yes,' I whisper back, but cannot look, for fear I'd make a holy show of myself.

Larry calls to me and beckons me with his hand to come closer to his perch, and when I look back, my soldier has gone. I glance all around, but he's disappeared like a thief in the night with my lust and love with him. I'm a horny old woman as I keep an eye out for my young lad like a dog on heat.

'Did you just tell Lady Chisellsworth that you're a whore who's been inside?' Larry has lines I haven't noticed before. Large furrowed wrinkles on his forehead that tell of his anger.

'I may have done.'

'For the love of God.' There's spittle in the corners of his mouth. 'Don't you know how to behave?' The spits are coming out thick and fast as he pulls on my arm. 'Have you no shame?'

My eyes fill with liquid. It's the shock. 'Who am I supposed to be? You tell me then. Am I a criminal queen or a fucking lady? 'I can tell he isn't sure of who he wants me to be. 'You told me to be Peggy Sheeran and to let the women of Dublin know who they're dealing with. That's what I've done. I'm not a mind reader, Larry. What is it you want?'

Bill and Ben are at my side. 'Take her home.' Larry points at me. I'm a dog that's come off its leash.

'I've someone to speak to –'

Larry grabs my arm hard. 'Get your fat ass home and stay there. I'll speak with you in the morning.'

I get bundled between the two yolks and poked repeatedly to move towards the door we came in. Herded like I might have done with Dora my cow, all those years ago. I am in the car before I let the tears fall.

'Did you do something?' my dark-haired minder asks.

I can't hold back the tears that are streaming now. It is frustration more than being upset. Anger at being made to leave. A fever in me at being told what to say and not being able to find my soldier.

'Larry likes to do all the talking. He isn't used to someone stealing his limelight. Not used to dealing with women.' Ben sounds almost sorry for me. 'Tiny will have to stay with you tonight. We've got to go back for the boss.'

'I want to be alone.'

The Dublin I want to be in speeds past me.

Tiny looms large over me in the kitchen as I put on the kettle.

'Cook left,' he says and grins, showing me his missing teeth. 'She said she's not coming back.'

'I'd forgotten I bashed her head off the table. 'The mugs are dirty, so I swirl the water from the kettle around them in the basin.

'She did mention it. Good job she's afraid of Larry.'

'Why didn't you tell me about him when you came to thirty-four?'

'Professor would've killed me if he found out I worked for Larry.'

'You could have told me.'

'Then it would have been Larry who would've got rid of me.'

'Have you worked for him long?'

'Before he went to America, he knew me. Then, the Professor took me on.'

'Do you know Sergeant Bushnell?'

Tiny nods now, sitting down and removing his cap. He wrings it like a cloth as he says, 'I like you, Peggy. I aim to keep you safe.'

'Thank you.' The back of my dress is sticking to me, and I'm sure he can see it in the bright light of the kitchen.

'They say you're having a baby?'

'Yes.'

'I'll look after it too.'

'Thanks.'

'I'm used to being the Big Lad no one thinks much of.' He stops wringing his cap as I turn to look at him. 'I've a lot going on in my head, you know. I'm not as thick as I look. The Professor didn't even think I knew English.'

'I remember.' I hear the kettle boil, but let it whistle for a moment. 'I'll need a good man, like you, to help me through all this. What does Larry want from me?'

Those large shoulders shrug. His eyes flit to the kettle, and he rises to lift it off the cooker.

'Does he want me to be a lady or a bad bitch?'

At the curse word, Tiny looks at me. 'You're no bitch.'

'I am. I hit a woman's face into a table.' The chair I slump into is hard and cool on my back.

'She deserved it. Thinks she's better than us all because she cooked for the queen or something.'

'Really?'

'Someone fancy. I didn't listen.'

I chuckle. 'Did I leave her with a big bruise?'

Tiny doesn't answer me.

'I've come only a few streets, but it seems a world away.'

'If anyone can make this work, you can.'

His cap gets set onto the table.

'Thanks.'

'Does Larry really control lots of Dublin?'

Tiny nods that big head.

'The Sheerans are in charge, then?'

'Yeah, and he wants to keep you here to…'

It's the way he stops. It makes me shiver. 'To what?'

'I dunno. I dunno what he's thinking. No one does.'

'You must know some things about him?' I ask and notice Tiny seems uncertain of what to say.

'No one knows Larry.'

'Didn't you learn much about him at all?'

'No one knows much. Makes him untouchable. No one to hurt him or be hurt. That's why he's not sure what to do with you. But he only has you.'

'He needs me?'

'He came home to take over and to find his family. That's what I thought.'

'Oh.'

'But no one knows what Larry thinks.'

'No one speaks to me. I cannot really go out, and the papers don't tell me anything much.'

'There's not much to tell. The Professor and the likes of him are gone. Larry has his ambassadors in place, and that's it. Larry's back on top, and all of Dublin knows it.'

'Where are you from? How did he find you?'

'I've worked for…people like Larry all my life. Not great at schooling, but my size came in handy.'

'Where are you from? Family?'

'All dead, and I'm from God knows where.'

'From where? Everyone comes from somewhere.'

Tiny smiles. I know he doesn't want to say, and that's the only time I wonder at his trustworthiness. I've always trusted him, even when he was a Russian, heavy sleeping in my kitchen, I trusted he wasn't bad at all.

'I'm used to being whoever people need me to be.'

'That doesn't answer my question.' I pull off my gloves and throw them on the table. 'No one is honest with me. I'm like a pawn in some chess game, and I hate this. I want out, and I'm getting out.'

Tiny reaches out to me across the table, but isn't near enough to touch me. 'You won't escape Larry Sheeran. And where are you going that would be better than this?'

'Better than what?' I throw my arms open and look around me. 'No one is as they seem. At least in number thirty-four people were honest and straightforward about what they wanted and who they were. Here, I don't know who I am anymore. Who the fuck am I?'

'You're Peggy. Damn fine Peggy.' He isn't lustful, he's more proud, like a brother might be. I can tell he does mean it.

'Thanks.'

'It's the baby too. My ma always said I wrecked her belly and brain.' His large hands take his cap back to wring it. 'She mentioned other parts, too, but we'll leave that alone.'

'I cannot place your accent. Is your mother alive?'

He shakes his head. 'Please don't ask. I promise though, Peggy, you can trust me. I'm a good man in here.' His thick finger points to his heart.

Is he trying to say he'd be a husband or father?

His hands go to his head, so his eyes are hidden from me. 'I meant, I'll protect you.'

'I see. I've a fella, you see…'

'Sergeant Bushnell?' He doesn't look cross or hurt.

'Sort of him. Sort of.'

'Stop worrying. You don't need to worry about me.'

I rub my belly as I think there was a flutter in there that wasn't from worry, nerves or annoying conversations.

'Who's the father?'

'I honestly don't know his name.'

The expression on his large face isn't disgusted. He smiles. 'You see. You've plenty of things to worry you. I'm not one of them.' He lifts his big frame off the chair and checks the lock on the back door. 'I'm checking the house now.'

'I'll go to bed.'

'Goodnight.' He's away to check the windows and doors, and it seems like that's an end to our conversation.

'I won't sleep,' he calls from the back scullery. 'No one will harm a hair on your head.'

'Thanks.'

The stairs are looming upwards towards the most comfortable bed I've ever known. There's nothing really to fear in this house, and I'm protected by the largest man, yet nothing seems real, certain or stable.

Why did Larry find me and take me in? What does he want from me? Nothing makes sense at all, and I feel I'm living in a lie.

I'm used to untruths. I'm good at being untruthful, but I'm not used to being uncertain of others and their truthfulness. Usually, Irish people are open, and if they're not, you know somehow their true nature will surface. Nothing can stay hidden in small towns, villages or counties. There's always someone who knows something. Someone who sees, hears or finds out the truth. The Irish definitely make the best detectives and couldn't be killers or hide from the law. No one can go anywhere in Ireland without seeing someone they know.

Sure, there was the one time I thought I'd run away from that beast of a husband. I'd taken the train to Dublin. I was trembling and worrying all the way. But in Maynooth who got on and sat in my carriage but Father Lavelle.

'Up seeing my nephew who's in training in the college. On to see the Cardinal and then home to Sligo.' His crooked smile bored into my soul. 'You're not thinking of leaving Sligo yourself, Peggy? Sure, where would a lass like you end up?' He looked at my tiny case and my bad-looking shoes. 'I'll have a word with himself, and he'll get you some nice new shoes and take you dancing. How's about that?'

He held my elbow and marched me up to the residence of the Cardinal where I had tea with the housekeeper in the kitchen until he could march me back to the train station and sit with me until we got to Collooney where we both got off, Father Lavelle saying now and again, 'Women like new shoes. You're a young woman now, and I know we should have seen that himself was buying you a few bits and bobs. That mother of yours spoilt you.'

I could've flung that fucking priest out of the window of the moving train, such was my hatred of him. The frustration I had at fate for putting him into my carriage and me finally running away. Himself did buy me the new shoes, but also battered me with them before he gave them to me all wrapped up again in their white tissue paper speckled with spots of red.

'I know life ain't easy on a woman. But you got to make the best of the things that God provides,' Father Lavelle said, when I muttered my misgivings. He ignored the marks I showed him at confession. 'I cannot see through the grille, Peggy. They can't be that bad and sure a man like Johnny just doesn't know how to tell you that he'd miss you. He's not used to dealing with a pretty girl and nice things. Are you being a good wife to him now? Children will bless you both soon enough. Give the Lord time. Have patience.'

'I pray I never give him any, Father.'

I'm sure he cursed at me then. Ranting uncontrollably through the box at me, he was. Saying my nature would be fulfilled by children and how my mother would be so disgusted if she knew I wasted my time with the Lord in asking for such vile things.

'I know your mother sacrificed a lot to give you a good home and bring you up in a community with Catholic values. She deserves to know you'll have a child and will raise it right, like she did. God love the creature, sure, this kind of talk would send her madder still. What an ungrateful lass you are.'

I can hear him still. If anyone would know about my past and who I am, Father Laval would. Whether he would tell me would be another thing and whether the bastard is alive to tell it, is crucial to my hatching plan.

The pillow is cool, and my breasts ache as I take them from my underwear. My tummy is swollen more, and the mirror tells me I have the glow other mothers have. I can see it, despite my tiredness and uncertainties. I like it. I love feeling the flutter inside me as I settle into the mattress and talk to my little one.

'All will be right, as long as I have you.' The baby must be sleeping, and I fall into the lull of the night to join her. It's a her inside me as only a female could survive all I've put her through.

Chapter 25

The pains wake me. Sharp, like a stab in the guts and in my right side mostly. They stop, and I close my eyes, hoping I'm dreaming. They come again, and I feel an ooze between my legs. My fingers tell me I'm wet there, and so I rise out of the sheets.

The light tells me I'm bleeding or at least there's a trickle of blood. Not much, but enough is there to make me shiver. The pains are duller but come and go. Like cramps at the monthly but odd, too. Like they aren't supposed to be coming and know they aren't right themselves.

I know it isn't good, but I also know some women bleed like a stuck pig and still hold on to their babies.

'Please stay.'

I whisper prayers to the angels in the hope they will protect us both. I place gauze from a drawer into my pants in the hope of stopping it all with sheer will. 'Please. You're wanted so much. I know I'm bad, but you can make me the best…'

I cannot say "mother" out loud. I gulp and cry solidly into the pillow, heaving my belly upwards with each convulse of self-pity. My arms encircle the little mound that is my future and all that I have, and we drift off in a haze of worry.

The gauze is white in the morning, and the pains are gone. I'm white, too, in the mirror, and my hair is brushed back from my face and held in a clasp. The crying has reddened my eyes, and they look foreign, swollen and sore with my self-pity.

Larry is at the dining table, but there's no sign of breakfast. 'Tiny tells me the cook left.'

'So I hear. I'll make us something. What would you like?'

'Scrambled eggs,' he says, looking at the paper. 'Why did she leave just like that?'

'No idea.'

'We need to talk about last night.'

'You mean, you need to explain what you want from me.'

I turn to leave the room, but he says, 'You were there to do your duty.'

'I didn't know why I was there…'

'There was an influential man there who needed some persuading. The type of work only a woman can do. We could've done with you being a little bit more discreet. 'His face is almost evil. It's as if he doesn't hear what he said or how it sounds.

'What?'

'You heard me.'

'You wanted me to whore for you?' I stand but know my shoulders are drooping like the lilies in the vase on the sideboard.

'I needed you to help a man see the error of his ways.'

'How was I to do that?' My hands are on my hips.

'Everything with you has to be a scene of some sort. Sally is not dead at all. There she stands before me. Again. I think we're not…'

'We're not what?'

'I can't work with you, Peggy. I thought when you came here we might find a common ground.'

'You haven't even given me a chance. I've no idea what you expect of me. There's plenty I can do, other than be a common harlot.'

'Really?' He doesn't try to hide his disgust then. I see it all over him. His eyes, his mouth, his hunched shoulders, the way he is half-turned away. 'Like mother, like daughter.'

'Mammy was no whore. Mammy was wonderful.'

'Was she now?'

'She raised me well. It was the Sheeran blood in my veins that was the trouble.'

'She didn't know the father of her child either. Tricked some poor prick into marriage, but he ran off. I need family, but I don't know if you're worth the hassle.'

'Fuck you.'

His eyes spring open and stare at me, those tiny glasses of his propped on his head as usual.

'I'm all you've got.'

His long fingernails scratch his bald patch. The silence from him confirms a great deal.

'So, you're going to have to put up with me. I'm no whore. I was in charge wherever I worked. I'll be in control of myself, where I go and what I do from now on. End of story.'

Larry is staring out the window.

'You need to tell me what you need of me.'

'Make me scrambled eggs.'

There's a pain in me. Deep in me it stabs, so I'm not sure if it is all physical. Before, when words came or actions from others, they didn't come from family. The hurt came from others, strangers or nameless folk, yet he is close to me. But he doesn't love me like a grandfather should. I rub my belly and look at the kitchen. The pots on the range are cold as the fire has been let go out. The eggs are propped on top of each other in the little basket and the bread hard but good enough for toast.

Tiny appears with sleep still in his eyes, scratching his head and heaving at his belt to close it.

'So much for you not sleeping,' I tease. 'Can you try to light the fire? I don't know where to find the kindling and the fuel.'

'Of course.' He smiles, and I set about the activities of a housewife, ignoring the fears in my heart about the baby. It still is very early days for life, and many a woman would have still come to me, hoping to be rid of the worry in her heart. But I want this worry to stay with me. I need it to be mine, to be healthy and happy and make me the same. I want this baby more than anything. The irony is not lost on me as I beat the eggs hard.

'I have pains,' I say aloud to Tiny's back by the range. I can hear the fire he's lighting crackling.

'The baby?' he asks, without turning around. I feel almost married to him, sharing my fears with a manly figure while making breakfast.

'Maybe.' I beat the eggs again harder.

'It's early days,' he says as if he can read my mind. 'You must rest.'

'It's the not knowing what's ahead.'

'Whatever it is, you can face it.'

His eyes never meet mine, but his voice is strong and calm. It is like he's always known me, and yet, I know nothing at all about him.

The smell of the cooking doesn't stir my stomach, and this bothers me. As much as I hated being sick, the lack of nausea is unsettling.

'I had to get the range lit, it had gone out,' I tell the dining room and the men in it.

'Why did cook leave?' Larry asks.

'I slammed her face into the table for calling me a whore.'

Neither he nor Bill or Ben say anything. They just look at each other.

'I want Tiny to be the lad that looks after me.'

I leave them to eat scrambled eggs and toast as the noise of them eating is irritating.

Chapter 26

'No, the Gardaí aren't looking for anyone,' Tiny confirms as we're walking free around the streets, me asking him about what's what and who's who. Some people take a longer glance than usual at the pair of us. The men touch their caps as if Tiny is in the military and is a rank above them.

'Hello,' a few men say to us both, but the women don't look for long and don't speak.

'Do they know who I am?'

'Dublin is a small place,' he adds, 'and, sure, there's always someone in control. For now, it's the Sheerans.'

'Who might try to take it?'

'The gypsies or the IRA, the list is a long one.'

'Does Larry not have them all sorted?'

'For now.'

His missing teeth always make me smile. 'Where's my place in all of this?'

'How about we collect the money from the ambassadors.'

'Money for what?'

'Money for money.'

We stop, and he raps on the door of the house next door to a shop and pub. A man appears in a vest and hands him a thick envelope. Neither man speaks, and the man in the vest disappears inside again. Tiny shoves the envelope into his inside pocket.

'Simple.' He grins again. 'It's their job to keep the land for the Sheerans and take up the taxes. They get a cut, and Larry makes sure all is well for their own business.'

'How many are there?'

'About twenty big boys Larry tolerates and a few new recruits who want in on the action.'

'Like the Professor, they are.'

'Yeah, some get the idea quick enough and start their own rackets. It's a matter then of keeping those boys in check. Keeping an ear to the ground. We'll have a quick one in here.'

He shoves the door open to the pub next door, and the smoke swirls as we enter. Women don't go into pubs much and especially not during the day, so the stares linger on me.

'Peggy Sheeran,' I tell the barman who hadn't been all that interested in who I was.

The glass he's wiping with a dirty rag gets put down, 'The usual, Tiny? Sheeran, eh?'

I prop myself up on the stool.

'They said Larry had a woman with him.' He talks loudly for the regulars around him and snorts. There's an air of humour lingering around him that I don't like.

'There's a woman in charge all right.' I point at the whiskey. 'One of those for me too.'

The hunched shoulders of a few men are lost in the sea of smoke from pipes, and there's a door that leads back into the shop on the right-hand side. One man tosses the last of the dredges in his glass and grunts something and leaves. All is very quiet for a time.

'Women are putting men off their pints,' the young barman says.

'Pity about them. They need to know that women like me are on the rise in Dublin.'

'Women do rise the men all right,' the barman quips, looking for laughter from his audience. Of course, he gets long guffaws from them. Tiny slurps on at his pint and gurgles amusement too.

'It might be dangerous to mess with the Sheeran women,' I say as the young barman puts down the whiskey in front of me. 'Anthony and the Professor tried to overpower me and look where it got them.'

His hand stops short of the rag, and he looks at me. He really looks at me. Fear seeps into his eyes, but he half snorts.

'The cook up at the house got her head smashed for being loose with her tongue too.'

There's a long silence.

'This whiskey isn't too bad.' I'm lying as it burns me all the way down to the lining of my stomach.

The barman wipes the dark wood before him and doesn't take me on at all. There are no more jokes or jibes. He thrusts an envelope at Tiny, saying, 'This was left for ya,' and Tiny nods for us to leave.

'We'll be back,' I tell the barman as Tiny puts some money on the counter. It gets pushed back near Tiny's big hands, and so he lifts it without protest. The barman doesn't look at me or answer, so I repeat it. 'We'll be back.'

'I hear ya.'

'That's if you're still here to see me.' I get off the stool, and I don't stop until I'm outside in the fresh air. There's a slight ache in my side, and Tiny takes a long look at me in the sunshine.

'You're made for this. That buck will be looking for bullets forever more.'

'He's a bad bollocks.'

'We've put our mark on this area anyhow.' Tiny waves to a man in a car. He pulls across the street, and Tiny holds open the back door. 'Get in. You're on a roll; we're going to O'Connell Street.'

I spend the day lording it about. 'Ladying isn't a word at all, is it?' I ask Tiny after the twelfth place we've visited and fiftieth time I've had to hold my own against the men in the room.

'You've a tongue on ya that would cut steel. They all know for sure you're not to be messed with.'

'If only I felt as big as I talk.' I think of his size and the fear of being shot is bigger than any of my words. 'I'm only allowed to say things because of who I am or who they think I am.'

'Doesn't matter. You play the part well. Larry will be pleased.'

I aim to say, 'Fuck Larry,' but at the end of the day, he's family and has given me this power, whatever way I look at it, I'm going to have to give him his due.

'There's to be a big meeting of the main ambassadors soon,' Tiny says when we are out of the car and at the front door. My feet are pinching and paining me. 'If you're like this with all of them, I think we could take over Ireland.' He empties his pockets out onto the dining room table. I take one bundle off the pile for myself.

'We need food,' Larry says as he enters. He frightens me with his quiet entrance. He's not usually around during the day. 'Did you see around?' he asks to the room in general, but I believe he's talking to me.

Tiny tells him where we've been, and all the people I threatened.

'She's strong, Boss. They're sure she's Sheeran, and by God, she's afraid of no one.'

'We need food,' Larry says again.

'I'll get us something.'

Tiny remains with him, and I can hear them counting as I reach the staircase and take my time on the steps. I hide the bundle and go to the toilet. There's a slight stain on the gauze in the pants, and I pray silently to St Brigid. 'Keep her safe inside me. Please. I beg of you.'

The kitchen cool store has rashers, sausages and puddings. They go into the pan with dripping, and the fried bread and eggs smell damn good. The coffee is thick as I'm not sure how to make it, but the pot of tea is piping hot on the trolley, and I holler for Tiny to push it to the dining room. Like a well-trained animal, he appears and does what is asked of him.

'Is this it?' I can hear Larry ask as the mounds of food are put on the table, and I cradle hot plates in my apron all the way from the kitchen.

'Yes.' My voice is as clipped and tired as I am.

'It'll have to do, I suppose. Until we can get a good cook.'

I ignore the prick as his fork bursts into a sausage. Ben and Bill are heaping the food onto their plates, and no one says much.

Tiny takes it as an opportunity to sing my praises. 'Peggy did a great job today.'

No one answers him, and Larry pours the coffee and wrinkles his nose.

'I'm tired. I'm going to bed.'

I take a plate and am about to put things on it when Larry says, 'Take your food and sit down.'

'I'm going to bed.'

'You'll do as your told.'

Having spent the day holding my own with the scum of the city, I stand now thinking a woman's work is never done. 'There's never an end to the shit is there?'

'Sit the fuck down,' Bill says and pulls out a chair.

I'm on the stairs when I feel the hand in my hair. The legs look like Bill's, and they drag me back into the dining room, and those evil hands toss me onto the chair. Tiny's mouth is open, and his eyes uncertain of where his loyalties lie. Larry isn't even taking in the scene before him and eats on. Ben is shocked, and his mouth is hanging open, uncertain of what to do.

'Eat,' Bill's fork points at me. My scalp hurts, and I feel violated and vulnerable.

'No.'

He rises off his seat again, and before I can move, he whacks the back of his hand off my jaw. I tumble sideways and land with a thud on the carpet. His hands are in my hair again, and the agony of the way he lifts me is huge. The chair is fumbled into an upright position with his other hand as I meekly waver in his grip. Like a rag doll, I am.

He throws me into the chair again and slaps the back of my head with his open palm. 'Sit the fuck down.'

I cannot look at the men in the room. I cannot move. I cannot brush my hair from my face so I can see them. My hand trembles as I touch my jaw.

'You're getting too big for your boots,' I hear Larry say as an explanation for the violence. 'Too big.'

I sit there and listen to the noises of them eating. I refuse to let the tears fall. They are so near the backs of my eyes I can taste them. I won't move or speak but hope my silence unnerves them. It doesn't. I can see Tiny's hands reaching for the plates through the mess of my hair. There are gurgles of hunger in my belly, and still, I won't move. Won't satisfy them to ask them to pass me anything or acknowledge my hurt. Won't ask them for thanks for cooking the meal or won't let them think this is the way to treat anyone.

'Eat,' Bill orders, shoving a plate in front of me.

I push my hair out of my face in case he launches another attack. The tremor in my hand makes the fork clatter off the plate. The sausage is slightly cold, like the atmosphere around me. I can feel the pain in my jaw as I chew awkwardly. The tears well up as the pain in my stomach rises too. I can feel the blood trickle. It's oozing out now from between my legs. I stop eating and swallow a large unchewed pile of meat. It sticks in my throat but somehow the muscles there move it down out of harm's way. There's sharp pains now, and much as I deny them to myself, they are insistent that they are there. Minutes pass, and I pray to St Brigid as the tears fall. I cannot move, cannot think of what's really happening to me, to my baby.

I hold my middle as the cramps are growing now, like waves in the sea, hurling upwards and outwards so I think my whole insides need out and away. I push back on my chair. Bending forward in my seat, I groan loudly. I don't want to give in to the pain, don't want to let any noise out of me, but it comes. The horror eases slightly so I can breathe, but against all my hopes, there's a pressure and a jab of agony and another, then another. The pains are heaped on each other and last longer, giving me little chance to breath or know what's happening inside me. I focus on the leg of Larry's chair, and through my fallen mop of hair, I mutter on to St Brigid.

Long groans leave me, and the wetness is greater now. It's too late for the bathroom. I can tell it's too late and scream, 'I need a towel or something.'

There's someone at my elbow, and there's a shuffling in the room.

'Lift her onto the tiles, for Christ's sake.' Larry's voice is shrill. 'If she's bleeding, she can lose it out on the tiles.'

The chair, with me on it, gets lifted, and I can feel gravity pulling my baby from me.

The chair lands on the tiles with a clunk, and I roll off it slowly, sliding my way to sit on the cold tiles. My legs open automatically, and the redness hits the white tiles and scares me. There's not a lot of blood, but it feels like a river and looks like it too. Tears are falling now, and I sense I'm on my own. There's no one there at all. My groans and the pains are closer together, and I utter prayers, but no one is listening. I'm up on my knees, holding on to the chair and breathing like a woman in labour does. The pains are sharp but easing now. I fumble my pants off and push them away from me. My skirt is sopping and stuck to my legs. There is the familiar smell of blood and the clots are large where I can see them.

'Get me a towel,' I roar into the emptiness of the hall. 'I'm bleeding.'

Every woman who has ever bled is with me then. They talk to me. Whisper to me of the strength I gave them. Even when I was cold to their agony, I held their hands or wiped their brow and their tears and told them, 'There, there. It's all right now. Let it all go. Let it go.' I feel them telling me I'm strong and can face this.

'It's a punishment,' Father Lavelle had said at me in the prison. 'For all the wrongs you do. Punishment comes back tenfold.'

'My baby never hurt no one. I wanted her so much,' I tell the hallway and see the newspaper on the stand. I drag it down and tear off the top few pages. I wipe it over the mess my baby and I have created on the tiles. It sweeps through it, and it makes it more real. I can see black through the redness. My hands are covered, and my fingernails are caked in my own blood.

'I'm sorry,' I whisper as I gather my skirt tails up and bunch them under my pelvis like a sack. I try to stand and wobble against the chair. 'I'm sorry,' I say now to the blood on the floor and the emptiness in me.

The steps on the stairs are like Everest, and the bath swirls with painful pink streaks. The bin is too small to take my skirt but the pillowcase from the bed heaves with the weight of it, and it all lies next to the toilet. I'll take it into the bath when I'm finished.

My head pounds, and the water is warm as I sink into it. I can hear my own pitiful mutterings even if I don't think them. My hand between my legs finds nothing unusual, yet nothing feels the same. I drain the bath with me in it and refill it again with the hottest water I can bear to sit in. I'm weak with fear and emotion.

'Maybe it was just blood,' I say to the invisible women in the steam around me.

'A mother knows the truth in her heart,' that matron had told me.

I grasp at my belly knowing it's empty, and the convulsions of tears add rivers of liquid to the bath. I hear myself howl and pant into the gulps of agony.

'You were my greatest gift.' Mammy's there in my mind, too, looking sorrowful, her knitting in her lap untouched and the wool pink and pretty. 'My greatest gift.'

'I cannot have another.' That Dorothy McKenzie is before me now, alive and sighing at having to have another child, when I can't even have one. Never before did I hate those women, never before did I think them ungrateful but I do now. For many minutes, I hate them all for not wanting what I need so badly.

'You saved me.' The Blonde Bitch who talked about me being her saviour. I'm not much of a saviour now for anyone. I should have asked her why she didn't want her baby. I should have asked them all. But I didn't care. I couldn't think of all their pains too. I could only think of the money. Money.

'Why did I want this baby?' I ask the invisible women in the steam. I ask them over and over. None of them answer me. I finally tell them. 'I wanted it for me. I wanted someone to love me.'

The water is growing cold with my thoughts and my tears. When all is dried and I'm in bed, it is like it was all a dream; a nightmare, a wish that disappeared in the steam. The only evidence of it lies down there in the hallway.

Chapter 27

No one comes to see if I'm all right. No one cleans the tiles in the hall. I fill a basin from the kettle on the range they've kept going and glance at the unwashed dishes on the low trolley with the squeaky wheels. The sponge from upstairs that I bought to bathe with mops up my hope off the tiles. I pour the basin into the enamel sink, and the hands that pour it shake uncontrollably. The reflection in the window is of a stranger with a swollen jaw and bloodshot eyes.

The dishes sink into the clean soapy water, and the kettle boils to make me tea. Somehow, all of this happens without any conscious thought from me. I feel numb to the world and to the duties I must perform. I see many numb women in my memories and understand now the expressions and the need to block out the fear.

'You can do this,' I tell the lady in the mirror in the hall as she touches her cheek. 'You always have. You always will.'

It's then I see Bill's legs. I glance down to my left and see them coming up the hall. It's the swagger of him.

'Larry says you're to stay indoors today.'

I don't answer him and freeze to the spot. I can feel the trickle down my leg. Luckily, my bladder is not too full; it just empties then and there at the sight of his legs. I shuffle my feet so he doesn't see the pool on my cleaned tiles. I cannot look at him. The feel of him near me is making me shake.

'I only meant to knock some sense into you...' he starts. The warmth of the liquid he feared out of me makes me cry. I just stand there with my head down with no control over my body. 'I didn't mean...' He stops. No excuse comes to him.

He can see I'm no help to him, and perhaps he smells the piss, but whatever it is, he turns and his trouser legs walk away. The newspaper lies in the little puddle at my feet, and the pee drains into it, staining the news. I just leave it sitting there unable to think of it until Mammy in my mind urges me to lift it.

As I'm changing my clothes, she talks me through making some potato and leek soup like she used to. I'm sipping at a cup of tea when I hear Tiny shuffle in. It's the amble walk of his and the uncertainty of his movements. My senses are coming around slowly, and the music from the radio is some company for me.

'Something smells good,' he says, sniffing like a dog.

'Don't you think you should have protected me?'

'I couldn't.' The bucket in his hand is full of coal for the range, and he shovels it in and stands back then to bask in the glow of the fire. 'I couldn't. It's a fine line you're walking.'

'I lost my baby.' The words get swallowed in a gulp, and I sink into the chair nearest the fire. The spoon sits in my lap on the apron, and I say it again as practice for myself. 'I lost my baby.'

'Sure it's all for the best,' he states like he's an expert. 'Sad for you, Peggy, but, sure, a woman like you doesn't need burdens now.'

'Burdens…'

The soup needs stirring, I know it does, so I rise to twist the spoon through the thick liquid. It smells wholesome and welcoming. The numbness comes again like a thick mist, and I listen to Tiny tell me about the business and the shipments of smuggled booze and cigarettes we have flooded into Dublin.

'Cleaning the streets, we are, and the whorehouses closed too. Larry took special interest in them.'

'Where'll those women go?'

He doesn't answer me as usual and mentions more of the business. The gambling houses on the payroll and the Gardaí in the pockets; names mentioned, ranks going right to the top. Males, the lot of them. There are no remarks about the livelihoods destroyed, and the enemies we are gathering.

'Joe Bushnell?' I ask.

'Died the other day,' he says it like he was a stray dog that he stepped over in the street. 'Yeah, dead all right. God rest his soul. He was weak as water.'

'I need a few days' rest.'

'Course.'

The soup thickens up with the silence between us, and I hear him clatter out with the bucket to the backyard and come in again with it full. My Joe is gone too. It sits there – the fear, the upset and the loss I feel. He was always there, and now, he's not. He's just gone. His son will miss him.

'I don't want Bill and Ben anywhere near me.'

'You won't have much choice...'

'If they lay their hands on me again...' I take a knife from the chopping board and hold it tightly. 'If they come near me again, I'll kill them.'

Tiny shows me his gums, but I don't smile back. 'You'll kill the two of them. Just like that?'

'Where is my rifle? I want it back.'

His face falls, and he takes off his cap to wring it in his hands.

'I want it back by tomorrow. And I don't want the whole world to know about it.'

'Yes,' Tiny says and surprises me with the meek look on him. 'All right, Peggy. You've been through a lot. All right.'

'I'm going out. I aim to get us a cook. Tell them that it is soup until I get back with a cook.'

'You're not to go out. I need to come with you.'

'No.'

He doesn't argue with me or the knife I'm shoving into the large satchel I drape over my shoulder.

The day is so cold that my shivering isn't noticed. The street sure is long and scary. Every man is a potential killer, but after a street or two, it all seems ridiculous. No one knows who I am. The knife is nestled in close to my side, and the place between my legs is bleeding like a monthly to add to my woes.

Number thirty-four looms above me, but the door below ground is where I'm headed, so I don't look at where I've come from at all.

A child opens the door, and the smell of dirty feet greets me. There's a few males who should be at work around the open fire in the one room, and mattresses are strewn about amongst the small children playing and lines of washing hanging from the ceiling.

'Peggy?' A woman I recognise appears at the open door.

'It's me, indeed.' I smile, despite my sore jaw. The bruise I know is more visible. She looks at it and moves her neck to reveal her own bruise going yellow. She sighs.

'I'm looking for Tess.' I acknowledge her honesty with my eyes and saying nothing about it openly. 'Tess that worked with me...'

'Yes, I know Tess. She's in Foley's. Cleaning some days. Mrs Foley takes great pleasure in telling us all that she has her in a few mornings a week.' She pulls on my sleeve and whispers, 'But she's sleeping rough, the poor lass.'

'Thanks, take care now.'

'It's yourself that needs to take care,' she says and closes the door. I still cannot look up at number thirty-four and simply march on to Foley's.

The owner is standing in his usual spot, looking up the street from the shop window, taking all in. He comes out from behind the counter to greet me. 'Peggy?' He grips my hand like a priest does to a long-lost sheep. 'Great to see ya, love.'

'It's Tess I'm after.'

Then, I hear a voice. 'We don't serve the likes of you no more...' Mrs Foley comes out from back where the pub joins the shop.

'Don't you know Peggy Sheeran?' her husband says. 'Sheeran.' He says it again louder this time to be sure she gets the whole picture. It stops her in her tracks, and her mouth stays open a little while.

'Hullo again.' I smile and ignore the pinch in the skin around my eyes.

'What do ya want?' Mrs Foley is as tight as the dress she has on. 'What can we do for Miss Peggy Sheeran?' She touches her own jaw and grins at my misfortune. This bitch is in need of a good slap.

'Tess. I'm looking for my Tess.'

'Tess Fitzgerald, is it?'

'You know rightly it is.'

'There's no need to be like that.'

'There's every need, when you're acting like a bitch.'

'Did you hear that, Liam Foley? This wan called me a bitch.'

'I heard her, Fionnula. Now, Peggy, there's no need…'

'Is Tess about? I want to see her.'

'I'll call her now for ya. We don't want any trouble.' Liam Foley scuttles into the pub, and from where I'm standing, I can see him swinging the back door of it open too.

Fionnula is standing with hands on her hips and looking down her nose at me. 'Soon as you have talked to her…on with ya now.' She grunts after the statement to give it merit, and I stare at her.

'That dress is about to burst.' I point to the buttons protruding on the front of it.

'You fucking cow,' Mrs Foley roars and attempts to lift the counter to come out through it to get at me, but Liam is back and holds her arm.

'That's Peggy Sheeran, Fionnula. She's Peggy Sheeran,' he hisses it at her. 'Do ya want to be killed where ya stand, woman?'

With that, Tess appears in the door of the shop. Her thick glasses and her crooked teeth are a welcome sight to me.

'Peggy,' she sighs, like I'm an ice cream on a hot day.

'Come with me.' I ignore the curses at my back from the Foley one.

'It's great to see you. The whole of Dublin is alive with the news. I didn't know what to think.'

'I came looking for you as soon as I could, Tess.'

'I know that, Peggy. Christ, what happened to your face?'

'The usual. I need you to work for me.'

'You know no one can say no to you.'

Her teeth and glasses are so dirty, but I hold her arm and hug it tightly to me. 'You can say no, if you'd rather work for that Foley bitch. But I'll have a bed for you and food too.'

'I'm coming with you.' She walks on with me, and I tell her of my "good fortune," lying about my luck and happiness at finding family of my own.

'So, you're the boss?' she asks me as we walk around the corner. 'Everyone says you're the only family he's got. God, it's like a fairy tale.'

'He's no angel, Tess. He definitely isn't a fairy godmother.'

'How could he be?' Her eyes are huge behind the glasses. 'He killed the Professor.'

'Any word of Molly?'

She shakes her head. 'Joe's dead,' she blurts out.

'I heard.'

'Died of his wounds. The bastards beat him bad. His wife was all mourning at the state funeral they gave him.'

I can't think of Joe in the ground. He didn't deserve to die. 'I don't want them to know we're friends, Tess.'

'All right. What work am I to do? I don't fancy the whoring.'

'It's cooking.'

She grins at me. 'Really?'

'Yes.'

'I love cooking.'

'I know. You're good at it and the hairdressing. You can keep me looking good.'

She skips ahead a little and looks back at me. 'Really, Peggy? Cooking?'

'Yes.'

'God, if I only knew this morning when I woke up…'

'I've some old clothes I can give you. Tiny works for Larry now, too, but he mightn't remember you. Our friendship has to be a secret. Do you hear me now, Tess? I need someone with me, but I need only for us to know.'

'Course, Peggy, I understand. Us women will stick together. I'll be as stum as you like, and I'll cook good too.'

'If you get asked any questions, you worked for the Foleys for a long time, and I stole you from them to piss the missus off.'

'Right so. No one will get much out of me. You know that, Peggy. Thanks for coming to save me.'

I feel so bad, and it's mainly for myself. The only friend I have in the world is a washed-up whore, who's sleeping rough, who I never had much time for.

Chapter 28

The next morning, Larry acts as if he didn't witness anything awful in his house the day before. He doesn't care who's in the kitchen, and only asks if Tess is trustworthy.

'She's a good cook and knows she's got a good job.'

'Does she know she'll die if she lets us down?'

'I didn't tell her that, no.'

'Maybe you should.'

The clip of his stick on the tiles is harsher than the words he just said.

'I lost my baby, and if any of those bastards lay a finger on me again, I'll kill them.'

'Be careful who you threaten.' But he does look frail to me, standing in the cold with his cardigan buttoned wrong. There's stubble on his chin that he missed.

'I'm not weak like you think I am.'

But he's gone into his study, and his door bangs closed.

Tiny appears from the kitchen looking all pleased. 'She's cooking chicken pies. My favourite. I put the rifle in your room.'

He doesn't mention seeing Tess before, and I say nothing as I put on my little hat. 'I'm going shopping. Get your coat.'

The shopping is done with the money from one of the larger envelopes I kept for myself the day we went out together. Larry never asked for it, and Tiny didn't miss it. He didn't take any for himself in front of me, but I wonder if his cut is bigger than Larry knows about.

'Are you feeling better?' he asks when we stop for coffee in Bewley's. People stare, but I don't care. His bulk is unusual, and then, of course, my new red hat is rather loud for a working day.

'I'll never be the same again.'

'They're feeling a bit sorry about what happened, you know.'

'Pity about them bastards.' A few ladies nearby whisper amongst themselves and point openly. 'Do you think the whole of Dublin are talking about me?'

'They talk about Larry.' Tiny munches on the cake and speaks with a full mouth, 'That meeting is tonight. All the ambassadors are coming to the house. Big security worries.'

'One bomb, eh?'

It's then, out of the corner of my eye, I spy a cup flying through the air. It smashes right at Tiny's feet. He leaps off the seat, his arms outstretched to shield me from further missiles, but none come. The manager or someone in charge bustles over with a brush, all apologies.

'No harm done.' But I'm a bit shaken. The shattering cup rings in my ears. 'Why are people so angry towards me?'

Tiny bundles up my bags to leave. 'People are scared.'

I don't like to say it out loud, but so am I.

Tess is in a tizzy when we return, having been given orders on what to make for the meeting in the evening and for the dinner before it. 'Is the Queen of Sheba coming?' she hisses through her horrid teeth.

'No, just all the gangsters in Dublin.'

'It was far from salmon mousse and sherry they were reared.'

'Someone threw a cup at me in Bewley's.'

'It's far from cup flinging in Bewley's you were reared.'

I have to smile at her. She's right. 'Be careful what you wish for, eh?'

'Many's a time in the evenings we would dream of having the time and money to have tea in town.'

'I miss Molly,' I say.

Tess is filling the kettle to put on the range. 'What notion did she take to kill that one from the country? Even Molly never felt the need to do them things that you did.'

'She was put away for cutting herself.'

'That poor McKenzie woman, God rest her soul. The priest had a run of it at Mass, preaching about the virtues of motherhood. And that family of hers sitting there, in a strange county, knowing it all was meant for them. It was tearful, it was. The Professor a few rows back. The blaggard and not a guilt kind on him. The whole place knowing.'

'I don't like Mass, never have.'

'Sure, that's the Protestant blood in you.'

I stare at her.

'Didn't ya know? Larry Sheeran is a Protestant.'

I'm not sure what to say now, other than, 'What?'

'They say he's got to be where he is because of the connections he has to the boyos up north.'

'But…'

'Didn't you know? You see, going to Mass gets you no information.'

'Not that religion matters.'

'Course it matters. Sure, you folk don't need the confessions nor nothing. You can get up to a heck of a lot more than us. That's why you always been different to the rest of us, Peggy.'

'But Mammy went to Mass.'

'Married yer father, didn't she?' She blesses herself.

'I've never believed much in religion. Even in school, the chants and the stories all seem so far-fetched to me. But I always liked St Brigid.'

'That's cause she was the feisty one that took on the Irish chieftains.'

'I didn't know you liked school?'

'You told me about Brigid. No teacher ever told me anything of any use.'

'I wonder what these bucks will be like tonight? Watch out for Bill and Ben. They like to use their fists.'

'I'll stay well clear of men. I've a kitchen now and plenty to keep me occupied.' She moves her glasses up on her nose. 'What's keeping you occupied?'

I have no answer for her.

'You need to find your place in all of this. You're used to being in charge, and I've never seen you let a man get the better of ya.'

I watch her wash the cups and saucers in the basin. 'I'll dry them.'

'Indeed, you will not. You're lady of the house now.'

'But I'm not.'

'Why aren't you?'

I don't want to tell her about the baby, the soldier and losing my heart on the hallway floor. I don't want to say I'm scared of my own family. Petrified of my own, like the man I married, I walked headlong into another evil, uncaring man and am stuck trembling inside.

'Why aren't you in charge?'

'Larry...'

'That frail fecker. Find out how it all works,' she glances around, 'and then get rid of him.' She pulls her finger across her throat.

'I couldn't. There'd be another inquest. I'd go inside.'

'For killing an old man?' Tess's whispering is propelling the spit out from between her teeth. 'For getting rid of a blaggard that no one in Dublin would blame you for killing?'

'He's my...'

'I could poison him slowly.' The grin on her is all the way up to her ears. 'No one would know. Sure, isn't he dying?'

'Whisht,' I whisper, getting up to check on the corridor from the kitchen and to look into the back pantry. 'You could kill us all trying that.'

'Give me some credit.' She turns around and checks on the pies in the oven. They smell delicious. Steam covers her glasses. 'I know a thing or two about poisons. My job in the factory was killing the rats. I'm good at killing rats.'

I'm back in my chair with my mind in a mess.

She goes on, all delighted with her plan. 'Sure, it wouldn't be a murder if I was killing a Protestant.' She laughs a good belly laugh and then looks at me. 'I don't know what you are…but you're not an Orange bitch anyhow. No way.'

'Thanks.'

'Still, I don't know how in the name of God the Fenians or bucks from the Liberties let a Protestant lord it over them.'

'Does a criminal's religion matter? A bad man is a bad man.'

'Protestant bastards are worse than anything.' She stops her stirring of something in a saucepan. 'Sorry, but they are.'

'I missed you.' I'm lying. But it is good for me to have her to talk to, even though she's talking about killing the only family I've got.

'No word of where Molly is?' she asks me, reading my mind.

I shake my head and feel my shoulders hunch.

'Her family must know.'

'Will they tell me?'

'Where do they live?' Tess is tasting the soup or sauce on a spoon, her face all scrunched up and looking more vulgar. 'Does anyone know anything about Molly? Dark horse, she is.'

'I've no idea. She told me very little.'

'Clever. Don't care what you say. She knew more than her prayers.'

'Don't talk badly of Molly.'

'Murdering, sex-mad wagon. That's what she was.' Tess is off on a rant.

'Don't. You're the one that thinks murdering is easy.'

'But there's mercy killings and killing when it's just, like in the war. And then…' She stops, knowing to go no further. 'I could've killed that Foley bitch, but I came with you, Peggy, cause even though you are a hard bitch, you're fair. I know where I stand. With that one, one day, I was the bee's knees, the next, I was a harlot. One day, she was all holy and posh, the next, she was down with the young ones that come into the shop, talking about women's lives and whatnot. There was no end to her faces; with you, there's only two.'

'Two?'

Tess grins. 'One for the men. And one for us women.'

'What's my man one like?'

'All sweetness and numb. Like a pretty stone, you are. Like nothing will weaken ya. Men don't like that, though. They need to feel stronger than us. Think that's why you never settled. Like myself, you're too independent.'

'I see.'

'And for the women, your face is more, "I know you're weaker than me and don't mess with Peggy Bowden."'

It's hearing my name that brings a tear to my eye.

She goes on. 'Yeah. That's it. But ya know where ya stand with ya. But that Foley one…' She rants on about the stuff she made her do and the groping Mr Foley did, which I don't really believe. But I'm not listening anyhow; I'm away back at home with Mammy and she's well, smiling at me, telling me all will be all right. 'See, I could never talk to no one like I talk to you, Peggy,' Tess goes on. 'I never had anyone I liked to talk to.'

I smile at her.

'Do you remember the day in the yard, and you telling us about your fella, and Molly slashed that young fella?'

'I do.'

'And his mother howling all around Mountjoy Square? Jesus, when ya think of it, we were lucky to escape her, weren't we?'

'Who? Molly?'

'Yeah.'

'Molly would never have hurt us.'

'Do you remember though the way she'd started to backchat at you? Saying nasty things and giving ya the evil eye? I'm telling ya, I saw that coming, you know. Saw it coming that she was turning…bad.'

'Did you now?'

'I did.'

'She didn't ever think of murdering anyone.'

'Didn't she? Sure, she was always hatching plans.' Tess takes the pies out of the oven. They look great and smell even better. 'She knew what she was doing.'

'She didn't set out to hurt anyone.' I rise from my chair and think of all the times Molly tried to love herself into a better life. 'I'm so like her. I never wanted any of this.'

'Well, you got it now and need to make the best of it.'

Tess has a way of irritating me like no other human. She never irks me enough to lash out at her but enough to make her like a fart. She is something awful that causes you pain and that you want rid of. Farty Tess.

'I'm here now,' she says, 'but I can only do me best as well. I know my place, and you need to take charge. Show them men who's boss. Plain and simple. That's all there is for it.'

I leave the kitchen, thinking I should slam her head into the table more than once.

Chapter 29

'The ambassadors are here!' Larry snaps at me in the hallway.
'I know. I heard them.'

He drags me by my elbow into the large parlour. We haven't used this room since the first time I visited. The time we played cards and happy families.

'Stay quiet and look pretty.'

I let a grunt fall from my lips just thinking of his act. A loving, frail man in need of family.

'Be nice,' he whispers as we walk on, and then, to the assembled men, he announces, 'This is Peggy.'

There are about six of them, varying in ages, shapes and sizes. Some acknowledge me with an ogle, but a few of them in the far corner ignore me altogether.

'Peggy will stay for the meeting.'

Larry sits in the large chair nearest the fire, and I find a high-backed, heavy chair brought in from the dining room nearer the door.

'Thank you all for coming,' he states grandly.

'Had we a choice?' someone asks to my left. The men in the far corner are listening now, but they don't seem keen.

'No.' Larry grins, and he looks so different to me again. I don't know him at all. He goes on, 'No. There's been no choice to all of this, but you all know it's good to have me back.'

Most of the six men are plain looking, bar one of the most earnest man in the far corner. None look overly bruised or battered from a life of crime. They seem well dressed, ordinary almost. One of them has a wrinkled brow and could be more weather beaten than criminal. None look scary or evil or men to fear.

'Does she have to be here?' says someone to my left again.

'Yes, I do.' It comes from my mouth before Larry answers. He puts his finger to his lips, but I say, 'And I've no intention of staying quiet either.'

The squinting starts from Larry as he tries to talk sense to me with his icy stare.

'I'm not comfortable with a woman knowing our business,' the man says again. 'Neither should you be.' He points at Larry.

'If she annoys you, all the better.' Larry doesn't stop for them to object. 'We need to discuss our revolution.'

'There's been a great acceptance to the rise of the Sheerans,' an older man says. 'We're delighted to have some control back.'

'The Professor and the likes were not looking after the right people. Only interested in petty dealings. The Sheerans know how to do big business.' Larry talks on. He oozes confidence. 'I aim to look after the big boys and keep the small ones in check.'

'Are you going to deal with the Fenians?' someone asks.

'If they bring good money to the table.'

'Guns from America is what they're after. That's all they want,' says the weather-beaten man with a northern accent. 'They're only interested in large-scale extortion and will leave the ports mainly to us if we rid them of the drug problem and the undercover Gardaí.'

'Done.'

Larry rises to refill his glass and nods to me to fill the others. I stay seated. Angrily, he passes the decanter around, and the men help themselves, and the conversation goes on to the division of the city and how well pleased they all are with their sections. Even those with lucrative areas have their barren patches, and there's talk of how to up revenue in those quarters. It seems there's some dissent amongst the gypsies and the loan sharks, but they're coming around. The conversations all cross over each other, and the men mingle for a time discussing the progress and how easy it all has been. A few troublemakers have been dealt with.

'The justice system sees the merits in one crime boss to deal with. The commissioner isn't on our books, though, and seems squeaky clean. The men of the cloth take the money, but we all shouldn't necessarily trust them either,' a tall man says with conviction.

'Is there anyone in any area showing signs of looking to take us on?' Larry asks, leaning in. He stamps his foot. 'They need to be stomped on promptly, even if they're family.' He points to a dark-haired man to his right. 'Hear me now, James?'

James nods. 'All sorted, Chief.'

'We heard herself here was doing the rounds with the Big Lad.' the weather-beaten one says. 'What's that for?'

'She needs to earn her keep,' Larry says. 'I have her on a tight leash.'

'I'm not a dog.'

Someone chuckles, and Larry ignores me by handing out envelopes from his pocket. Each has a name on the front, and when I open mine, there is one hundred pounds. I cannot see what the others got as they didn't open theirs but shoved them into their inside jacket pockets.

'Let's eat,' Larry states, and they all make their way into the dining room.

'I'm tired,' I say to Larry as he passes my chair. 'I need rest.'

'Are you not pleased with the money?' His glasses perch on his bald head, and he looks at me intently. 'Spend it wisely.'

'Thank you.' I touch his arm, needing for him to show the tenderness I saw in this room before.

'You did well finding this cook. But you're going to have to learn that men are in charge, and always will be.'

'But you said to them...'

'That's just to keep them on their toes. You need to learn men are in charge. This has been your ruin until now.'

I look at the envelope. 'You have no one else, and I can do great things.'

'You've done fuck all great up until now.'

Then, someone calls, 'Chief, we need you.'

Chapter 30

'Tess says they liked the food last night.' Tiny is shovelling in the scrambled eggs.

'Good.' I wonder if she has started her poisoning.

'I like you eating with us.' He sprays scrambled eggs from his gums.

I'm at the kitchen table, and Tess is whirring around the kitchen, beaming like a Cheshire cat.

'What's for midday?' Tiny asks and winks at Tess. 'I've an eye for a woman that can cook.'

I gawp at the two of them. 'Surely you don't have a notion of Tess?' It comes out of my mouth before I can stop it.

She thumps down a saucepan. 'And why would that be such a strange thing? You've always been cross if anyone gets more attention than yourself.'

The way she says it makes it very obvious we know each other.

'Were you a girl from thirty-four?' Tiny points between us both.

Tess resumes her clunking around, and I put my finger up to my lips. 'Shh.'

'Right.' Tiny nods and puts on his cap. 'You need fuel?' He directs this at Tess, and she grunts at him. 'Right,' he says again and disappears out the back with the coal scuttle.

'We're not great at the pretending,' Tess says, chopping at onions.

'No.'

'It's silly anyhow.'

'I don't know what I was thinking. I think I just wanted to feel like I had a plan, had secrets, had options. I don't know why

I'm even here. Nothing is working out, and I'm not a woman at all anyhow.'

'You're not a woman at all?' Tess stares at me. 'What kind of nonsense is that? And you with a fanny between your legs like the rest of us.'

I'm on my feet marching about the kitchen. Tess has been busy tidying and scrubbing. Things look nice. 'You've made a good job of this kitchen.'

'Cause I love it. And I've a bed and board to boot, and a man that likes me.' She winks at Tiny as he comes back in the door from the little backyard. 'You need to find what makes you happy.'

'As if I will ever find that and be allowed to do it.'

Tess twirls on the spot and raises her arms. 'Look around you. If I can find my heaven on earth, so can you.'

'I'll have to ask St Brigid.'

'Go to Mass. Even a Protestant like you can light a candle.' She nudges me, teasing me. 'They say there's a new priest, and he doesn't preach hell and damnation. He is full of time for those in peril. Got me the job with the Foleys. It was him who got the female students to give me clothes. I'd go with ya, but the midday meal is on, and I've the supper in me head to start. Go now and talk to your St Brigid. Tiny will take ya.'

'I can drop you off and collect you. I've a bit of business in the convent across the street.' Tiny follows me into the hallway and hands me my coat. 'You need out into the fresh air. It's a lovely morning and time in a church will be good for your soul and your…belly.'

I'm glad he mentioned my loss to me. Glad of the sympathy in his eyes. 'All right, but I'm bothering with no nuns.'

'You leave them girls to me.'

It's a good dander to the chapel, but the day is fresh. I don't bother asking Tiny what he's at going to a convent. We know no one, and when I reach the steps up into St Agatha's, Tiny nods and says, 'Back in half an hour or so.'

The chapel door is open, but it is dark enough inside for some of the large lights hanging from the vaulted ceiling to be lit. The candles are flickering on the stand, and there's a tiny box with a slot in it.

I find I do want to light a candle for the baby I lost.

'It wasn't a baby at all,' I can hear myself thinking, and yet, I want to think of her and what might have been. St Brigid seems a long way from me, but Mammy smiles in my mind, and I thank her for coming to be with me. I stretch to light one candle off another and place it in a nice row at the front. I bless myself and start to say a rosary.

'Holy Mary Mother of God...'

My mind wanders as I mouth the words. *Imagine being the mother of a God. How do we know there is a God at all? Was there a Jesus and a Mary? Men told us there was.*

'Huh,' I blurt out, and the candle in front of me blows clean out. I've extinguished a flame of someone else's hope. 'Typical.' Tears fall, and the snotters run out of me. 'Sorry,' I say to the candle, which is looking very sorry for itself and smoking from its tiny wick.

My shoulders shudder, and I pull on the scarf tied at my chin to take it off to dry my tears. I blow my nose into it and gulp a few convulsions of self-pity into the nice fabric. I'm lost in my own terrible thoughts and tears for a little while when I feel a soft hand on my shoulder.

'Are you all right, my child?' a voice says, and I can see the hem of a black cassock and plain black shoes.

No words come out as the male shoes walk me backwards towards a pew, and the kind hand helps me sit on the cool wood.

I blow again into my scarf and feel silly like a child. There's nothing said, and I compose myself for a few seconds. 'Sorry, Father.'

He says nothing at all, and I breathe in and out and am glad that the tears stop. I sniff and wipe my eyes with both hands, letting the scarf sit in my lap. Wet and pathetic, that scarf looks, as I stare at it rather than into the face of the religion I probably no longer belong to.

'Better?' the voice asks.

'A bit.'

'Good,' he says, and it's then I look into his face. That familiar, handsome farmer's face that I loved with all my heart all those years ago.

'Mick?'

'Hello, Peggy.'

I just gawp at him. His wonderful nose and smile, the twinkling eyes that were made for reading, and the cheeks I kissed when he slept.

'Holy fucking hell!' I breathe out.

Mick holds out his hand formally for me to shake it. I cannot believe it is him. My Mick Moran. I find it hard to think, form words, move or smile.

'Peggy... Married Peggy, is it now?'

I point to my tweed jacket and to my heart that doesn't feel like a Peggy at all. 'No. Not married, but I'm Peggy Sheeran now. That's me...I suppose.'

'Don't you know yourself?'

'No.' I smile, despite the agony that's dripping off me.

'Larry Sheeran's Peggy?'

'Yes, I suppose I am.'

'It is good to see you.' He reaches out for my hand and holds it. How nice his skin is against mine. Something deep inside me makes me pull away from his grasp.

'I want to throw my arms around you, and sure...'

'Man of the cloth now.' He points to his collar. 'I...'

The door of the chapel bangs loudly.

'You're probably very busy...' I go to get off the seat, although I want to stay and stare at my Mick's dimples forever.

'Please don't go just yet.'

His hands are still big but look soft and unworked. The feel of him is familiar, and suddenly, I lean into his chest and rest my head there. It feels wrong and yet right to do it, and then, his arm encircles me.

'I missed you,' he says softly. I think he kisses my hair, and I sob a little into his collar.

The door bangs again, and I take my head from the crook in his neck. 'Sorry. My God, you're a priest.'

'I'm one a long time now, and that's the first cuddle I've had in many a long year.'

'Me too. I needed it.'

'Yes.'

We sit side by side, and the church organ starts up.

'She's probably seen us. The organist. I got one for the church, I missed the one we had in my last parish. But that organist sees everything,' Mick moves a little down the seat and swivels in the seat to look around.

'I'm sorry if I brought any trouble with me.'

'I was comforting an old friend,' Mick says in his old way and winks at me.

'Less of the old, if you please.'

'So, you're Peggy Sheeran now?'

'Apparently so. And you're Father Moran?'

'Yes, I am.'

The organ music is irritating. Not a tune I know.

'I'd no idea you were anything to Larry Sheeran.'

'Neither did I.'

'He always talked of a Sally. I never dreamed it would be the mother you always talked of. Never thought of her being your mother Sally.'

'Why would you?' I sniff and stare at the pew in front of me. 'How do you know Larry?'

'I met him in my parish in Hell's Kitchen.'

'Hell's Kitchen?'

'I worked there when I was ordained.'

'In America?'

'You know Ireland. I needed a new freedom, a life.'

'Free of me.'

'Well, free from gossip.'

'So, you went to America?'

'Yes.'

'God All fucking Mighty.'

'Don't curse in the house of the Lord, Peggy. Please.'

'I cannot believe we were so close, and yet, oceans apart.' I look at his shoes, as I cannot stomach those wonderful holy eyes of his.

'Maybe it's God's will that we're brought together in this way.'

'God's will?'

'Larry's a great man for charitable works. He looked after all my projects in Hell's Kitchen and talked to the bishop about me returning to Dublin. He's a great man. If you're family to him, we'll do great works together in the name of the Lord.'

'Is Larry not a Protestant? Am I not one?'

'You're here now.' His lovely arm points to the candles. 'Larry doesn't practice much, but he and I have had many theological discussions.'

'I bet he's a great theologian.'

'Don't you think this is a miracle? Us meeting like this, after all these years?'

'I don't like St Brigid's sense of humour or her flipping timing. As if I wasn't fucked up enough.'

Mick's eyes are on fire with annoyance.

'So, you think Larry is a great man?' I ask.

'Don't you?'

'Does he know of our past?'

'I doubt it.'

'I bet he does.'

'How would he?'

'He knows a great deal.' I'm overcome with emotion. My head is so sore, and my heart is aching to hold Mick and hit him at the same time.

'He's a hard man, but has a good heart. Wait until you know him.'

I touch the bruise on the left-hand side of my face and wonder does he see the mark in the dark church. 'Do you know why he's back in Dublin? And why he's insisted you come back here? How do you help him?'

'I know he wanted to find his family…heirs.'

'He's disappointed so.'

'He has you. And he has businesses here. He brought me back to his parish to help the poor of Dublin and to start projects like we have in Hell's Kitchen.'

'I see.'

'Tell me why you were crying. Do you want confession?'

'No.'

'Don't be so angry. I remember there was a tender Peggy in there somewhere. She used to show herself to me sometimes.'

The tears come, and I try to look at him through them. 'Prison broke me. I built myself up only to be knocked down again and again. God is a bastard, Mick. Your God is a bastard. I cannot believe he stole you too.'

'Arrah, now…'

'It's true. I loved you. I dreamed of finding you. I did. I thought you'd love me still and…' I get off the seat. 'I need to go.'

His hand pulls me to sit very close to him on the wooden seat. 'Larry has great plans for you, Peggy. He told me of the great business he will leave to his family. It was me who encouraged him to make amends. Don't be hard on him. His only daughter let him down and got pregnant with you. He was a God-fearing man and threw her out. He regrets it still. Let him make it up to you.'

'Is that what he told you?'

Mick nods and smiles at me like a priest. I want to thump the sanctimonious head off him – but I do still love the very bones of him.

'Father, I need to talk to you about the music…' a voice says, and the bruised face of the cook from the house appears into the light of the candles. '*You!*'

'Nora, this is…'

'I know who and what she is, Father.' Her eyes are on fire in the flickering light.

I rise off the seat and mumble, 'I know Nora. Everyone knows everyone in Ireland, Mick.'

Mick takes in the obvious hostility between us.

Nora whispers, 'She's a bad one, Father. And she did this to me.' She points to her well-bruised eye and forehead.

Mick's mouth opens, and he looks at me to deny it.

'Ask Nora about your precious Larry Sheeran and why he's back in Dublin. She'll tell you all.'

I don't see how Mick is as I leave, because I'm thundering my heels down the aisle, suffocating in the incense and the air around me until I break through the heavy doors and out into the sunshine.

Tiny's sitting on the steps eating an ice cream. 'Feeling better?' he asks, with some cream on his chin.

Chapter 31

'You weren't long at the convent. There's ice cream on your chin.'

He rubs at it with his dirty sleeve and grins at me. 'Not better, then?'

'No, worse.'

'I know what would make you feel better. We could go tackle the nuns?' Tiny grins. 'They've refused to do Larry's laundry, and he isn't best pleased. They send it to the outskirts of Dublin. I think you could persuade them, and he would be pleased with that.'

'You want me to do your job?'

'Yip.'

'Lead the way and don't look back.'

'Them candles did work miracles,' he says, and we march over the road and down the street towards the large pillars and railings that tower high over the footpath. There's a formidable building off the street a few paces with bicycles sitting out to the right-hand side of the door and a large statue of Our Lady in the other alcove to the left.

The door heaves open, and there stands a big-busted woman in a huge habit, her face aglow. She points at Tiny. 'We told you to leave.'

My palm is on the door, and my feet over the lintel before she registers that I'm even there.

'I saw you coming again,' she says and then looks at me, sweeping her eyes from the ground up to my scarf that's newly tied over my hair. 'He was told no…' She looks at me intently, her gaze and tone less aggressive with each passing second. 'Don't I know you?'

'You probably do.' I remove my palm from the door, but leave my foot wedged against the bottom of it. 'You probably do. I'm Peggy Sheeran.'

'Ah.' The large lady heaves her bosom up to make herself seem even more ludicrously large. 'The Sheerans don't own…'

'But, yes, we do. We own all of Dublin now. Including your precious convent and Father Moran's church.'

'How dare…'

My glove comes off in one strong pull, and I slap her square across the face with it. It's a loud crack. It shocks Tiny, he stumbles slightly. The large black figure before me also shuffles on her flat feet and looks stunned.

'Let me be clear.' I take her by the throat. The skin of it ripples under my grasp, and it takes me my two hands to get a tight grip on her person. The other gloved hand is on her arm. I shove her back into the hallway and up against the inner door. 'I'm afraid of no one. Least of all a big, fat fuck like you. So, unless you want me back again, you will take the Sheeran laundry for fucking free and do a damn fine job of it.'

Her red face and jowls wobble in agreement.

'Good.' I let go of her and walk away. 'Tiny will drop it off tomorrow.'

I'm around the next corner before I stop walking, and I bend over to hold my knees, which are trembling. Tiny has to run to catch up with me.

'Good God, woman! Even I don't manhandle a nun!' His face is agog, and his mouth is hanging open.

'They're only women. And sure, us women get manhandled when it suits. Those fucking nuns have the right idea. I think I need to spend some time following their good example.'

Tiny is bemused, and my mind races on the way back to the house.

Tess is busy, but I stay in the kitchen, making some notes.

'What are you at?' Tess asks, looking over my shoulder. 'Uniform, red hats. Mission…'

'I think we need a female army.' I suck on the pencil.

'You sound like them students who tried to save me from myself.' Tess is all flour down the front of her apron. 'God love them, they tried to make me see I needed an education. Me? Who can barely add up my whoring money.' She chuckles.

'What do they sound like, these women?'

'All high and mighty. You'd fit in with them, come to think of it.'

'Could I meet them?'

'They mightn't want to talk to the likes of you…' she starts and fusses at the pastry she's rolling, 'you being a Sheeran.'

'Am I not an educated woman?' I bite the pencil and think Tess's teeth look cleaner. 'Could I not talk with them for a few minutes?'

'They give out soup and clothes to the working girls of a Tuesday. If you can stand to listen to them.'

'I think I'd like to talk to them.'

Tess arranges for me to meet them in Connolly's pub in one of the snugs. The place is near where they were doing their charity work. There's a good bunch of them, and they seem strong lassies, rather than the weakling librarians I had in my imagination.

They stare at my red hat as I take it off and lay it on the table. I order a glass of whiskey for them all, and we stare at each other for a few seconds. I look into the eyes of each one of them in turn.

'I need an army, ladies. A quiet army to start with.' I whisper this, and they all lean in. 'One that can help me take on the men of Dublin, then Ireland.'

The snug is compact, but there's a good murmur outside, so I figure what I say is unheard.

'I'm Peggy Sheeran, as you all know, and I aim to use my position to help the women of Ireland.'

Some of their eyes bulge, and then, one of them says, 'You aim to do this how?'

'All in good time. But I need to spread the word quietly that there's a women's revolution starting. Are you with me?'

'What will you revolt against?' the same one asks. But her cheeks are red, and her eyes sharp.

'It all.'

'All?' She looks at her fellow students. 'All what?'

'The tyranny of men.' One chokes on her whiskey, and there's a shuffling of uncertainty as I go on. 'I aim to start slowly. We take over in small ways and support each other.'

'What could we take over?'

'Leave that to me. I'm going to need women in all walks of life to work together. Like the nuns or these secret male orders, we can and will get respect and have our own methods. We must only tell women we trust to keep the faith.'

'Keep the faith?'

'Yes. Keep the Faith in Women.'

'Faith in Women?' Tess looks confused.

'We'll wear red with pride and know each other with a secret wink.' I wink at a few of the girls before me. They wink back. 'Faith in Women,' I whisper.

They wink at each other and whisper, 'Faith in Women.'

'That's it,' I exclaim like a proud mother. 'We'll all revolt together.'

'Cheers,' Tess shouts, and we all raise our glasses. 'Faith in Women.' She winks and laughs. 'Cheers, everyone.'

Chapter 32

In the kitchen a few days later, Tess is howling with laughter while pounding some dough into the table. 'The woman across the street scuttled over to me and waved her red scarf at me and winked,' Tess tells me as soon as she sees me. "Faith in Women," she whispered. I laughed at her, and she said, "Haven't you heard about the revolution? Spread the word."'

'Who was she?'

'The doctor's wife from up the street. She barely looked at me before. The amount of red I'm seeing on the streets, Peggy. Do ya know what you've started?'

I sip my tea.

'Women are in need of leaders, all right. Sweet Jesus, I told you to take charge of the men in this house. Not take charge of the whole of Dublin's women.'

'We might need them.'

'I was talking to the working girls that go to the docks. They're all with ya.'

I glance at her.

'The women in the factory too. I was up there to get something, and those that are still there were asking me about the revolution.'

'Really?'

'There's great excitement.'

'Lord God.'

'I know. I went in with them to the bingo, and the place was littered in red bits and bobs.'

'It's spreading…'

'This loud one got up after the fella had said goodnight to the bingo goers, and she shouts, "We all know to spread the word now, ladies, don't we?" There was applause – at the bingo.'

'Larry wouldn't let me out. Said there was trouble. Did you see any?'

'No. But if Larry finds out about your revolution – maybe that's the trouble he means.' She howls laughing. 'What's it all for?'

'To be in control, I'll need support. Women need to be like them feckin' nuns. They all stick together and get away with all sorts.'

'The nuns?' Tess stops her work. 'I don't want to be like them.'

I can't help but laugh.

'The whole of Dublin will know about this.' Tess kneads away at the dough. 'Hope the men don't get wind of it.'

'Larry...' I mutter.

'Don't you worry about him. I'll fix him.'

I don't move, can't speak and freeze to the spot. She doesn't stop what she's doing, and my eyes follow her around the room, to the range stove and back to the sink.

'It won't come to that,' I manage to say at last.

She pushes her glasses up on her nose and says in all seriousness, 'It always comes to that, Peggy. Surely you know that with all your schooling. Survival of the fittest.'

The men don't come into the kitchen much, except Tiny. Bill and Ben have almost been promoted since they lashed out at me. Got a new air about them and don't look at me at all. I'm glad of it; I almost feel faint if I think they will hurt me again. It's all the old nightmares returning, Him standing laughing at me pissing on the floor when he took the handle of the broom from its hiding place.

Even thinking of it now, He did little with the broom handle, thankfully, as the beast would have killed me for sure. But he left it in the corner just to torture and torment me. The animals even hated Him, and then the drinking... No one loved the bastard,

225

and when he "fell" and didn't get up, there was more than me who breathed a sigh of relief. Larry would be the same, surely? No one, not even me, would miss him. He likes to torment me too, doesn't he?

'A blessing,' one of the nicest neighbours said as she nudged me when she sympathised with me at His wake. 'Sometimes, the angels look over us. Be guided by them.'

I'd listened, and after the inquest, I sold everything, and the angels saw me right. When did the bad luck start?

'I cannot bring this baby home,' a young one's aunt had told me. 'Her parents think she's working hard in my shop – they know nothing of this baba.'

This woman was a well-to-do grocery shop owner, and she had bundled her niece into me when she was showing and said, 'She's hid this. What will I do? It happened to her in Dublin, she tells me. My brother will hold me responsible. It's too late for the boat to anywhere respectable. I'll pay you to hide her here somewhere in this big house, and when her time comes, I'll pay you to help us get rid of the child.'

With the bank loan looming and my marriage to Mick on the cards, I'd seen a way of making a nest egg for myself, in case Mick made me leave my work. It wasn't going to be for long. The young one had done a good job hiding the truth, and I knew how others got homes for the little ones. Hadn't I watched the nuns from afar or sent girls to them before?

I had decided it would be a once off. I wouldn't do it again. I told myself this over and over. But the money was easy as sin, and both the aunt and the girl were grateful. There were only one or two after that who caused a fuss and reneged on our deal. God love them, they changed their minds when they held their babies.

Women are strong. We know when things must be done. I remember one wanted to keep her baby after all. A boy, it was. Families always want the boys. God bless her, she kept him, thinking he'd get the farm and all sorts, but her family threw her out good and proper. She was back on my doorstep with him

when he was really too old to sell to anyone, so we found the way
of the Moses in the bulrushes. It was Joe who'd been whimpering
on about abandoned babies, and well, that was as easy as sin too.
I'd made a decent cash pot, and things looked so grand.

'I got greedy, Tess,' I say to the steam and heat in the kitchen.
'I got greedy all those years ago and look at me now.'

'Yes, look at you. One of the wealthiest women in Ireland and
most probably the head of a revolution,' she scoffs, 'and educated
and pretty. Rich. Did I say rich?'

'Not for the right reasons. It's not for the good works, like the
nuns.'

'You and the feckin' nuns.'

'They're known for good works and good living. I'm a…'

'Will ya listen to yourself. Do you really care? Honestly, do ya?
You're making something of yourself. And mark my words, I was
sent to them nuns and, well, enough said.'

'Sure, they got me put inside.'

'There you go.'

'Greed is the worst thing.'

'You're right. There was Molly. She got greedy. Stealing all the
men for herself and trying to take on your work on the side too.'

I stay silent.

'Was too greedy, that's what it was.'

With that, the back door flings open, and Tiny arrives looking
all battered and bruised. There's a large gash above his eye and
him carrying a bloodied stump of wood. His ear is half hanging
off and there's a pile of blood on his neck and the side of his head
still dripping.

'Lord God Almighty!' Tess shouts and runs with a tea towel to
paste to the side of his head.

'Do you need a doctor?'

'Call the doc. He'll come.'

The doctor does a lot of tutting, and Tiny does a lot of
moaning. Myself and Tess act like nurses. Tess holds Tiny's hand,
and I lift and lay out what the doc needs to put in the stitches.

'God, that's sore,' Tiny yelps for the fiftieth time.

'It's a good job it's not the men who have babies,' Tess says.

'You're a big lad,' the doctor jests. 'You'll live. But I daren't think of the other fella.'

Tiny doesn't answer. The stump of wood lying on the floor looks hard. 'They'll live. More's the pity,' Tiny says.

'Who?'

'I fell into the chapel, and Father Moran brought me here. He's just got a new car, and I think I left it in a right mess.'

'Don't you worry about a priest's car. He'll have some woman to clean it for him.'

'He was more interested in how you were, Peggy. Were you safe.'

'So, you met him the other day?' Tess asks, leaving Tiny's hand down. The doctor is almost finished, and she's about to make tea.

'I met Father Moran, yes.'

'Isn't he the loveliest man?' Tess says, and Tiny squeals at the doctor for putting on the bandage too tightly.

I take this as a sign the conversation can move on, but Tess remains on the subject. 'Lovely man – for a priest. Handsome, if a man of the cloth is supposed to be handsome.'

'There's no need to go that far,' Tiny says. 'Father Moran has been asking about you all right, Peggy. Father Mick told me he knows you from years ago.'

'Mick? Mick Moran?' Tess squeals. 'Mick? Your Mick?' She points at me. 'But he's a priest? Ya dirty mare.'

'I knew him before he was a priest. I'm not a dirty anything.'

The doctor is smiling. Tiny touches the white wrapping on his head and doesn't pay much attention now his Tess is no longer involved.

'He and I were engaged long ago.'

'Jesus, the romance of it. He couldn't have ya and ran off to the priesthood.'

I hadn't thought of it like that.

'Speaking of romance…' The doctor nods at Tess to go upstairs.

She shakes her head and tries to look at him in disgust.

'I need paid.'

Tiny slaps a good few pounds on the table and grunts. 'Take that.'

'I'll need more…'

'You're just playing us now, Doc. You'll get no more and keep that mouth shut.' I zip my lips closed and try to look fierce. It must work as he scuttles for the back door.

'Goodnight to you all.'

'Engaged to Father Moran?' Tess is still on a roll.

'What did that doctor mean about romance?' Tiny asks, and we ignore him as I start recounting instead the time myself and the priest started courting all those years ago. Tess sniggers and laughs when Larry shouts around the door.

'Is Peggy in there?'

It's as if he's too good for the kitchen, so I leave my place at the table and make my way into the hallway.

I can sense Bill and Ben are there, too, before they step out of the shadows.

'So, tell us about this revolution, Peggy?' Larry says, and he scratches the top of his bald head as I feel the dread rise in me.

Chapter 33

I freeze. I'm struck dumb like I was in prison. I look at the black-and-white tiles and inwardly ask Mammy and St Brigid to keep me safe again.

'Answer me,' Larry whispers. 'Come on now. Tell us of your revolution.' Bill takes my arm and drags me up the corridor and into the front hallway where I see two pairs of female legs. I look up as I hear Larry add, 'Martha and Nora here have plenty to tell me.'

Martha's smug face hasn't got any prettier. She's ghastly thin in her ordinary tweed skirt and her overcoat like a sack around her silly frame. The cook looks worried under her little hat with a fringe, and her reddened hands are gripping the handle of her handbag.

'Let's all go into the sitting room,' he announces as if it will be a nice affair in there. 'We'll all sit down.'

Sitting will mean I will wet his chair, but I don't protest, and I pull at the hem of my skirt as I sit; my eyes don't leave the floor.

'She's getting all the women to stand up to the menfolk,' Martha starts before the rest are even sitting.

'When does she do this?' Ben asks. 'She's rarely out of the house.'

'That one has been out long enough to try to seduce Father Moran,' Nora adds.

I can sense Larry's amusement at this as he chuckles softly.

Martha pipes up, 'She's getting the women to wear red, wink at each other, whisper and all sorts of secrets. She's the devil, I tell you. The devil.'

'The devil, eh?' Larry asks, and the tone in his voice is harsh. Martha must sense it. She adds quickly, 'Or so they say, sir.'

'They?'

'The women.'

'So, Peggy here is seducing priests and starting revolutions on the few occasions she's been allowed out of this house?' Thankfully, there's an air of disbelief in the room.

'Mrs Foley says she's always been evil and can make men do all sorts for her.' The organist plays all the instruments in her repertoire now, as she can sense I'm weak at the minute.

'All sorts? What does she get them to do?' Larry asks.

'Kill babies, sell them, hide bodies – like that poor woman up from the country.' Martha adds on a few grunts for flavour.

'You don't need the likes of her, Mr Sheeran,' the older woman says with a flourish. 'Women who don't know their place are dangerous to us all.'

'Indeed, they are. Indeed, they are.' Larry is looking at me; I can sense it. 'What do you have to say, Peggy?'

'I want them out of this house.' I cough and say it louder. 'I want them out of this house.'

'Are they telling us the truth?'

I look up at him and see him for the first time in days. He looks pale and drawn. 'What do you think?' My voice cracks, and my mouth is dry.

'I think you're right, Peggy. These ladies need to leave.'

I don't look at the bitches, but can tell they are shocked to be asked to leave. They stand, but I look again at the floor. I'm not sure I want to alone with these men. What made me say I wanted the women out? At least with them here, I'm safe.

'I don't think you understand…' Martha starts.

But there's a shuffling, and Bill and Ben are obviously moving the women to the door.

'Did you honestly think all the women of Dublin would stay quiet and go along with whatever scheme you're pulling against me?'

I shake my head. 'It's not against you. I heard you say you wanted the women of Dublin with us.' I steal a glance at him. He's mopping his forehead and looks feverish.

'We're family and you should…' He stops talking and grabs his throat. I look down and wait for him to go on. 'I'm in pain. I can't deal with you now.'

'There's nothing to deal with.'

'There's no trouble from anyone in the whole of the city. My return to the top was so easy. The only person who's caused any major fuss is…'

I peek at him. He's leaning over in his chair, obviously unwell, when the two yolks arrive back into the room.

'Take me upstairs,' he whispers.

'When an old man is out doing his business, and he's attacked by a group of women who announce they're sent from his own – it's no wonder the man is sick,' Bill spits at me.

When I do look into his angry face, he has a gash over his left eye. I'm left in the room shivering in the draught from the open door.

Chapter 34

Tiny won't answer me or Tess about who attacked them.
'Was it women?'

Tess stares at me over his hunched bandaged head.

'Let's just say Bill and Ben were of little help. Bundled Larry into the car and left me to fend for myself. The bastards. I had to get the mob off me. Larry has had to call in reinforcements to guard the house.' He nods to the back door, 'Men guarding the house until we figure out what's going on. They blamed you, Peggy, and Father Moran is worried.'

'Larry isn't well with it all.'

'A mob of women?' Tess seems gleeful.

'Said that the women of Dublin were on the rise, and that they wouldn't stand for the likes of Larry no more.'

'It shook him,' I say, sipping at the tea with a dash of whiskey, my damp skirt a reminder that I'm no rebel.

Tess makes big eyes at me and fumbles in her apron pocket. Tiny is staring into the open door of the range at the fire sparking away, with no concern for the world. From her pocket, Tess holds up a little bottle, and her teeth and lips make a grimace.

'Sweet Jesus,' I whisper at her as she makes her way round to my side of the table. Tiny is picking dried blood off his wrist and jacket sleeve and isn't paying any heed to us.

'I thought I'd help,' she whispers, and I catch another small glimpse of the bottle. I cannot believe what she's trying to tell me. 'Tiny, would you get us more fuel out the back? I don't want any men out there to think I'm the enemy.'

His bulk rises slowly off the stool, and he ambles to the coal scuttle and disappears.

'Poison?'

'Shh,' She grins her awful teeth at me. 'It's only poison if you or I take it. It is medicine for that bad bastard.'

It won't sink in, what she's saying.

'Been at it a few days now. Slow and easy does it.' She chuckles. 'No one will be any the wiser.'

'But what if…?'

'What if an old man dies? Will anyone in Dublin miss the likes of Larry Sheeran? Think of the way he treats you. His own flesh and blood. What must he truly be like? This is for you, Peggy.' She throws her arms around me and hugs me to her. She smells of baking and lavender. She smells almost like Mammy used to.

'If he dies, though…Dublin will be taken over by…'

'You, Peggy. Dublin will be taken over by you. And the women will be glad.'

'But, sure, I couldn't take over anything. I just meant for us to support each other…and me, I suppose.'

'Support you under the likes of Larry Sheeran?' Tess is close to my nose. 'Sure, he won't even let you out of the house. The women are fighting already. They're hungry for change. Give it to them.'

I stare at Tess. 'Not ten minutes ago, I pissed myself with fear, and now, you want me to lead the women of Dublin in a revolution.'

'You're no weakling. I've seen you take your rifle to a house full of men. Saw you work the gangsters of Dublin before now and play with the police. There's no one better than you to do this and, sure, with the army of women you are –'

Tiny comes back in, complaining. 'It's lashing down. The men say they're all still marching and hollering around O'Connell Street, their husbands pulled out of pubs and all sorts.'

'The papers will be good to read in the morning,' Tess says. 'Maybe someone should bring Larry his hot milk?' She winks at me, and I sink into the chair she's got by the fire and watch her pour milk into the saucepan. 'Help him sleep.'

'I'm not taking it to him.' I watch the milk bubble up the saucepan.

'I'll do it myself.' Tess winks. 'I do it every night this last while. I'm still waiting on a thank you.'

'Larry doesn't say thanks,' Tiny says, picking at the chicken leg he's found somewhere.

'Someone might need to teach him some manners, then.' Tess is gone with her little silver tray of milk and biscuits, and I presume the little bottle tucked in her apron pocket.

Chapter 35

'We'll need to call the undertaker,' the Big Lad says over the old man who was my grandfather. 'It was quick in the finish.'

'He had a strong heart.' Tess blesses herself. 'He's left a list of things to do. Myself and Peggy saw to it that he got all his last wishes put down on paper.'

'I told Tommy that the boys outside would be welcome in to help eat all the sandwiches the local ladies sent in,' Tiny says. 'Hope that's all right. Everything has calmed down in the city, and everyone is in mourning.'

'Women are asking if they can wear red to the church,' Tess says.

Father Mick nods and looks at the list. 'His signature is clear as a bell, God bless him. He was so precise to the very end. Even down to the prayers and hymns…all laid out for me, like he promised. I've to allow the clergyman to say a few words, and he's asked here for you to give his eulogy, Peggy.'

'What's that?' I ask meekly, even though I looked up how to spell it, taking time from my forging.

'A few words on the great man that he was.' Mick puts his beautiful hand on my arm. 'The church he will be laid out in doesn't know Larry at all, and the clergyman asked me to say a few words. It will be a great day with the whole of Dublin out to welcome him home now, to rest in peace here forever.'

'If you'll excuse me, Father. There's a few people downstairs I must speak to.'

'Of course, Tess and I can stay with the remains until the undertaker gets here.'

'Thank you.'

'I know that Larry was kind enough to send me a copy of his latest will last week. Bill and Ben brought it over. They never mentioned they were leaving. Imagine him knowing to send those men home before he died. It's almost as if he knew he hadn't long left.'

'Yes.'

Mick touches his collar. 'Maybe they didn't realise they were taking me his last wishes in the box with the whiskey bottle.'

Tess nods.

'I'm surprised they went back to America, knowing he was so ill and all.'

'We insisted,' I say as I leave the room. 'A rifle can be very persuasive,' I mutter as I descend the staircase.

The ambassadors have all arrived and are in the sitting room. A hush falls on them as I enter the room, and I don't speak until I reach the fireplace.

'Thank you for coming, gentlemen.'

'We would all like to sympathise with you on your loss,' the weather-beaten one says. 'All of the city knows its place now. And the people will be out in force to pay their respects, whether they like it or not. I've spoken to the union men, and all is set for an almost official day of mourning.'

'Thank you.'

'We're here to also ask you to quench the fires of the women's revolution.' James gets to the point.

'I aim to bury my grandfather and make sure his last wishes are completed. I also believe that I'm now in charge of his… dealings in the city.'

'You are not,' someone says, and I raise my hand.

'This is not a meeting. This is me telling you how things will be. Peggy Sheeran is in charge, and all business will be run through me in future.'

'We won't stand for —' the voice starts again.

I look at the far wall and say loudly, 'Peggy Sheeran is now in charge. Anyone with a problem can leave this house now.'

Two men get up to leave and look at the others in the room. No one else moves.

'You don't have the manpower to keep this act up for long,' one of the men on his feet says, pulling at his jacket. 'You're only a… You don't know the first thing about being in charge of anything.'

'Tommy?' I say, and my blond-haired bodyguard walks from his place by the door. 'Take this man out and show him what we do to those who don't listen to reason.'

Tommy marches over and hauls him towards the door. He, of course, struggles, and Tommy headbutts him and drags him out into the hallway. There's a scuffling sound and a little whimper from behind the closed door.

I address the assembled men. 'Tell his family if they need funds to come to me. Otherwise, take it that he will be buried around the same time as Larry.'

The gasps in the room are loud.

'All of your wives are to wear a splash of red to the funeral, and if I summon you here in a few days' time, I expect your full support.'

I don't look at them as I feel I may crack the mask I'm wearing or may fall to my knees in fear. 'Thank you for coming. And there will be a good display of mourning for the funeral.'

I leave the room and click the door closed. There's not a sound, and there's blood on the tiles. I stand there, reminding myself of my own blood that spilt here and how weak I was then. How frightened and scared I felt. I cannot and will not go back there.

Tommy comes into the kitchen with Tiny, and both just look at me like they did when Bill and Ben didn't want to leave the house too.

Tess gives them both a large slice of cake and a big glass of beer. We don't speak for quite a few minutes

'The solicitor thinks he may be able to find Molly,' I announce to the room. 'It was on the list of Larry's last requests.'

Tommy stops eating the cake; he touches the scar on his face. 'Larry wanted you to find her in the finish?' he asks.

'Asked the solicitor himself. He was a bit weak then, but he said, "Find Molly."'

'God rest his soul.' Tommy blesses himself. 'He knew you loved her, that's why.'

'Gave us a good laugh, though – it sounded more like "Kill Molly" at the time,' Tess says and winks at me. 'Poor solicitor had a time of it making it out. Good job we were there.'

'Yes, lucky, too, that the doc could witness the will.'

Tiny throws a shovel of coal into the range. 'It'll be a big funeral for the city. The Gardaí want to call to sort out a few things.'

'The army have been told to be on standby, in case the women get out of hand,' Tommy adds. 'What a sight that would be – the army up against women.'

'The papers say we'll have to ask them to be peaceful. Ireland has enough troubles, but they haven't seen half of it yet,' I say, trying to sound braver than I am. The kitchen and the house feel so different now.

'There'll be those who try to take over now,' Tommy says. 'Men all around are not happy at you being a woman, but even in their own homes, they daren't say that.'

'Afraid of being poisoned, are they?' Tess chuckles, and I see the men looking intently at their cake and beers. I glare at her, but she's enjoying the power. Tess is becoming a big liability.

'Men better get used to it,' I add to the speech I'm preparing in my head.

'Father Mick says it will all blow over,' Tommy chips in.

'Does he now?' I'm getting fed up with Mick hanging around me, giving out mixed messages. His face is always all holy, and yet, the air around him is less than priestly. I know he wants me. I can feel it off him. He wants me the way I want him. He uses the excuse of Larry dying to stick around the house and only goes when he needs to say Mass. I know he'll be back later saying, 'I'm worried about you. Your soul is on my conscience.'

'I think he's still has a notion for you, Peggy. It's the way he looks at you. He goes on about your soul.' Tommy laughs. 'I don't think it's your soul he's after.'

I can't help grinning.

'It's a mortal sin to think of a priest that way,' Tiny announces.

'My soul is well fucked, then.'

Everyone laughs, and I like the sound of it.

Chapter 36

There's an uneasiness in Merrion Square. Everyone is saying there's a tension in the whole of Dublin. Women pitted against their menfolk in most houses, the children sense tension in the air and stay off the streets, huddling in alleyways watching for the future.

I haven't strayed far, dealing with callers and figuring out which bad bastard I can trust and going through the itinerary with Tiny about who needs sorting or who will sort out issues for old favours.

'That Garda got a shock when he saw ya,' Tess says as she swings in with the tea. 'Didn't stay long. Gone before he even got a cuppa. He's a fine man all the same. What is it about uniforms?'

'He says he's putting army boys in plain clothes to look after me today and tomorrow.'

'Myself and Tommy could've done that,' Tiny says, sliding into Larry's favourite chair by the fire.

'Tommy knows nothing. He's only a child himself. He's all into the power being with Peggy is bringing him, but he's no army.'

'Is Tommy being silly?' I ask Tiny and Tess. Tiny shrugs it off. 'Do I need to talk to him?'

'He's a loyal pup,' Tiny says when he can see I'm not convinced. 'He's still determined he's going to get Molly back.'

'Screw loose, he has, Peggy. You'll need shot of him before long. You don't need that madwoman back.' Tess pokes at the fire. My mouth opens, and I close it. I look at Tess and the supper sandwiches from the women on the street. She hasn't had to cook in days. I'm happy to eat their food.

'More food from the people on the street?'

She nods and helps herself to some whiskey from the decanter. This will all have to stop.

'Tell Tommy I want him and everyone in the house tonight. Tomorrow will be a big day.'

'You should've had Larry here,' Tess starts. 'Him lying up in the church with the guards looking out for him, well, he's going to turn in his grave.'

'Let him. Now, out. I need peace.'

Neither look all that pleased to leave, and I'm about to say it again when a drunk Tommy arrives with Father Mick propping him up.

Tiny takes Tommy towards the stairs and leaves Mick redundant in the doorway. We're alone. Alone for the first time since the chapel when we met.

'Come in or go out. The room's getting cold.'

He clicks the door shut.

'Tommy misbehaving, was he?' I ask, pointing to the chair for him to sit.

'He just needs a sensible shoulder to lean on.'

'Sit down. Tell me what's happening in the world.' I used to say that to him when he came to Ranelagh. When I was stuck inside the walls of the maternity house.

'Like always, Peggy, I think you don't see or understand what's really happening.'

'But you're going to tell me.'

He sits in the nearest chair and leans in. 'I just think you're blinded or blinkered. You only think about yourself. No one else matters.'

'You mattered to me…once.'

This throws him off his train of thought. He stops and isn't sure where to resume.

I help him. 'I learned to depend on no one but myself.'

'Did you care for me at all?' He stops, but doesn't let me say anything. He takes a breath and goes on. 'If you did care, would you have been doing illegal things? If I mattered? You knew I was a man to do everything the correct way. I couldn't stomach the thought of violence or going against the law.'

'I did a few little things to earn us more money.'

'Money.' He shakes his head. 'The root of all evil.'

Looking at him, in his black attire and his hair all slicked back and his face all nice in the glow of the fire, I'm conflicted. 'Do I want to slap you or kiss you?'

His eyes pretend they're shocked, but he seems pleased. There's the makings of a wry smile.

'Money's important to the church, too.'

He nods. 'It isn't all it's cracked up to be, that's for sure.'

'Crisis of faith, Father?'

'No.' He sighs and looks at the fire. 'Just like you, I need to find out what I want.'

'Do you want me?'

'Yes, I do.' It is like a statement he'd make in church. 'But that's not important now.'

'What is?'

'Let me speak.' He isn't cross, just definite. 'I came here to ask you to look around you tomorrow. Somehow, the people of Dublin see you as a saviour, or a person who will rescue them from their lives.'

I sit forward in my chair.

'Huddled away in here, you don't seem to realise the impact the Faith in Women nonsense has had. The papers haven't come or the normal deliveries because of the death, but, Peggy, the whole place is waiting on you to take charge. After tomorrow, it'll be a different Dublin for all of us.'

He sits back and looks at me. I can see him as he was all those years ago, his eyes brimming with tears and looking at me in prison. Is he proud now though?

He speaks again, and I try not to see him beside me in bed. 'The women of Dublin have started a whole movement with their meetings. One gathering was outside the GPO stopped the city for at least an hour. Another was over the other side, and they refused to disperse until the Taoiseach promised to meet with you, Peggy.'

'Me? I had no idea.'

'Didn't Tiny tell you?'

'I suppose he mentioned it but he made it sound like just more business. He didn't mention the politics, or the Taoiseach. Who is the Taoiseach these days? I'm not meeting prime ministers. I'm a criminal.'

'Are you, Peggy? Is that really what you want to be?'

'Sure, politicians are blaggards too.'

Mick smiles. 'As a woman, which role would be best? There's many a woman now looking into being a spokesman for their community.'

'Spokesman?'

'Yes,' he goes on, not noticing my point. 'You could get elected on the strength of the feeling. There's an election soon enough, and I'm sure any party you choose would be persuaded to take you.'

'What do I know about politics?'

'What did you know about midwifery? You learned.'

There's a crackling in the fire, and we both watch it for a time. My mind is racing and not taking in anything at all. It's all in a muddle at the bottom of my stomach with grief, fear and hope.

'Didn't you marry again?' he asks me then, and I have to look into those eyes of his. He wipes his nose with the back of his hand.

'No.'

'Did you not want children?' he asks, and then remembers something. 'Or wouldn't they let you?'

'I thought maybe I couldn't have any. But I...'

The blood on the tiles, the longing to have someone of my own, the fear, the pain is so near the surface. I choke on a sob and grab my mouth to stop me from telling him.

'You lost a child?' he asks with a priest's knowledge of things women hide or can't say. 'I've seen that kind of look before. Many cannot talk about it.'

I gulp back the tears, looking at the patterned carpet. 'I know it's hard to lose what you want most. I just didn't know how hard it would be. I cannot think of it or all the women who tried to explain the emotions over the years.'

'Yes.'

'Some were relieved. I understood that, I still do. But I wanted my own, and I wasn't allowed that love. Probably punishment for all my past sins. But many do nothing wrong at all and suffer this. I don't think there's a God above at all, Mick. There may be a devil, but there's no one looking after me.'

'Of course there is.'

'Don't preach to me, Mick. You haven't seen what I've seen. If there was a God, it wouldn't happen.'

'I won't preach.'

We both stare at the fire.

'The child's father. Did...do you love him?'

'I don't want to talk about that.'

'The fire is nice,' Mick says, uncomfortable in his chair as he crosses and uncrosses his legs. 'Tomorrow will be a sad day for you.'

For an instant, I forgot about Larry laying in the church. 'He was a stranger to me. Didn't understand about real feelings. He was too –'

'Criminal?'

'Perhaps. He tried in the beginning, but he wasn't sure what to do with me. He didn't know how to...love.'

'Like you, maybe he didn't allow himself to.'

The fire and the carpet take my attention. 'You're not allowed to love?'

'I'm allowed that. Just not allowed to...'

'Be a man?'

We watch the flames leap up as they eat at the logs. There's a long silence, and my eyes feel heavy.

'Have you thought about what kind of a life you'll have in this house now?' Mick asks, his voice soft and low. 'Have you thought of how you may be a prisoner in your own home if you go on a certain path?'

'Larry wasn't a prisoner.'

'He was in ways.'

'Aren't we all prisoners of our choices?'

'He was lonely. He had no one. Do you want to be like that?'

'Aren't you describing yourself?' I glance at him, and his expression is pained. I've stabbed him with the truth. 'Don't you live in a lovely house? Big, no doubt, and all alone. No one to love except your God, who's invisible and cruel.'

His face is red, and I wait, watching the logs let the fire take more of them.

'I know you don't respect me. You never have,' he says.

'I did. I do respect you. I just didn't think you'd run off to America and hide…'

'I didn't run off anywhere.'

'If you say so.'

'I saw a new life for myself. An adventure. A time to do God's work.'

'Maybe now I see a new life. An adventure and a time to do work for Peggy.'

'Selfish, as usual.'

'Respect is earned. Hiding – that's what you're doing. Hiding behind that cloth you wear.'

'I'm not hiding. You hide behind the walls of everywhere. Cowering and doing evil and seducing good men.'

I laugh out loud then. It bursts out and hangs in the air between us, erasing any niceness. I chuckle again and pull at my blouse. 'Who doesn't respect who?'

'You're an impossible woman.' Mick rises to his feet. 'Impossible.'

'I'm only impossible, because you know I'm right.'

'Do what is right tomorrow. That's all I ask.'

'I'll do what is best tomorrow, don't you fear.'

'For Dublin or for Peggy?'

'For both.'

'I'm not sure that's possible.'

'But sure, I'm impossible? Wasn't it yourself that said it?'

'I'll pray for you.' He isn't sure whether to leave or not, so I rise off the seat to show him out. We get to the door of the room, and he turns towards me. I reach for the handle because he doesn't, and we're quite close. I can feel the heat from him and sense he wants to touch me as much as I want to touch him.

'Don't waste any prayers on me.' I look up at him and into his blue eyes. 'My soul is fucked too many times already.'

I grin at his disgust at the curse and lean in to peck him lightly on the lips. He lets me. His eyes are still closed when I say, 'Goodnight, Mick.'

He seems reluctant to move as I pull the door towards us and let him out into the hallway. We stand almost on the very spot I lost my baby, and he looks down on me. 'You're a great woman. But don't...'

'Get too big, I know.' I open the front door and let in the cold air.

He steps into the night, and I close him out. All is so quiet.

Chapter 37

'The army boyos are here, Peggy,' Tess calls through the bedroom door. 'No uniforms, though.'

I come out to her, and she whistles at my red hat.

'You look nice, too, Tess. Black suits you.'

Tiny is at the bottom of the stairs with a heap of men. There's no sign of my soldier, and I'm disappointed. I can see they are shocked at my hat.

'Larry bought this for me.' I touch it proudly, and the oldest of the men still looks unimpressed.

'There's a big crowd outside along the route and at the church. All is peaceful enough.'

'Us Irish respect the dead,' Tiny says, and I see him take Tess's hand and give it a squeeze. 'Father Mick and all will be waiting.' His big head nods towards the street as the men file out and stand either side of the little path.

The air has a chill, and a breeze flutters the feathers in my hat, but the gasps from the people on the street might have done that as well.

The car seems odd without Bill and Ben in it, and I acknowledge the people with a small wave as I get into the back of the car.

'You could hear a pin drop,' one of the men says as we settle ourselves into the seats. 'There's a great respect for you in that silence, Peggy.'

I notice a flow of people in the streets, walking towards the church. A few men remove their hats if they realise we are stopped beside them, and I see an odd flash of red as we sweep through the traffic.

The throngs of people at the church are only moved by the car. There's barely room for the car and people are hustling to and fro to get a glimpse of me.

'Where are the others?' I ask the men in the car, all strangers sent to protect me. From what, I'm not sure. 'Where's Tiny?'

'They're behind us somewhere. Right now, we need to get you inside.'

'Are you worried they'll attack me?'

The oldest man in the car glances over his shoulder and laughs. 'These people are here to show their respect. The government just wanted to make sure no one tries to take a pot-shot at the greatest woman in Ireland right now. It wouldn't look good.'

I pull at the collar of my black coat. 'Are you serious?'

'Yes.'

'I'm a nothing, a nobody, a woman from…'

'It doesn't matter what you were. It's what you are now that matters, my girl.'

'This is us,' the old man says. 'Are you all right?' he asks me. I'm uncertain of what or who I am at all.

'Father Mick is waiting for you at the door, and we'll walk behind you and to the left and right. No one will harm you. The people wouldn't like it.'

'The people?'

'Your people, Peggy.' He bows his head to get out, and they all jump from their places. When I stick the red hat out of the car, I can tell we are at the foot of the steps. There's a small patch of space on the steps, and people are blessing themselves; men remove their hats and caps, and all eyes are on me as I look to the top of the gap between the people to see Mick standing there looking sombre. He blesses himself and holds out his hand to welcome me into his world.

I can't look anywhere but at him. I glance only once or twice at the steps to assess where they are. The people are so close I can hear them muttering and shuffling. The army boys are closer still. One has his hand on my elbow, like Larry used to do. When I get to the top, I smile at Mick, and he doesn't return it; he looks to my right, and a man I know steps forward.

'Father Lavelle?' I gasp, and his grey head under his small silly church hat bows at me.

'I'm sorry for your loss. I offered to be here to represent your poor mother.' His handshake is limp and unfeeling. I cannot believe he's here, and my heart sinks as I see the church laden with too many figures, all facing front. All these strangers here out of fear for Larry or because of some lie or nonsense that I've created. Father Lavelle and all these people are here because I'm from trouble and have created trouble.

The walk to the top pew is like a never-ending journey. My shoes make noise on the tiles, and I'm glad the organist isn't Nora. The thought of her head hitting the table actually brings me a little bit of confidence as I sit and look at the altar.

The service is a blur, the hymns horrendous. I picked the longest and most awful ones, but now I'm desperately sorry that I did. The church is so stuffy, despite the cold day, and my feet are sore in my fancy shoes. The hat is totally unsuitable, but there's nowhere to set it, and it will have flattened my hair.

Waiting on Mick's voice sustains me through the prayers. The clergyman is insignificant looking, tiny, but his voice drones like a car engine, and Father Lavelle starts an odd time, and his voice is disgustingly loud and familiar. He must always be clearer and bolder than the rest. I close my eyes when he speaks, and I'm back there, where he made all of this start with his demon ideas. There's a bishop at the top in some sort of a funny hat. Like me, he looks uncomfortable in it and is half sleeping until his head droops, and he wakes himself with a jolt.

As the procedure goes on and on, I find Mammy in my head. She's looking on me with pride. I picture our life in the cottage and Daddy in the garden out the back with the potatoes. His face isn't too clear, but I can hear him call me. I see Mick dancing me around the Gresham. I feel the wind in my hair from the MG. I can see Mick naked in our bed and hear him pant with pleasure in my ear. The soldier is between my legs, and his baby is in my belly. Other things, like the gaol and the messes of blood on the floors, try to seep into my perfectly formed dream, but I don't let them. Molly smiles at me, and I hope now that I'll find her. I'm in Mick's arms, and he tells me he loves me, instead of God. I stand before a crowd full of women, and I tell them everything will be all right.I believe it, and they believe me. I don't have to tell men to get rid of Tommy, Tess or Tiny. They're loyal and kind. We live in Merrion Square, and people bring us food, and the coal man rings his bell for us to get the coal in. All is perfect. I don't have to make hard or harsh decisions. I'm respected and loved, without ever going out or doing anything.

Then, back in the now, Mick's urging me with his eyes to come forward. It is time for the eulogy. It must be.

I take my time leaving the seat and getting past the men in the row. As I stand at the lectern, I wonder will I take a bullet, or if the army boyos are good runners. I glance into the crowds of faces and feel hot and uncomfortable. They're waiting on me to speak. To say something great about a man I should care for.

'We are gathered here today to mourn the passing of Larry Sheeran, my grandfather. Larry was a man I barely got a chance to know. Time and life conspired against us, and we had very little time together.' I breathe and look for eyes I might know. I can feel Father Lavelle's piercing eyes into my red hat from behind me.

'Like Larry, I know the law from an unusual angle.' There's a slight amused murmuring in the crowd. 'They say an apple doesn't fall far from the tree, and even though Larry was in America for a good part of his life, we walked similar paths.'

I clear my throat and fix my hat a little, pushing it tighter onto my head.

'No one knows much about Larry's life, and that's the way he liked it. Married to Peggy, they had one daughter, Sally. Sally was my mother, of course, and when Larry was in America, I remember us sending many letters over the ocean. Larry was a hard man to get to know, and I think me being a woman didn't suit him. My mother had been a strong woman, and he found her and me difficult to deal with. Larry was used to being in charge, but I know he'll be pleased to leave all his businesses to me, as I like to think that I was "his favourite woman." He was adamant in his last days that I should continue his legacy. Larry liked to have a tight grasp on everything, but he was learning to share. He made a large list of demands with the help of his dedicated workers, and we aim to see these through. I also know how proud Larry was of the Faith in Women movement. He managed to sit up in bed in his final hours and voiced strong feelings about women standing together.'

The crowd likes this; there's a barely audible clap from somewhere.

'As a great leader, he was starting to understand the value of women and their role in society. Larry knew how to see the best in people. His great talents came in encouraging us all to be strong and to live well.'

I love that I can lie to a packed church, and I take time to savour the atmosphere before I go on.

'I want to thank the people of Dublin for coming out in such numbers. Larry would be proud of the depth of feeling people have for the Sheerans, and he should rest in peace now knowing his memory will live on. We pray now that Larry Sheeran will rest in peace with his daughter, Sally, and his fine wife, Peggy.'

'You've a gift for speaking,' someone whispers to me when I return to my seat.

I see Molly smirking at me in my mind's eye and her saying, 'Aye, and a gift for lying too.'

Chapter 38

'The Shelbourne is delighted to welcome you,' a manager says as I take off my hat and look around at the splendid décor. 'It's a sad day for Dublin and for the family, but please, just let us know if we can do anything at all to make it easier for you.'

'Thank you. Please make sure the army men are fed something other than sandwiches. We're all rather sick of sandwiches.'

'Of course.' He shuffles off, and someone hands me a whiskey.

'I don't want anyone to disturb me for a while,' I say to Tiny who is flitting around Tess like a schoolboy. She's done her hair and looks slim and prim in her new clothes.

'What a speech,' Tess whistles. 'What a load of lies.'

'Be quiet.' I move to settle into a lovely chair with its back to the people who are entering the function room.

'The ambassadors organised this send-off,' Tiny says.

'I don't want to talk to anyone for a while. I'm tired.'

'Not even me?' Mick is standing there with Father Lavelle at his side like a puppy.

'Not even you. Go get some food and drink. You and I can talk later.'

'Father Lavelle wanted a quick word,' Mick whispers. 'He's going home then.'

But Father Lavelle is already in the chair opposite me. People leave us alone, and my whiskey seems very welcome.

'You've done well,' he says.

'Are you sneering at me?' I look at his shoes. They need polishing. It isn't like the Father Lavelle I knew to have under-polished shoes.

'You've landed on your feet again, Peggy. Like you always do.'

'What do you want?'

'Father Moran seems to be aware of some of your past. Does he know all of it?'

'I don't know. I care little about what priests know.'

'He cares very deeply about you.'

I glance at him and then at my whiskey. I sip from it. 'What do you know about me?' I ask.

'You're not to ruin that good man. Do you hear me now, Peggy?'

'What do you know of my past? I've questions for you too.'

'Promise me that you're not going to be like your mother.'

I stare at him. 'Mammy?'

'You're not to take on and ruin a good man, just because you can.'

'Ruin a good man.' My voice is high. I know it's loud. 'Ruin a good man?'

He doesn't seem embarrassed. 'We both know Father Moran has feelings for you.'

'We were engaged when times were good.'

'Those times are gone.'

'Yes.'

'Don't ruin the man.'

'Why is it that you're talking to me? Did you say this to him?'

'I didn't need to. He's a man of the cloth. He knows his duty. But I know you. Let the man be.'

'So, you think I'm trying to destroy him?'

'Didn't you destroy every man in your life?'

I gulp at my whiskey and think of how right he is. 'I never set out to destroy any man.'

'Stop your lying. Women like you won't be content until every man is tortured by your tongue, your body, your evil ways.'

'The men in my life made their choices. I had to work with what a man's world gave me. I did and do damn well, and that worries the likes of you.' I point my finger at him and whisper, 'You who hide away.'

'Hear, hear,' Tess says from behind me. 'Faith in Women, Father. Have you no faith in women?'

'I have faith in God, and he's a damn sight more powerful than Peggy Bowden.' Lavelle's up and off his seat.

'Tess, give us one more minute, please?' I ask her, and reluctantly, she sidles over beside Tiny, who is standing near the bar.

'Before you go,' I say to Father Lavelle, 'who was my father?'

'Gordon Bowden.'

'Was Mammy not pregnant before she married him?'

'Of course she was. They ran away from the Sheeran life, but, sure, no Protestant church would marry them or christen you. The country is too small, and their clergy is not one for forgiving. Gordon was braver than most and willing to lose all to take her on.'

'So, Gordon was my father?'

'He loved your mother. God rest his soul. Had to try to control the madness she brought into his life. Ruined him, she did, in the finish.'

'He chose to go to war.'

'There was little of his life left. His own were unhappy at him taking on a woman like Sally. All he had left was his sense of duty. He thought war would make him a man again.'

'So, he was…'

'Too good for your mother. Although she kept up her chin for long enough.'

'He loved her.'

'I need to catch my train. Don't be like your mother.'

'If I'm half the woman my mother was, I'd be proud.'

He tuts and mumbles under his breath, 'They should've kept you locked up like they kept her.'

'Mammy is free now, and so am I,' I fling the whiskey into my mouth, but my hand trembles as I watch him go.

'Fighting is so hard,' I tell Tess as she hands me another whiskey.

'The army boys are leaving. That soldier from thirty-four is here.'

'What?'

'I know. Jesus, he's a hard boyo to forget. Was asking about ya.'

'Really?'

'I told him you had big things happening, and he was all impressed. Those eyes on him out on stalks. Got called away then to stand to attention someplace.'

'Is he gone?' My heart is in some dither, thinking I might see him.

'Now, you don't need to be bothering with youngsters like him now, Peggy.'

'No.'

'Anyways, the likes of that young buck wouldn't be seen with the likes of us in public.'

'No.'

'Well that's what he said, more or less. Says he's scared of ya,' she sniggers. 'Says you made him go all funny. He won't come near ya again, in case you get to him again.'

'For fuck sake.'

'You're wild pale all of a sudden, Peggy.'

'I asked for a rest to myself. That priest from my past would send anyone pale.'

'Sit and take your ease, then. I'll get us another whiskey.'

Chapter 39

There are flowers everywhere in the house, in bunches and vases. The smell of lilies is stifling. I cannot bear for any room to be cold. I want all the rooms to feel good and for the house to feel as free as I do.

The to-do-list the last few mornings has been very long. Meetings and letters, meeting everyone from the delivery boys to Larry's ambassadors, to real ambassadors. There have been a few letters from politicians and even one from some Deacon in the Protestant church. All full of fake sympathy and looking to connect with Faith in Women.

'A great movement for the rights of all humans,' I read somewhere in the paper, quoted from someone important.

I've had two large meetings of my followers. These have told me there's an appetite for the movement all right. Tess is not sure she likes the new me and yet sings, 'They love it all, Peggy. Lap it up. Forget all the bad shite.'

I've spoken to the women about the way forward and got a standing ovation at both meetings, while sweat ran from my pits and vomit rose in my throat with the sight of the fevered women. Scary, they looked, those eyes ablaze with the coming glory they want. Power hungry, like the menfolk. They are very forgetful, as Tess says, of my past shames.

It took me a long time to get home and to sleep afterwards, my head bursting with future plans, long lists of rhetoric and the faces of Mammy, Molly and many women before me. Then, I'd slept for hours.

The criminal side to the business is fine. Tiny seems happy, and Tommy is in charge of protection for some of the older ambassadors and is loving it all. All monies owed are coming in, and we've sold most of our shipments. The arms for the Fenians have come. They seem pleased and off doing whatever they do. My telephone calls with the Hell's Kitchen side of things were promising, with them suggesting I come to the United States of America.

Fionn in Cavan was on my list, so Tommy went to take him back to us the day after the funeral. Mainly, we felt safer, and he could take the car. Anyhow, these days when I venture out, I like taking the bus. I get to display my red gloves or shoes, and all the women acknowledge me. There's an air of hope. No one slings cups at me, and we smile at each other and giggle sometimes. I forget that the army warned me that the Gardaí would be no good to me if there was a crisis.

'They won't come to you, if there's trouble, Peggy. They think you got rid of their own. Joe Bushnell. Ring a bell?' the older army fellow mentioned on leaving Merrion Square. 'We'll be sent only in a national emergency. You won't make one for us now, will ya?'

He was handsome for a man of his years, and I had wanted him to be more than an arm to lean on. My liking for soldiers raised its head, and my heart fluttered when he looked at me. But his duty only extended to his job. I got no opportunity to try my Peggy charms on him.

Tommy comes back, saying, 'There's no Fionn. Family shipped him off to America or Australia when they heard about his mother and you being a Sheeran. They were scared stiff of me. But the man of the house stuffed some of your money back into my shirt.'

'Keep that money, Tommy. The solicitor's still knee deep in trying to find our Molly. Her family remain tight-lipped, despite the bribes.'

'She's not going to be the Molly you know, anyhow,' Tess says to poor Tommy. 'Those places change folk. She's going to be even madder than she went in.'

He bangs the door in his stumble out to the back yard. I follow him. I can tell he's crying facing into the pile of turf we've taken as payment for a job.

'That's fine turf.' I pretend I haven't seen his tears.

He scrubs his face with his hands. 'I miss her.'

'I know.'

'With Fionn gone, that'll kill her. I just knew something wasn't right. Did she know they'd sent him away?'

'You said they sent him away when they heard about all of this.'

'Do I trust them? Looking for the money, they were. Thought they'd get away with not keeping the poor mite. Maybe that's why Molly hurt herself?'

'She'd lost everything.'

'But you were still there.'

'I wasn't good to her, not like I should've been.'

'You were. You were the best to her.'

'Molly needed someone like you.'

'I left her. They all told me she was no good. That I...' He cries now like a child, and I go to take him in my arms. He snuffles into me and wets my neck with his tears. He moans on about his love for her and his need for her, his mouth and breath on my skin warm and wet. I pat his back, and he sinks into my shoulder. We stay like that for a time, and he feels manlier in my arms. His muscles are strong under his shirt and his body tight against mine.

He moves a little and doesn't let go. I pat his back and say, 'There now. You'll be all right.'

He sniffs and lifts his head. His hair is all floppy onto his reddened face, his eyes all teared and swollen. The back of his hand rubs under his nose, and he moves out of my arms. 'Thanks, Peggy.'

Those big boots of his move a few steps towards the house. I'm walking behind him, but he stops, and I don't realise. He turns, and I walk straight into his chest. His arms reach out to steady me and himself. I shout, 'Sorry,' but his chin hits my forehead with a crack.

We both groan and stumble. He tries to assess the damage his chin has caused, but my eyes are scrunched tightly closed with the pain. He's apologising now over and over.

'Shit. Sorry, sorry. Are you all right?'

His lips kiss my forehead. I feel them. Soft. My eyes shoot open. He's here, all young, and there's a want in his eyes as he touches my face, and his thumb moves to trace over my lips. I'm there in his arms.

'I'm old.'

'You're lovely.' His thumb sinks between my lips, and I'm not sure what he's doing. My tongue touches it, and he moves my hair with his other hand. 'Lovely,' he says. With that, he moves his face towards mine, and he clamps his mouth to mine.

There's stubble on his top lip and chin, but the lips of him are nicely warm. They touch mine a few times quickly. I like them doing that. I need it. Our skin sticks to each other making nice familiar smacking sounds. He shifts his arms so they encircle me, and his mouth opens, letting his tongue out and into mine. My feet are between his. The whole of him is pressed against me. The need of us both is strong, quick and longing.

My mouth is just as urgent as his until I think about what I'm doing. I pull away, and he seems to think for a second too. We both stop, and our eyes open.

'This is wrong.'

'Yeah.' He fixes his hair back, stepping away totally now. 'Sorry. Yeah.'

'We'll say no more about it.'

'Yeah.' His back is to me, and he's opening the handle to go inside. 'Sorry.'

There are lilies on the kitchen table, and the smell off them is powerful. Tommy isn't certain of how to be now.

'We'll say no more about it. It's been a hard few days.'

'Course.'

'We both miss Molly.'

He pulls on a jumper and an overcoat without answering me.

I'm nervous. 'How does it all seem now in the world of Faith in Women? The papers seem to think we've an army of our own,' I ask him for something to say. Proud, too, of where I am and trying to forget my sin with him.

'It's mad the way it all rose up.' He stops and looks at me. 'It's mad the power you have over people.'

I'm not sure he's being all that complimentary.

'People are fickle, my Ma said. She's right.' He pulls at the collar of his coat.

'Fickle?'

'I kissed you.'

'It's a mistake is all. We were upset.'

'I dunno. Something came over me. Like a spell or something. Like when you speak. It's that mouth of yours.' He checks his pockets and looks set to leave. 'Father Lavelle told Father Moran you are like a modern day...' There's no more words from him, and he fidgets at the buttons doing them up.

'Modern day what?'

'They call you... It doesn't matter.'

'Call me what? What are you trying to say?'

'You got me to do the worst things in the world. You didn't bat an eyelid. Why would stealing Molly's man be anything to you?'

'I did what?' I slam the tea towel down on the table and then wring it in my hands. 'I got you to do nothing.'

'I've damned my soul forever, and yet, you wanted more of me.'

'Get out.' I can't listen to him anymore.

'You cast your spell on me.'

'You kissed me. You did all that other stuff to be a big Sheeran man, and you got paid for it. Don't make out I forced you to do anything.'

'They'll find my Molly, and I'm taking her away.' He looks all cross and high and mighty.

'Get out.'

I think of Larry, and how he never wanted Tommy here, and how right he was.

Chapter 40

Tiny and Tess are in my living room. I know they've been to evening Mass already, but I couldn't face watching Father Mick with me thinking impure thoughts. Tess looks the picture of comfort with a rug around her knees and them both with my whiskey in crystal glasses.

'You both look at home.'

'It's a night for the fire.' Tess fixes the rug, not taking on my annoyance.

'Where's Tommy?' Tiny asks.

'I don't know.' I pour myself a whiskey. It smells nice. I swirl it in the glass and feel the heat off the fire.

'He might have caught a chill in the back yard earlier and him in his shirt sleeves.' Tess drinks at her whiskey, and I ignore her. But she doesn't stop. 'But he had the heat off you, I suppose.'

I glare at her. Tiny shuffles in his chair.

'He's Molly's man, and, of course, you want him.' Tess swigs again from the glass.

'I don't.'

'So, sucking his face isn't wantin', then? It looked to us like ya wanted the young fella.'

She's right, I did want it for all of five seconds. I'm lonely; it's that simple. But I'm not telling Tess that.

'I know it's been a long time for ya and all, but couldn't ya leave the poor young fella alone?'

'You know how to annoy me.' I sit facing the fire, wishing she would just go away.

'So, you didn't fuck him?' Tess says.

'That's none of your business.'

'Just like you not telling me about the baby?'

I glare at Tiny, and he bends to tie his boot.

'Yes, Tiny told me. Or at least he said he saw you bleed on the tiles in the hall.'

It's the tone. She doesn't believe it or is doubting some of it. Like she's doubting me. A bubble of grief surfaces. I've mainly blocked out the torture and the nightmares all of the past brings me. I pretend it never happened, and I don't allow myself to feel sad.

'I lost a baby. Yes.'

'You killed it?'

'No! I did not.'

'Who was the father?'

I don't want her around me. I cannot have her talk of my baby like that. 'That's none of your business.'

'Not my Tiny?'

Tiny reacts first, howling a loud, definite, 'No.'

'Don't be silly.' I sip the whiskey. The flames are high in the chimney. My head and heart hurt. 'I lost my baby.'

'And who was it who killed the woman from down the country? Tiny says he got rid of the body for you.'

I gulp down the mouthful and want to throttle Tiny. I don't speak.

Tess resumes her tirade. 'Now that I think about it, Molly wouldn't be near the likes of that one. She was too flighty and stupid. No woman would let Molly near their bits down there.'

I don't answer.

'Did Molly know you killed that woman? Is that what happened?'

Tess is like a parasite, gnawing at me.

'Did you hurt Molly?' Her eyes are all big behind those glasses of hers.

'I'd never hurt my Molly.'

'You never tell me things that matter.'

'Oh, shut up.'

'You don't trust me.'

'This is what happens when you know things. Questions. Silliness.'

'I just want to know if I'm living and working for a murderer.'

'There's not much work out there for the likes of you. Get used to it.'

I notice Tiny's gone. The door is standing ajar, letting in a draught.

'I should know things. I'm supposed to be your right-hand woman.' She sighs loudly. 'You told that halfwit everything, for God's sake. And her not well in the head.'

I want to leave the room, too, but can't.

'Who got you up the duff?' The glass in Tess's hand clinks onto the little table Larry used. I can see him grinning in his grave. Enjoying that we're divided over a man now.

'I don't know his name.'

'One of the regulars at thirty-four?' Tess has her nose all curled up, thinking. I can't bear for her to taint it all with her terrible questions. 'Who?' She's adamant in the way she is unbending as usual.

'It doesn't matter.'

'It wasn't Tommy?' The rug comes off her knees.

'Christ, no.'

'Who? I'm not giving up. Joe?'

I stay quiet, hoping she thinks it was Joe.

'No,' she ponders. 'It was someone else, and you didn't know his name.' I can almost hear the cogs in her brain working.

'The soldier! Our gorgeous soldier?' She leaps to her feet. 'It was him!'

I finish the whiskey in my glass. 'What does it matter?'

'It matters. Sweet Jesus, it matters. You never told us it was you who had him. We all blamed Molly. You never said. And all the fuss we made over it and all the bad feeling that went on.'

'Exactly.'

'You let us think Molly took him.'

'No one took him. It was a whorehouse.'

'You took him, Peggy, and you never said. It was only you that could've seen to him. Not a word out of you. You're some piece of work.'

'Look who's talking! I don't poison people,' I whisper this as loudly as I dare, glancing at the door all the time afraid of what she did and how near to the surface it is.

'I did it for you. But I think it was you who killed that one up from the country.'

She comes around the chair and over to me by the fire. Onto her hunkers she goes, looking right into my face. 'Did you kill her, Peggy?'

'Molly did it,' I say like lightning. 'She didn't mean to. Does it matter?'

'Course it matters. Tommy plans to get her out. None of us are safe in our beds.'

'Don't exaggerate.'

'They won't let her out.' Tess sinks back into the chair. 'They can't let her out.'

'You don't know what it's like to be locked away.'

'Is that why you love her best? Cause she was with you in the gaol?'

'I suppose.'

'Everyone loved Molly best.'

I want to say no one, only Tiny, could love a bitch like Tess.

'The Gardaí think you had Joe done in.'

'I heard.'

'Did you?'

'Course not.'

She stares at me uncertain of whether to believe me. 'You hadn't much bother letting me do away with Larry.'

I can see the hot milk and the biscuits and the way he died.

'Your own grandfather?'

'He deserved it. He didn't care for anyone.'

'Do you care for anyone?'

'I care for lots of people.'

Tess pulls the rug around her legs again and stares into the fire.

Chapter 41

The theatre is full to the gills again. All sizes, shapes and classes of women wearing flashes of red. All of them have come to see and hear me. Some are looking defiant, many muttering together, but most are looking expectantly at the stage.

'Waiting on you, they are. Silly fuckers.' Tess leans into me to peek through the curtain. 'Tommy has told me that the gangs around Mountjoy Square need sorted soon. The bastards. Don't they remember who they should be loyal to?'

'It's the likes of Mrs Foley, Martha and the fucking cook, Nora, who resent me now.' I take in all of Tess, watching her reaction to my words. She doesn't seem resentful, but Father Mick has asked if she is "still good" to me.

'A few bitches.' Tess spits a bit when she curses. 'There's masses out there, and they aren't here to see Mrs Foley or fuckin' Martha.'

'I'm not cut out for this life.' I have to admit it. I'm afraid that my knees won't let me stay upright. They've taken to wobbling on their own. 'I don't like the spotlight. I need back behind the walls or pissing in back alleys.'

'Get away with ya. You've always been one for the fancy life. Women are in need of power, and you've always been giving it to us. Even in number thirty-four. You made us stronger, Peggy.'

'Did I?' I can feel a pride returning. 'Where's Tiny?' I look around.

'Checking on things.'

I can sense after a few seconds that Tess is watching me. 'What?'

'It's almost time,' she says and still doesn't take her eyes off me. 'You aren't evil, like they say. I always feel bigger, better and stronger around you. I do things I'd never be able to do when you're with me. That's how these women feel too.'

'Will you stop.' I'm not sure what else to say to this unusual Tess before me. 'Who says I'm evil?'

'No one, Peg.' But she looks fearful suddenly. 'No one at all. We don't need you hurting anyone else. The crowds wouldn't like it.'

'I don't hurt anyone.'

'Anyone who speaks out against you – well, the ambassadors see they're kept quiet.'

'Really?'

'Mrs Foley is in the hospital. Nora has disappeared.'

'That's not my fault.'

Tess doesn't answer me.

'I don't hurt anyone.'

'Well, the ambassadors are whispering, blaming you for plenty. They say you get others to do it.'

'Bastards!'

'There's a need to put those boyos in their place.'

'How? I can't kill them all.'

'I don't know. They're scared only of the public. It's the only thing that's keeping them from touching you. But they don't like it. They're starting the rumours.'

'Rumours?'

'Don't fret about that now. It's important to keep the public with you.'

I peer through the curtain. 'The crowd looks smaller tonight. Do you think?'

She stops as Tiny comes up the back stairs and onto the boards to join us behind the curtain.

All is fine and hushed, despite me staggering out onto the stage. I grip the podium and try not to look at the faces before me. I look at the pages I've scribbled some sentences onto and lean more on the wood as I breathe in and out slowly. I say a silent pray to Mammy and start.

'Ladies…' I pause. 'Welcome, ladies. I doubt there are many gentlemen here.'

There's a roar of applause. I wait for it to stop and go on. 'I'm Peggy Sheeran, and I'm delighted to see so many fine women here tonight.'

Somehow, I get through the pages before me. Promising them all a better future with more respect and greater power over their lives. Afterwards, the noise is loud, and women queue to shake my hand and get me to sign their leaflets. Like Marilyn, I sign each one, and Tiny moves them on as best he can. I hear a few comments. 'We love your respect for us. We're delighted there's finally a woman in charge. Keep going, Peggy.'

I'm on a cloud when we leave.

It takes Tess to bring me crashing to earth. 'When are you going to do what you say?'

I fix my lipstick and shrug.

'You'll have to do something to fill those promises.' Her voice is insistent. 'Put those men in their boxes. Sort things out. It's no good making empty statements over and over.'

'I'm meeting with the ambassadors tomorrow. I'll talk to them about giving some of the most capable women roles in helping us around Dublin.'

Tiny coughs loudly from the front seat. Tess looks unconvinced. The silence in the car helps me picture the faces of the gangsters of Dublin when I suggest fitting women into our plans.

Their faces aren't actually as bad as their voices when I do mention it the following evening.

'Madness! Women can't run anything in our business.'

'I think they can.'

The dark-haired one from the north says, 'You give us a nice story for the papers. Political Peggy – but apart from that, you're of little use. And you don't scare me. Tommy isn't here to cart anyone off for you anymore.'

'I'm Peggy Sheeran.' I state it as clearly as I can with my breath caught in my throat. 'I'm like the pirate queen of the Liffey.'

The guffaws from them are loud.

'You're a puppet. You'll do as you're told,' he says. 'We should murder you here and now, but then, you'd become a martyr.'

I stand tall in the room full of treacherous bastards. 'You've no respect. I've given you all of this. Freedom from Larry. Your slice of a capital city.'

I cannot hear the bastard now as he goes on and on about my past and how I'm far from someone who could do anything great. Each sentence is like a knife in my gut. I can't take it. I feel each word like a punishing blow.

Then, I hear, 'Women that don't obey their husbands are freaks. You're a murdering whore. Sure, you're a queer with that halfwit they locked up.'

I don't hear anything more from him and don't remember making the decision to leave to get my rifle. The only thing that brings me back into the present is the noise, and the smoke around me, and me shouting, 'You will respect me!'

The bullet stops his ranting, and his chest sinks inward immediately with the metal. A little mark lets blood seep out. His features go from angry to shocked in a blink. Men leap back and over each other in the clamber and squeal to get out of the room.

The dark-haired bastard sinks to his knees and grabs at his heart, gulping and cursing. Then calls for mercy. I feel no pity. In my head, I can hear him still defiling my love for Molly and saying I'm a butcher. I can see the face of Him and Father Lavelle mists into his features. I pull the trigger again and then again. The shots seem so much louder. I'm not even sure if those shots hit him as I squeeze my eyes closed and pray to Mammy to keep me safe.

When I open my eyes, all that's left in the room with me is a bleeding dead man.

Chapter 42

'What have you to say for yourself?' It's Martha's father. The brute of a Garda who worked with Sergeant Joe Bushnell and who was there the day they took my Molly away. He's a male version of ugly Martha, only he has a bulbous nose over a thinning, grey moustache.

The room in the station is cold. Even the hairs coming from the tip of the brute's bulbous nose are grey, like the paint on the walls. 'Dancing in the Gresham like some sort of queen, she was, when the lads picked her up.' Martha's father directs this to the others in the room.

I ignore him. I also don't heed a slight nudge from the solicitor. They've provided me with one maybe slightly older than my soldier. Where might my soldier be now?

'Murder, Peggy,' the brute says loudly, so I look at him. There's only us and chairs in the room. The walls are bare, like my soul. There's some other yolk in a male uniform and of course the solicitor, too, but it's the brute that speaks again. 'You might as well talk. Tiny was caught with the body, and him and his lovebird are singing away like canaries.'

I'm cold.

'They talk of other bodies too. Killed your own baby, apparently. And your own feeble grandfather. Oh, and that lovely McKenzie woman. Joe, one of our own, of course, God rest him. The list goes on, Peggy. And you dancing like a lunatic in the Gresham?'

I cannot look at him. But I hold my head high.

'My Martha says you're vicious. That you attacked Nora by trying to bash in her skull and were abusive to old Larry. Thank

Christ Martha left when she did. God knows what you would have done to an innocent girl.'

I fix the hair behind my ear and stare at the chip of paint peeling from the wall above his head.

'They say your mother went mad.'

My solicitor coughs and touches my arm, urging me to speak.

'They say you were one of them lesbians with that Molly McCarthy.'

I swing in Mick's arms around the dance floor and leave this brute to his ramblings. I've no rifle to silence him. They took that off me as well. I've nothing left.

'Maybe you slit the wrists of that Molly one?' He almost shouts this.

I ignore him, watching Mammy in her rocking chair.

'They say you're a witch and can cast spells on people. That you murdered countless babies and children.'

I hold my tummy and listen to Molly singing in my head.

'That you seduced a priest and hundreds of married men. That you got men to do all sorts for you, and tried to take over the criminals' activities in Dublin. That you tried to bed and bribe Gardaí and members of the defence forces.'

'Seduced a priest, did I?' I smirk at that.

'Find it funny? Did you all see that? This bitch thinks she's funny. Good men, women and children are dead because of you, and you're laughing about it.' He blesses himself and sits back in his chair. 'Filthy whore like you has the cheek to laugh at such evil.'

The meadow's grass is long, and Dora leans into me as I walk around her.

'An inquest into your first husband's death. Wait for it – it was deemed an accident. In light of all that we know now Peggy, it was murder. We know that now. This list goes on and on.'

'I did think of killing him, all right,' I admit to the room, 'but he fell.'

'Course he did.' The brute laughs at me. 'Course he fell. Like the businessman from the north just fell over onto your rifle in your parlour.'

'I shot him.'

I like seeing the shock in the brute's eyes. 'A confession?'

'Were there witnesses?' the solicitor asks.

'A few have come forward.'

'Did they say why they were in my parlour?'

'Does it matter? You killed a man and admitted to it.'

'Yes.'

The peeling paint is an odd shape. Even when I turn my head to the side, it looks odd.

'Inciting violence at your political meetings, you were. The Fenians aren't too happy with you either. But someone tells us that you get them guns. We might be able to prove that soon enough. You're a woman of many talents, Peggy.'

I smile. I cannot help it. The paint might look like a heart if you stare at it long enough.

'Why were you struck off as a midwife?'

'The feckin' nuns did that.'

'Why were you struck off, Peggy?'

'They said I sold babies.'

My solicitor flicks through his file.

'Where did Molly McCarthy's baby go? Tommy's very concerned about him.'

'Cavan.'

'We checked, and he isn't there.'

'He was left with those feckers. And they sent him off to America or Australia.'

'Did they now? They say they don't remember you or any baby called Fionn McCarthy.'

'They told Tommy they sent him away.'

'They don't say that now.'

There's indeed a lot of shit to wade through. But this brute is doing a good job of throwing it.

'Did you attack that cook who worked in Merrion Square?' He goes to look for her name.

'Yes, I bashed Nora's face off a table.'

'Where is Nora now?'

I shrug.

'Did you have Joe Bushnell beat up?'

'No.'

'Did you kill the Professor and his many followers?'

'No.'

'You expect us to believe you?'

'I do what I can with what I'm given,' is my reply. The pen of my solicitor is screeching across the paper.

'Tess Fitzgerald tells us that you poisoned Larry Sheeran?'

'No.'

'That you murdered Dot McKenzie.'

'No.'

'That you performed abortions and ran a whorehouse for many years in Mountjoy Square. We've found some women who will testify to you ruining their pregnancies.'

I cannot answer him as the peeling paint looks more like the head of a dragon now.

'Tess Fitzgerald says you rented out women. You manipulated halfwits into working for you. Sold good girls to any man who came along. That even that halfwit, Molly, had her body used by common criminals to keep you moving up in the world.'

I sigh loudly.

'Mrs Foley stood up to you, and she's still in hospital. That young fellow Tommy with the scar says you got him to do all sorts and got Molly killed, as he can't find her. Father Lavelle has an interesting opinion of you. And, sure, we know what you did to poor Father Mick.'

I sniff up the liquid that comes into my nose and wipe the tear off my cheek.

'You needn't start crying. You better start talking. We know you did time before, so you know what's ahead. Make it easy on us and admit it all. You're an evil cow, that's what you are.'

The drips from my nose wet the back of my hand.

'Does anyone have a good word to say about you? Anyone respect the pirate queen of Dublin?'

I shake my head. 'I thought too big. No one wants a woman to think too much of herself.'

'Don't start your preaching in here. Do you know what the women are at now? Out marching on most Gardaí stations, baying for your blood. Trying to find you. They feel cheated. Like you cast a spell on them, and they've all finally woken up. We should just turn you out for them to find. They'd give you the right kind of justice.'

'I didn't cast any spells. That's ridiculous.'

'They've realised what you are.'

'I'm just Peggy.'

'Don't play the vulnerable country lass card on me.'

'I've only done my best.'

The men in the room shuffle together, like they are at a loss what more to say or do.

'Is that all you've got to say?' the brute with no name asks.

'Yes.'

'That's your reason for all of this?' He flaps the pages in front of him. There's a lot of them. I look at them thinking of how easy paper takes ink.

'That's all. That's it. It's over.'

'You won't defend yourself at all?'

'That bastard was threatening to kill me.'

'Had he a gun?'

'No.'

The brute sighs.

'I was mad.'

'What kind of mad?'

'Crazy or cross?' someone else asks.

The peeling paint looks like a face now. Mammy smiles and nods at me. I know what she wants me to do.

'I hear voices. Like Mammy did. I hear them clear as a bell.'

My solicitor stops writing. 'Someone needs to assess my client...?' He flicks a few pages.

'Peggy! My name is Peggy.'

His young eyes open wide. 'We must stop this immediately and get her seen to. One of those head doctors needs a look at her.'

The shuffling and banging of doors knocks the paint peel off the wall a bit more. It's hanging there taunting me with its shape – what is it?

A few hours pass, and I lay my head on the table and close my eyes. No dreams come, but the knock on the door is loud, and I come back into the cold, grey Gardaí station.

There before me, in a fancy pair of high shoes, is the Blonde Bitch. The one who started all the bad luck in number thirty-four. Her hair is all curled like in the movies. In her hand is a wad of paper, and I can see a pen tucked behind her ear. Beside her is the brute and my solicitor and some other men who sit at the far wall. All eyes are on me, and I want to cry. But here isn't the place to wail about my lot.

'Peggy Sheeran?' she asks and sits down.

'Yes.'

Those blue eyes dart a look at me, like a mother does to silence a child. 'I'm Dr Fowler. I'm here to assess you, Peggy.'

I look at her tight jacket and skirt that is too short.

'I'm a psychologist.'

I blink back the tears. 'You're a country lass?'

'I was. Like yourself. I've researched a good deal about you.'

'Where are you from?'

'I could say I'm from Sligo. Then, you might feel an affinity towards me and be good to me.'

I smile, it seems I was right about seeing her again. 'Let's pretend that you're from there, then.'

'Let's.'

The room feels warmer, and my mind whirrs with her being here. The anger I felt for her comes and goes as I look into those pitying eyes.

She opens that pretty mouth. 'I'm here...'

'To see if I'm mad.'

Her curls dance a little. 'I'm here to talk with you and ask how you're feeling.'

'Could we be alone?' I ask.

'That would be ideal, Peggy. I agree. Could you give us a few minutes?'

No one seems in any hurry to leave us. They look at each other, and then, the brute says, 'Five minutes. If you're a doctor at all.' He sniffs at the Blonde Bitch on the way past.

She winks at me. 'You've a good memory, Peggy, but let's talk as if they're still listening.' She winks again. Her smile is new and lights up her whole face. 'Do you understand?'

'Yes.'

'Do you know why you're here?'

I wipe my nose with the back of my hand.

'I've researched you a great deal, Peggy. Your time in Mountjoy, and all that's happened since. I looked at the woman you were and have followed the papers recently. Women who visited you knew all about you. And you were good to them.'

'I tried.'

'Women should look out for one another. Isn't that what you believe?'

I grunt again. My eyes are hurting me with tears and tiredness.

She goes on. 'They tell me you keep repeating, "I do what I can with what I'm given."'

'Yes.'

'What happened, Peggy? Were you given too much?'

'What do you want me to say?'

'I'm here to save you.'

'You're not here to keep me quiet?'

'Many women came to you, and you never knew who they were.'

The tears flow as she talks on.

'This is about you, Peggy. Only you.'

'I did my best.'

'Are you a good woman?'

'I try to be.'

'You do what you can with what you're given.'

'Yes.'

'Are you a witch?'

'I dunno.'

'Did you shoot that man?'

'He was talking about killing me. Next minute, he was dead.'

She doesn't seem shocked. Her curls are beautiful.

'I'm going to prison,' I cry at her.

'I can save you, or you can save yourself.'

I feel her touch my hand.

'You're mad. Aren't you, Peggy? Aren't you mad?'

'Maybe I am...I do hear Mammy sometimes. I feel like I'm insane most of the time.' A sob leaves me. It starts a convulsion of noises. I try to stop them.

'Boys?' she shouts, and people enter. I can't look at them. I bury my head in my hands and wail into them. 'She needs medication,' I hear the blonde one say, 'I need the paperwork, and we need to get her looked after.'

'Looked after?' the brute roars. 'This whore!'

'My name is Peggy,' I shout and swing over and back in my chair. 'I do the best I can with what I've been given.'

'She's taking the piss,' the brute shouts. He's worried now, I can tell. His eyes are darting to all the others in the room. 'She's taking the piss.' Finally, his gaze stops at me.

I make the wailing noise Mammy made and whine, 'I wanted too much. I just wanted too much. I've done my best. Someone make it all better. Make it all go away. Make these fuckers all go away. I need away from here, because the doc here agrees that I'm as mad as fuck. Mad as fuck.'

The End

Acknowledgements

Many of you know there's a special magic which brings me to write everyday. Without this magic, my love for writing might never have been realised. I thank and love this magic with all of my heart.

I acknowledge all those who've taken me this far along the writing road. Those who've pointed me in the right direction and brought me to this destination. Even if you're not specifically mentioned, I am grateful for every read, act or kind word.

Carmel Harrington, the Irish Times best-selling author, took me into her online writing group Imagine, Write, Inspire (IWI). Carmel has been with me from the start and from under her fairy H-mother wings, this has happened. Benji Bennet told me to write and let the rest happen. Thank you Benji for my new direction.

To all the IWIers who've read most of the words I've ever written. Thank you to ALL of you, for your support, encouragement and friendship. I've never met you Catherine Power Evans but you keep me motivated with messages and are a powerful writer.

Vanessa Fox O Loughlin, who believed in me and forged me on when I was in shock that others might actually read my words. Thank you for everything Vanessa.

Mona Deery, for being one of my first printers, readers and shoulders to lean on. Heather Norris for being the 'bestest' friend and to my sister Aishling for her unwavering support.

Claire Horan, Collette Kielt, Eileen McLaughlin, Brian McDermott and all those who listened to me talking about book ideas for hours. Little did we know it would end up here. My teachers through the years who gave me a love of reading and writing. Danny McCarthy who answered the emails which started all of this publishing lark. Also gratitude to Ivan Mulcahy for his time and feedback in the early days.

To my writing doc, Liam Farrell - thank you for supporting me in the dark days on twitter and for listening still today when I ramble on about all things #WritersWise.

To all of the contributors on our #WritersWise tweet-chats. Massive shout-out to all those who trend and chat regularly with us on #WritersWise Thursdays.

Alana Kirk, Hazel Gaynor, Louise Phillips, Elizabeth Rose Murray, Lorna Sixsmith, Catherine Ryan Howard, Andrea Mara and all of the other wonderful guest-hosts on our tweet-chats. Huge thank you to all the literary world who give free advice and writing tips so readily. To all those who told me to keep writing; thank you Siobhan Davis, Sue Leonard, Mary McCauley and also the Big Smoke Writing Factory course tutors.

When I needed strength there were special women out in the internet world who kept me going, Bernadene Byrne, Mary McLaughlin, Sam Hogan-Villena and all on The Extra Special Kids Facebook page.

To Rian Magee at Twinbrush, for design and branding (and being there from the beginning).

I wouldn't have continued without the guidance from my beta-readers (especially Linda Green and editor Jean O'Sullivan) and my own new Readers Involved Project deserves a mention here too. The encouragement from various aspiring authors and book bloggers on social media forums/events was invaluable.

I'm forever grateful to all of the publications and literary journals who gave me readers and confidence. Also to Rachel McLaughlin and the Donegal Woman website for allowing me to have fun with Woman's Words every Sunday.

Thank you to Tracy Brennan, my wonderful agent and to all at Trace Literary Agency. Nicola Cassidy, Sheila Forsey, Caroline Busher and Adele O'Neil are just some of the powerful writers who I'm honoured to communicate with. To the team at Bloodhound

Books who believe in Peggy as a character and me as a writer. I cannot thank Bloodhound Books enough for making my dream come true and I wish to give a special mention to my editor Lesley Jones.

To my friends, family and community who've waited patiently with me as I talked about nudges about books. For my husband Brian I save the biggest mention. You helped me gain the time, space and courage to write. You're a saint really.

Made in the USA
Middletown, DE
08 February 2020